DOWN WITH THE SUN

Also by Marc D. Hasbrouck

Stable Affairs
Horse Scents

DOWN WITH THE SUN

A NOVEL IN THREE ACTS

MARC D. HASBROUCK

DOWN WITH THE SUN
A NOVEL IN THREE ACTS

iUniverse books may be ordered through booksellers or by contacting:

iUniverse
1663 Liberty Drive
Bloomington, IN 47403
www.iuniverse.com
844-349-9409

ISBN: 978-1-6632-1762-2 (sc)
ISBN: 978-1-6632-1763-9 (e)

Library of Congress Control Number: 2021902770

Print information available on the last page.

iUniverse rev. date: 02/10/2021

AUTHOR'S NOTE

In ancient Roman mythology, *Janus* is the god of beginnings, changes, transitions and endings. He is depicted as having two faces, since he looks to the future and to the past. The first month in our calendar year is named for him.

"Behind every mask there is a face, and behind that a story."

Marty Rubin

INTRODUCTION

I love the theater. Sitting in the audience, waiting for something exciting, frightening, enticing, enlightening, and entertaining to begin. Ever since Thespis first stepped out upon a stage way back in the 6th century B.C. we have been enthralled by the magic of the spoken word and actions from a multitude of characters, with a variety of voices and opinions. When the overture begins or when the house lights begin to dim the thrill of anticipation is heightened. The curtain rises. A series of scenes begins to weave a story into a cohesive whole. We, as the audience, meet new characters. We learn new things. Scene by scene, from one act to the next, we are transported and transfixed. We share laughter, tears, perhaps gasps of surprise and, yes, sometimes anger. A story is being told. We are also critics. Will there be a rousing standing ovation at the end? Merely polite applause? Will there be booing and hissing, or will we all file out disappointed and silent?

The anticipation is building…the house lights are dimming…

ACT ONE

NOW AND THEN

"We write to taste life twice; in the moment and in retrospect."

Anais Nin

1

NOW: I can't remember when I told my first lie, but I must have been very young. Oh, hell, we all tell lies when we're little kids, don't we? *"Not me"…"I didn't do it"…"It was Timmy. He broke it."* Some of us may never outgrow it. Perhaps I have. One lie is reason enough to question every one of your truths. But lies can protect us. Lies can preserve the feelings of others. And some lies can be destructive. Be that as it may, I have always been keenly aware of others' reactions to whatever I say or do. What I *wasn't* aware of, however, as I was growing up were the subtle influences that would shape my entire life. Frankly, *most* of us aren't aware of them. We're not paying attention then. We're not taking notes. We either ignore them or can't recognize and acknowledge them, right? Sometimes we do. And sometimes it's too late. I read somewhere, and sometime ago, that we are all creators of our own lives. Every person or every experience that forms our lives have been drawn into our reality by…drumroll, please… ourselves. Bear in mind, though, that while we're creating our own reality, others are creating theirs. Our destiny, therefore, is determined by choice, not chance. In other words, there are no coincidences. Actually, I think there *are*. Someone famous once said: All the world's a stage, and all the men and women merely players; they have their exits and their entrances, and one man in his time plays many parts. Yes, that may very well be true, but sometimes life goes off script.

A sunset in one place is a sunrise in another.

THEN: Just call me Bax. Baxter is my name, though. Great name, huh? Don't know how my parents came up with that one but I sorta like it. Baxter Janus. I'm seven years old, tall for my age and I heard somebody say that I'm towheaded. I think that means my hair is so blond it looks white. My Gram said I have hair the same color as Jean Harlow, whatever that means. I have no idea who he is. My Mom always has her radio playing when my Dad's not home. He doesn't like music so much. My favorite song is that Johnny Mercer guy singing "Ac-Cent-Tchu-Ate the Positive". I'm gonna make that my theme song when I grow up. My Dad got home from some kinda war or something over in someplace called Europe not too long ago and my Mom said he was gonna get a purple heart. I really never knew what color hearts were but I thought they might be sort of red and bloody. Anyway, she was proud of his purple heart. My dad doesn't like to talk about it.

We live in a big old house in someplace called New Jersey. The town is Dover. At the end of my street, down a short hill, are railroad tracks. Sometimes whenever I hear a big train blowing its whistle I run down to watch it go by, with a lot of noise and steam coming out of its smokestack on top of the engine. I have a dog named Laddie and he looks just like that dog in the movies named Lassie. My Mom's parents, Gram and Gramp, live a couple blocks away. Mom and I are always happy to see them whenever they come for a visit. My Dad doesn't seem to like it that much. I can tell by the look on his face and he mumbles something I can't understand.

NOW: Obviously at that time I had no idea what was going on with the emotions between my father and my grandparents. Why that feeling of coldness and, possibly, distrust? What had happened? Sooner or later, I hoped to find out.

And, sooner or later, I *will* find out.

After all these years, I still have very fond memories of that big old Victorian house we lived in. Hours were spent on the wrap-around front porch with half a dozen large wooden rocking chairs. My grandparents' house was even bigger and grander. Of course, memories have a tendency to make things bigger…and grander. Moms and grandmothers dressed much differently way back then. Never any slacks or shorts. My mom, Olivia, mostly wore what she called housedresses. Simple and plain, never anything too fancy. She always seemed to smell like soap. Perhaps it was because she was constantly cleaning the house. Even when it didn't need it. And Gram, Lillian Freemont, was always smartly dressed, with stylish skirts and blouses and, more often than not, some kind of jewelry, costume or otherwise. She always smelled so nice and fresh; Arpege. I know, because that's what Mom bought for her every Christmas. Gram never looked old or frumpy like some of the other grandmothers I saw. She was on the tall side, about five-eight, with salt and pepper hair and sparkling bright blue eyes. She also had a sarcastic wit that could be devastating. With an arch to her eyebrow, I could tell that she was catching me in a lie or far-fetched story. Gramp, Chester Freemont, was a very successful lawyer and dressed the part, even at home. He smoked cigars and, at times, a sweet-smelling pipe. Yes, it was Prince Albert…in a can. I loved that aroma. He always smelled of Bay Rum. I know, because that's what Mom bought for him every Christmas. He often whispered into my ear that I was his favorite grandson. I was his *only* grandson.

THEN: Last year, for my sixth birthday, my mom gave me a couple of small flags as a present. They were on little black sticks with a gold pointy thing on top that looked like a spear or something. "This one is Germany and this one is France," she told me, holding up the flags. "That's where Daddy was fighting in the war. I'll show you in the atlas where they are and you can learn about them if you'd like." I liked that. We read about the countries together and I asked about other flags and other countries. My Gram and Gramp thought that was a great idea and they bought more flags for me. Every time they came to visit, like every week or something, they brought a couple more flags. Now I have about thirty flags and I know every country. They can pick up any flag and I can tell them what country it is. They think I am so smart. Well, I am. Someday I'm going to visit all those countries. I hope I will anyway.

My very best friend, Ant, lives next door. His name is Anthony but he pronounces it like Ant-nee, so I just call him Ant. Anthony Bertoli. There are always great smells coming from his house around suppertime every night. My

Mom says his family is Eyetalian and they make the best meatballs and stuff like that. I showed Ant my little flag of Italy and he told me they had a much larger one hanging in a frame in their living room. He's about a couple months younger than me and a lot shorter, but he is a faster runner than me.

Every afternoon Ant asks if I want to come in and watch television with him. We don't have one, just a radio. I like to listen to a lot of kid shows and my favorite is about Baby Snooks, but Ant thinks it's a stupid show. I guess it's not really a show for kids but it makes me laugh anyway. His favorite television show is Junior Frolics *with Uncle Fred. He's not really our uncle, that's just his name on television. He shows cartoons and talks a lot.*

"Baxter," Ant's mom called to me this one time. "Want to stay for supper tonight? We're having lasagna and that's Anthony's favorite meal. You can run over and ask your mom if it's okay."

"Oh, I can't," I lied, "my Gram and Gramp are coming for supper at our place and I should be going home by now." I had no idea what that lasagna stuff was but it didn't sound good to me. Probably had a lot of vegetables in it. Yuck! I also hoped that Ant's mom wasn't watching out the window to see that Gram and Gramp really didn't come to our place that night for supper. I worried about that for several days, but I'm usually not caught in any of my lies.

NOW: In all honesty, very few of my lies went undetected. I also wasn't aware of the fact that I was spending more and more time with my grandparents and less and less time with my parents. Frankly, my parents were boring and my Gram and Gramp were anything but! I later discovered that Gram and Gramp helped my mother financially while my father was fighting in the war to ensure that we could remain in that big, beautiful house. While my dad was gone, my mother and one of her friends worked at the nearby Picatinny Arsenal making munitions. The facility hired over 18,000 workers and ran three shifts daily. She also worked part time as a librarian. She really didn't like to read that much, but Gram and Gramp sure did! They were always bringing me new little books to read and that habit of reading voraciously stayed with me to this day. When my dad came home, he took advantage of the new GI Bill to further his education and enjoy the supplemental cost-of-living stipends. He had been a draftsman before the war and a couple years following his return he was working at one of the best architectural firms in Morris County. Mom quit both of her jobs to stay home and take care of us like a good housewife at that time did. Long before women's lib, mind you.

THEN: *On the other side of Ant's house was a cemetery with a big fence around it. I don't know why they have a fence around a place where they bury dead people. Are they afraid they might wake up and get out at night or something? Running along the back of the cemetery is a path through some woods. My mom tells me to be careful walking there. Sometimes there are hobos who camp along that path and who knows what they might do to little boys. This is where Ant and I have to walk when we go to school. It's a little old school up on a hill and it has a large playground. We like to play on the monkey bars but we stay away from the swings and the teeter-totters. There are two twin boys in our class, redheaded Tom and Jerry Wallace. They look exactly alike and they're mean as snakes. They tease all the girls and shove kids off the swings. I was on a teeter-totter once and was up while Ant was down, sitting on the other end. Tom...or Jerry...can't tell them apart...pushed Ant off and I came crashing down and knocked the wind outta me when I hit the ground. The big brat just laughed and laughed. They always do bad stuff like that when the teachers aren't looking. They never get caught.*

NOW: My favorite books, at that time, were about Uncle Wiggily, a kindly old rabbit gentleman with rheumatism. There was a big bully in these stories, the Pipsisewah and his sidekick Skeezicks. The Pipsisewah is an ugly creature, sort of looking like a rhinoceros, with two horns on his snout and hooves for feet. Skeezicks looks like a skinny crow. I imagined that these two were the bullies Tom and Jerry. And I imagined that my mother was Nurse Jane Fuzzy Wuzzy.

I thought that Uncle Wiggily was brave and very wise, the way he handled the bully.

THEN: *I don't know why I did this. Why I felt so brave on this particular day. It was before the school bell rang in the morning and we were out in the playground. One of the twins was all by himself. They are never apart and they do mean things side by side. Something came over me. I was carrying a little bag of cookies my mom had given me for recess. I went up behind Tom...*

or Jerry…and started beating him with my bag of cookies. He was so surprised by this and tried to stop me but I kept swinging. The bully tried to back away but I followed him just kept hitting him that that little bag. Well, we both ended up in the principal's office and she just glared at me. Miss Scott always looks like she's mad at something or somebody.

"What were you thinking, young man?" she demanded, with her hands on her big fat hips. She smelled like an old girdle and cigarette smoke. "Why did you just attack that poor little boy like that?"

"He hit me first," I lied. "He came up behind me and pushed me and tried to trip me. And then he punched me in the back. It made me mad."

"Well," she said, "we don't go around hitting each other like that. Are you sure he didn't trip you by accident? I'm sure he didn't mean to, did you, Jerry?"

"I'm Tom, Miss Scott. No, ma'am, but I didn't…" he stopped for just a second…"I didn't mean to trip him." Tom must have been lying too. "I must have stumbled or something." He stared at me with fire in his eyes, but the principle didn't see that.

"You two boys shake hands and make up. Then go back to your classroom. Baxter Janus, I will send a note home for your parents to sign. And this will go in your record. I'm surprised at you. This is not like you at all. Shame." Our teacher marched us back to our class and I sat in silence for the rest of the day. At recess I ate my bag of smashed crumbs.

After school Ant and I started walking toward that little path through the woods. He was happy that I had hit Tom and laughed and laughed about it. All of a sudden Tom appeared from behind a tree and he had a long stick in his hand.

"Okay, kiddo," he snarled as he came toward us. "I'm gonna beat the tar outta ya and your greaseball friend, too! That'll look like an accident, too, just wait and see!"

We started running as fast as we could go. Ant was faster than me but I was faster than Tom. Halfway through the woods I saw two hobos cooking something over a small fire.

"Help!" I yelled to them without even thinking. "Help us. There's a big bully chasing us and he's gonna kill us he says!" And we kept going.

A minute later I heard one of the hobos call out "Hey, punk. Stop right there!" Ant and me just kept running.

NOW: Sometimes a lie and the truth are so close together that it's difficult to really know what's what.

THEN: My mom scolded me when she read the note from the principal. My dad just shook his head and laughed. I tried to explain why I did what I did. I may have stretched the truth a little bit here, as well.

"I guess I should be upset with you," my dad said, "losing your temper is never the best route to take but, on the other hand, I'm proud of you for bullying that bully. Maybe taught him who not to mess with."

I guess I was sort of brave for doing that. Or stupid. Maybe I will get a purple heart. But I don't know how to tell if it changes color. I'm not so sure I taught Tom, or his bratty brother, about messing with me. Maybe I made things worse. But I don't know what those hobo guys did or said to him. Maybe they killed him and cooked him on their fire for supper. Ant told me that's what they do sometimes.

NOW: Call them hobos, call them itinerant workers, gypsies, or just bums; whatever you call them they have been around for centuries, I suppose. Unless they were lost somewhere along the Donner Pass, it's doubtful they have ever had to resort to cannibalism, though!

THEN: Ant and I were scared to walk down that path through the woods to go to school the next day. Were the hobos still there and what did they do to Tom? We passed the little place where they had the fire going but it was out and they were gone. No sign of anybody. No little boy bones in the ashes of the fire. When we got to the playground, we saw him. And his brother. They saw us but didn't do anything or even try to come in our direction. I saw that Tom (or Jerry) was sneaking up behind little Becky Henley. She sits in front of me in class and the twins are always teasing her. Pulling her hair…pushing her… calling her names. I wanted to warn her but I was too afraid, I guess. It was Tom and he was almost right up behind her, ready to do something when she turned around real fast and looked him right in the eye.

"Oh, no you don't!" she yelled at him. "No more, you big bully. I saw what Bax did to you yesterday and I laughed and laughed. All of us kids laughed at you."

And she kicked him right in the knee…and then she stomped right on his foot. Hard, too. Ant and I just stood there. Our eyes were wide open and my mouth hung open in surprise. And then, guess what? Tom started to cry. What? He was really crying. All the other kids started to laugh and clap. Becky turned and looked right at Jerry who was on the other side of the playground. She looked him right in the eye too and held up her fist, shaking it at him. He turned and ran away. Well, that's just great. Now I'm afraid of Becky Henley.

NOW: Actually, Becky and I became good friends after that incident and remained so for many years. We even went out on a couple of dates when we were in high school. At recess that day she shared one of the cookies her mother had freshly baked. A chocolate chip cookie. I had never had one of those before and, for some reason, that has been my absolute favorite cookie since then. As for Tom and Jerry Wallace? Their bullying seemed to taper off and they weren't nearly as aggressive about it as in the past. But we were still cautious around them and confronted them with what little bravery we could muster. We, as young students, had not been aware of the bruises that appeared on one or the other of them from time to time, but the teachers at school had been. As it turned out, they were the victims of an extremely abusive mother and they were simply taking out their own aggressions on their classmates. A perfect example of psychological determinism. Ironically, Tom was able to overcome that aspect of his personality and grew up to become a popular police chief in Dover. He was the loving father to three redheaded sons, two of which were identical twins. Jerry, on the other hand, was killed in a street fight in Newark at the age of 17. Apparently he had sexually molested a fifteen-year-old girl and forced her to perform fellatio on him. Her older brother, with several of his friends, tracked him down. His body was found in the gutter along South Broad Street, with 15 stab wounds, one for every year of the young girl's life. His penis, however, was never found.

2

THEN: *Mom and Dad went to some meeting that was almost just across the street, in the American Legion Hall, but Gram and Gramp were babysitting for me so I wouldn't be alone. We were all sitting in the living room. Gramp was reading his newspaper and was smoking a big cigar. Smoke was floating over his head like a big cloud.*

"I see they're playing 'Adam's Rib' down at the Baker," said Gramp as he looked at his newspaper. "It's a comedy about lawyers with Hepburn and Tracy. I think we ought to see it."

Gram didn't answer him, she just nodded. She was reading a book with a funny name. Well, it wasn't a name, really, just looked like a number to me. "1984". Laddie was lying down on the floor next to me as I was reading a new Uncle Wiggily book that Gram had brought for me.

"I thought I saw the Pipsisewah hiding behind a tree this morning when Ant and I were walking to school. It was on that path behind the cemetery."

Gram turned to me with a strange look on her face and put down her book. She turned her head just a bit to the side and squinted at me. "Really?' she asked me.

I slowly nodded my head. "Uh-huh."

"Well, now. I find that very difficult to believe, Baxter. And what time would that have been?"

"I think it was around 8 o'clock. Maybe," I said.

"Oh, no, now I know you're mistaken. Because I saw him at around that time poking through the flower boxes on our front porch."

I stared at her with my mouth open. I didn't know what to say.

"Poppycock! You're both crazy," said Gramp, looking up from his newspaper and brushing some ashes off of his lap.

I turned to look at him as he was shaking his head.

"No, you are both wrong, because I was backing my car out of the garage to head to my office at that very time and I nearly hit him."

There was silence as both Gram and Gramp stared at me. They were both smiling.

"Well, then," said Gram, "Obviously someone is not telling the truth. Who might that be?" And she winked at me.

I was getting ready to say something when I heard the front door opening. Laddie got up and ran into the front hall to greet my mom and dad as they came in. My mother saw us in the living room and motioned for me to come kiss her. She was wearing the prettiest dress I had ever seen her in and had some dead animals around her neck. She said it was a mink stole but she didn't tell me who she stole it from. Or why. I thought it was kinda creepy.

"Corey, get in here," my mom called to my dad. "Show Bax what you got tonight."

My dad slowly came into the living room and glanced at Gram and Gramp. They looked at him too but they weren't smiling, just sorta staring. Dad was wearing his army uniform and he looked so handsome.

"Well, bend over, silly, so Bax can see it," Mom said to Dad.

He walked over to me and bent over, pointing to something that was pinned to his chest.

"He finally got his Purple Heart tonight. A stupid little snafu held it up. Bax, aren't you so proud of your dad?" asked Mom.

Then I saw it. So that's what a Purple Heart was! It wasn't a bloody messy thing, just something purple with a gold picture of some man on it.

NOW: The Purple Heart, the very first U.S. military decoration, was actually designed (and designated) by George Washington back in 1782. It's an award that no military person wants to receive. It means that you've either been wounded in action or killed. It's a beautifully designed heart-shaped medallion, in purple, with a bronze profile of George Washington in the middle. Several actors and famous authors have been awarded this honor, with only one U.S. President being so honored: John F. Kennedy. Even some animals have been awarded this medal…Sergeant Stubby the dog, for example and Sergeant Reckless the horse. One brave (and perhaps reckless) man, Curry T. Haynes holds the honor of having the most Purple Hearts awarded: ten.

It wasn't until years later that I understood that strange word Mom had said at the time: *snafu*. A popular military phrase…an acronym for Situation Normal. All Fucked Up.

Just a couple weeks after Halloween Dad drove Mom and me into a big city. We had to go through a long, stinky tunnel to get there. Mom said that we were going under some river. I hoped the tunnel wouldn't collapse. We parked up on top of some building and then walked a lot of long blocks to where a parade was going to be. Dad said he really liked parades. I almost laughed because he doesn't like anything. I have never seen so many people, all of them standing along a big street. Pretty soon I heard a lot of music. Sounded like drums. Then I saw the biggest balloon I had ever seen! It was floating above the street and some men were trying to keep it from blowing away, I guess, by holding onto long ropes. Dad lifted me up and put me on his shoulders so I could see over everybody and watch the parade. That was the best parade ever. Even Santa Claus was in it. After the parade was over we had to walk all the way back to the car. We drove back through that stinky tunnel and went to Gram and Gramps house. Gram had cooked a great big old turkey and it smelled so good when we went into their house.

I ate so much I thought I would explode. Mom helped Gram wash the dishes and Gramp and I went into the living room. He lit up a cigar and Dad fell asleep on the couch. I guess I fell asleep too, because when I woke up I was in my own bed at home.

A couple weeks later we went back into the city again. This time Gramp was driving, but Dad stayed home. We parked on top of that same building after going through that dumb old tunnel, but this time we took a taxi to someplace where there was the tallest Christmas tree I had ever seen. Below the tree was a small place where people were ice-skating. Right in the middle of the big city. Wow! We looked at the tree for a while, and then we stood in a long line of people and went into a building that had a sign on it that said Music Hall. I think it was a movie theater. Sure was a fancy one. When the lights went out a lot of people came out onto a stage and there was all kinds of music. A whole bunch of pretty ladies were dancing in a line, kicking up there legs at the same time. Looked like they were wearing bathing suits, sort of like Santa's elves. Everybody in the audience must have liked that because they started clapping and clapping.

After all that singing and dancing was over, a big curtain came down and then went right back up again with a movie screen behind it. The lights went out and a movie started. I don't even know what the movie was because I fell asleep almost as soon as it started. Mom woke me up when it was over. Before we went home, we all had supper at a restaurant where all the waiters seemed to know Gram and Gramp. All I wanted was something called a shrimp cocktail. I fell asleep again in the car on the way back home. I don't even remember going through that tunnel.

NOW: This trip into New York City for the holiday festivities became a tradition for the next several years. The city was always so magical at that time of year. All of the department store windows along 5th Avenue were turned into strange, enticing wonderlands. And that huge Christmas tree at Rockefeller Center never failed to be impressive. To top everything off, Becky Henley, my grade school classmate who stood up to the bullying twins Tom and Jerry Wallace, grew up to be one of those high-kicking dancers on that big stage. For some reason, every time I rode through the Lincoln Tunnel and smelled the exhaust fumes, even as an adult, Christmas always came to mind. Great memories can be triggered so easily by the olfactory senses.

THEN: *Christmas Eve, and I can't fall asleep. Guess I'm too excited. Mom and Dad had put the tree up in the living room, but Santa always decorates it when he comes. He must be really tired out by the time he gets back home to the North Pole in the morning. I heard some noises downstairs but I knew it was too early for Santa to get here. Mom and Dad were still up. I almost yelled down to them to go to bed. If Santa sees anybody, I think he'll* *skip the house. Laddie jumped up on the bed with me. I put my arm around him and almost started to fall asleep. I closed my eyes.*

All of a sudden there was a very loud crash and it sounded like something broke. Now I was scared. Really scared! Oh, no, did Santa crash on our roof? Did the reindeer come through a window? Is Santa dead? I pulled the covers up over my head and closed my eyes real tight. I couldn't hear anything. I kept my eyes closed and pulled the covers tighter around my head.

I guess I fell asleep then.

Before I knew it, the sun was coming up. I was almost afraid to go downstairs, but I heard Mom and Dad down there and I could smell their coffee. I slowly opened my bedroom door, Laddie ran down the stairs and I carefully followed him.

"Well, Merry Christmas, sleepyhead," Mom said as I peeked into the living room. "You must have been really tired, Bax, you're usually up at the crack of dawn on Christmas morning."

The Christmas tree was beautiful! All decorated and my favorites, the bubble lights, were bubbling like crazy. Tinsel hung all over the tree and the lights reflected off of it. I looked all around but I didn't see anything broken. Dad was sitting in his big chair with his leg up on a hassock. Mom brought him a cup of coffee and they both looked at me and smiled. I couldn't believe all the presents under the tree. Santa really brought a lot. I hope he didn't hurt himself.

There were several boxes all shaped the exact same that Santa brought for me. That was strange. That never happened before. I opened the first and my eyes popped wide open. It was part of an electric train set. All the other boxes had more train cars, including a big steam engine, just like the ones I like to watch at the bottom of our street. A larger box had a lot of tracks that had to be put together and another box had the control thing that would make the train go. I was so excited I almost peed myself. There were a few more packages for me, but they just had clothes in them. I pretended I liked my new shirts and pants, but they were boring. I loved that train set!

Mom opened a present from Dad and it was a very sparkly necklace and earrings. She cried when she saw them and gave Dad a great big hug and a kiss. Yuck. Then Dad opened his gift from Mom and it was a big gold wristwatch.

He gasped when he saw it and gave Mom a great big hug and a kiss. Another yuck! There even was a present from Santa for Laddie. It was a big box of dog cookies shaped like bones. He wagged his tail and barked until Mom opened the box and gave him one. He ran off into another room to eat it. I guess he didn't want any of us to get it from him and eat it.

When Gram and Gramp came over for dinner they brought more gifts for everyone. One gift for me was a subscription to National Geographic. *I love that magazine. Another present for me was a big book about the Seven Wonders of the World. The strangest present was a little wooden sign that looked like Gramp had made himself. It said* Baxter Janus Railways. *It was like those billboard things that we always see along the road. But how did they know I got a train set from Santa?*

NOW: I didn't discover until a couple years later about that loud crash. Dad had tripped coming out of the attic with the tree decorations and fell down a few steps, dropping the box and twisting his ankle. The following Christmas Mom suggested that we help Santa and decorate the tree in advance. "He's gotten so busy, Bax," my Mom had said, "I'm sure he would appreciate our help."

That was a very special Christmas. Dad treasured that beautiful gold Rolex watch until the day he died. Mom constantly wore those sparkly diamond earrings. To this day I subscribe to National Geographic. And I still have that Lionel set. The orange and blue boxes are a little tattered and worn, but the Baxter Janus Railways still run.

3

THEN: One Saturday afternoon Mom asked me to run over and return a big cook book to Gram. She had borrowed it and made a whole lot of new stuff for dinner. It was only a couple of blocks and I didn't have to cross any busy streets or anything. I don't ever have to knock on the door whenever I go there. They just let me walk in. I opened the front door and heard some loud music and a lady screaming something. It scared me and I just stood there. The lady stopped screaming. The music stopped. Then a man started screaming and the music started again. I ran down the long hallway to the living room, where the lady had been screaming. Gram was sitting in a chair, leaning her head back, and she was crying. Gramp was lying flat on his back on the floor at Gram's feet. I rushed over to them and she looked up, surprised to see me.

"Oh, Bax, you scared me half to death, you little devil," she said, wiping the tears from her eyes. "What a nice surprise."

"Why are you crying, Gram and why were you screaming like that?" I asked, almost afraid to know what was happening. She started laughing so hard more tears came to her eyes. Gramp sat up.

"That wasn't me, Baxter. Ha! If only I could scream like that. It's the opera, Bax. On the radio." She leaned over and turned it off. "Broadcast live from the Metropolitan Opera House in New York City. We listen to it every

week. This was a very sad opera and the music is so beautiful it makes me weep…oh, do you even know what opera is?"

I shook my head. Then she told me. I didn't understand how music and screaming was so wonderful. I just like happy music like the kind Mom plays on her radio.

"Why were you on the floor, Gramp?" I asked, still a little worried about what I just saw.

"I find it very comforting and relaxing, Bax," he answered, "and if I fall asleep at least I won't fall out of my chair and land on the floor with a thump," and he laughed.

Sometimes old people don't make sense to me.

NOW: Gramp had connections. I don't know how he did it, but when the old Metropolitan Opera House was demolished he somehow managed to purchase two of the old seats (from center orchestra, no less) before they were carted off to the old-seat-graveyard. They were delivered to their house, cleaned and set up in a prominent spot in their living room. From that point on, Gram and Gramp sat in their very own "private" seats and listened to the opera every Saturday afternoon coming live from the Met… now at Lincoln Center.

~

THEN: *Gramp was very proud of his big vegetable garden in their back yard. He grew a lot of stuff that I didn't like. He had a big chicken coop back there, too, and he would let me and Ant feed them whenever we came over to visit. It was weird. I knew he had ten chickens in the early summer but every now and then when I fed them one more was missing.*

"She flew south for the winter," Gram said when I mentioned it. I was confused because it was still summer.

Gramp paid us ten cents for helping him weed his garden every couple of weeks. The only things that he grew that I liked were those big, red tomatoes.

NOW: Anyone from New Jersey will tell you that there is *nothing* better than a Jersey tomato. Oh, how I miss them.

THEN: Gram came out to the garden with a big basket with a handle on it and started picking some of the vegetables.

"Take these home to your mother, Anthony," she said, "I just know she'll make something delicious with them. Mister Freemont grows far too much for the two of us to eat. I'll fix a basket for you, too, Bax, to take home. Now, don't you dare turn up your nose at me, young man," she scolded. "You need to eat some of these delicious vegetables."

Sometimes when we pulled up a bunch of weeds there were wiggly worms attached to the roots. Gramp told us to either leave them be, because they were good for the soil, or throw a couple in to the chickens so they could have a nice treat. I just let them be.

"Well, we've done enough for today," Gramp said, "it's probably time for you to get back home, Bax, before your Mom calls and scolds us for keeping you here so late. The streetlights will be coming on soon."

The light was fading quickly as we walked back to their house. Ant had already headed for home with his basket full of vegetables. There were tomatoes, and string beans, and cucumbers, a couple of carrots, and some big purple thing that Gram called an eggplant. I didn't know that eggs could grow on plants as well as those things that come from chickens. Laddie ran ahead of us, wagging his tail and sniffing the ground. Probably on the lookout for rabbits. I've seen him chase them before but he never catches any. A few lightning bugs were starting to twinkle around us. Gram had been holding my hand when she suddenly dropped it, looking up and pointing at the sky.

"Fledermaus," she exclaimed excitedly, "fledermaus!"

I scrunched up my face and looked up at her. "What?" I asked. "What kind of word is that? I never heard that word before."

Gram laughed and pointed up to the sky again. "Look, can you see them?"

"Those little birds flying around? I can't hardly see 'em."

"Can *hardly* see them," she corrected. "No, no," Gram said, laughing again. "Those are not birds, they're beautiful little bats. Haven't you heard about bats before? Even at Halloween? Surely you must have."

I shook my head, looking back up toward the sight of five or six swirling things swooping through the sky, sometimes dipping down very fast. "But what was that word you said? That strange word."

Gram laughed again and hugged me tightly. "I was being funny when I *said that word, little man. My favorite operetta is* "Die Fledermaus"*…The Bat…and I love to see those amazing little creatures dipping and swooping through the evening skies. They are on the hunt for all those nasty, irritating little bugs that fly around up there in the sky. Especially mosquitoes. Bats are our friends. Yes, that word, fledermaus, is German. I guess it sort of means flying mouse and that's exactly what the bats look like. Come on inside and I'll show you in the encyclopedia."*

I looked back up at the bats flying overhead. Why hadn't I ever noticed them before? I guess I never looked up to see them. Gram opened my eyes to so many things. She sure is smart for an old lady.

NOW: Ever since then, whenever I'm outside around dusk I can't help but look up, hoping to see a bat or two swooping though the air. "Fledermaus," I whisper to myself, "fledermaus."

4

THEN: *Ant couldn't wait to show me some new comic books he got. Flash Gordon! Gee whiz, these are great. I'm too old, now, for those Uncle Wiggily books. Kid stuff. But, wow, Flash Gordon is so grown up. Of course, I picture myself as Flash. Becky, from school, is Dale Arden, Ant is Dr. Zarkov, and my grumpy old dad is Ming, the Merciless. I'd like to zap him with a ray gun.*

    NOW: In retrospect, this wasn't really fair to my father. The blame for his attitude towards me was partly on my own shoulders. I wasn't the kind of son that my dad had hoped for, I guess. I didn't care much for sports. I liked to read. A lot. I liked to learn about …well, just about everything. He was always criticizing me about…well, just about everything. He'd find fault in the tiniest of things and then dwell on it. I also think that he was extremely jealous of my close relationship with Gram and Gramp who always showed me love and gave me lots of encouragement. It's strange, but looking back now I can't ever recall my father telling me that he loved me. Where I was concerned he was simply aloof. Was he affected by fighting in the war? Was it something else? Who knows? Mom made up for it, though, with lots of hugs and kisses.

    Meanwhile, back to Flash Gordon…I watched those old films with Buster Crabbe whenever I could. We still didn't have a television but Ant and I watched them at his house and were transfixed. Here comes a little movie trivia: In the early 1970s George Lucas tried to buy the film rights to Flash Gordon to do a remake. He failed to do so. Instead, he decided to create a little something called "*Star Wars*."

THEN: *I knew immediately that something was wrong with my arm. I was running through the back yard chasing lightning bugs, with Ant and a few other kids from around the block following close behind. I guess because it was getting dark I never saw the hole in the ground. It was little, but just big enough for me to trip and fall when my foot hit it. The other kids were too close to me and, one by one, they fell on top of me. Ant was the first one to try to help me up, but he looked at my right arm and his eyes grew large.*

"Oh, no," he exclaimed, pointing at my arm and scrunching up his face. "I think you broke something, Bax!"

He was right, of course. I stood up and looked at my arm. It was bent at a funny angle and looked like it was longer than it should be. But there was no pain. I didn't feel anything there. Gram and Gramp had been out for a walk on this nice springtime evening and they were sitting on our front porch with Mom and Dad drinking iced tea. I ran around to the front of the house and up onto the porch.

"I think I did something to my arm," I said, almost afraid that I was going to get scolded.

They all looked at me, then at my arm. All the rocking chairs seemed to stop rocking at the same time. Mom and Gram gasped and Gramp fainted. Dad ran into the house to get his car keys, and then he picked me up and ran with me to the car. I really can't even remember the ride, maybe I fainted too, but it seemed that we were at the hospital in a flash. As it turned out, I had really done some damage to my elbow, breaking it in a horrible way.

I was in a big, white room and a nurse or somebody put a rubber thing over my nose. It smelled funny and then I went to sleep and had some very weird dreams. A pin was placed in my elbow. And then my arm was in a cast for the remainder of the summer. The doctors weren't very encouraging…they told Mom and Dad that I might never be able to bend my arm again…but all I got out of it when the cast was removed was a strange, slight bend to my arm and not much strength. But at least I could bend it. Perhaps not in the normal way, but it worked.

NOW: That slight "deformity" (and a note from my doctor about my asthma…it was a mild form but just enough, obviously) kept me out of the military draft when the time came.

"Good," my father sneered when he found out about my 1-Y classification. "They'd have chewed you up and spit you out!"

A man of compassion.

THEN: *It's a struggle, with my right arm in a sling, learning to do things throughout the summer with my left hand. Mom helps me get dressed every morning. Just like a baby. And every Saturday night she gives me a bath. Whenever I'm out playing, if my shoe comes untied Ant ties it for me. He is such a good friend. He feels really bad about falling on top of me, but he couldn't help it.*

Mom's good friend has a big house up on Lake Hopatcong. I was looking forward to going up there again this summer and swim off her big dock. I guess that won't happen. I call her Aunt Sophie, but she's not really my aunt or anything. She taught Ant and me to swim last year and how to paddle a canoe. Ant was disappointed, too.

"No swimming this year for us, I guess," he said as we were sitting in the grass looking for four-leaf clovers.

"You could swim if you want," I told him. "We're going to visit Aunt Sophie on Sunday. Want me to ask if you can come along?"

"Okey-dokey!" he said with a big smile on his face.

Mom and Gram don't know how to drive a car. They said they don't even want to learn. They're scaredy-cats. So Gramp drives all of us up to the lake. Dad stayed home by himself. He doesn't like Aunt Sophie. He doesn't like a lot of people. The sun is shining but it's very windy. We can see a lot of sailboats out on the lake when we park at Aunt Sophie's house and, gee whiz, they are moving so fast! I think Aunt Sophie's husband got killed in that war that Dad fought in and she doesn't have any kids, so she's always so happy to see Ant and me when we come to visit. I think she's really pretty and has bright red hair. Gram says it comes out of a bottle, but I never saw any hair being sold in bottles before.

"Well, slugger, just look at you," she said as she saw my arm in a sling. "Let me give you a great big hug." And she did. "Ant, I swear, looks like you've grown a foot since last summer." He hadn't. He's still shorter than me. "And you're just getting handsomer and handsomer. You'll be a lady-killer in a couple of years!" That one scared me. A lady killer? Ant wouldn't hurt a fly. Well, unless he falls on you. And breaks your arm.

Mom brought her little Brownie camera and she let me take some pictures of everybody. It was a little tricky with my arm in a sling, but I take it down to the dock and take pictures of the sailboats. Ant wants to get in some of the pictures too and he poses like a goofy person, making funny faces. He makes me laugh. I love him like a brother, but I can't ever tell him that. That would be weird.

Gramp and Ant go into the house to change into their bathing suits. Ant comes running out as fast as he can and takes a big jump off the dock. Gramp comes out a couple minutes later and takes his time getting down to the dock. He takes a slow dive off and makes a huge splash. All the ladies laugh at that. I sit on the edge of the dock and just watch as Ant and Gramp swim out to the raft that's far out in the lake. Gram and Mom don't swim either. They never learned. Mom says she's afraid of water and Gram said it's too late to teach old dogs new tricks. I thought dogs already know how to swim without being taught. I watch as the guys swim around a little bit and try to splash each other with water. It makes me sad that I can't be in there with them having fun. After they get back out of the water and dry off, we all have a big picnic lunch on a big wooden table on the lawn. It's still very windy so we have to watch that things don't blow away. After the lunch all the adults sit on big wooden chairs on the lawn and talk. Adults sure can talk a lot. Gramp makes them laugh from time to time. Ant goes back in for a swim and I just sit, again, on the edge of the dock watching him. I want to get in that water so bad!

The sun was setting behind the hills across the lake. A few lights were starting to come on and I can see that the sailboats that are still out there are not moving so fast now. Mom lets me take a few more pictures with her camera. I can hear some music and people laughing off in the distance, across the lake. I know that's Bertrand Island, an amusement park that we'll be going to before the summer finally ends. Mom and Dad usually wait until school almost starts again before we come here. Like it's sort of a prize or something to help make me look forward to going back to school. I don't need a prize. I like school. I walk back up to all the grownups, still talking, still sitting in those chairs, on the lawn. Ant has fallen asleep on a blanket on the grass. We'll be heading for home soon. I can feel that the wind has almost stopped.

"Hey, look, everybody!" I call out. "Can you feel it? The wind is dying down now."

Gram looks at me and smiles. "It'll be back. If the wind goes down with the sun, it will come up with the sun."

Something caught my eye. "Hey, Gram," I said as I pointed up to the sky. "Look!"

She did and then she laughed and laughed, clapping her hands.

"Fledermaus," we both said together. "Fledermaus!"

It was finally Halloween again. My favorite night. Candy, candy and more candy! We waited until after dark before going out. I was dressed in a costume that was supposed to be a tiger; it even had a long tail, although it really just looked like I was wearing yellow pajamas with a couple orange and brown stripes on them. Ant was dressed in a Casper the ghost costume. It was difficult to see and sometimes even breathe in our scratchy masks and we stumbled a few times on the uneven sidewalks as we walked around the neighborhood. We passed a lot of our other friends running and laughing along the way. I wanted Gram and Gramp's house to be one of the last ones on our route. There were just a couple more houses left after theirs. We both carried pillowcases for our loot and they were becoming heavier as they quickly filled up with candy and a couple of apples. Neighbors who knew us would drop in a penny or two along with the candy. The front porch light was on when we reached Gram and Gramp's house but we almost tripped going up the steps to the front porch. Those masks kept slipping. I rang the doorbell and stood back a little bit. The door slowly opened but nobody was there. It was really dark inside the house. Nothing happened. Ant and I looked at each other.

All of a sudden, Gram's head popped out from behind the door and she was wearing the scariest old witch mask I had ever seen.

"GAAARRGH!"

We both jumped and I let out a little scream.

"Gotcha!" she hooted again loudly. She lifted off her mask and laughed with a witch's cackle. "Sorry, boys. Hope I didn't scare you too much. Here you go...and happy Halloween to you both." She dropped a handful of candy bars into each pillowcase and we both got a quarter dropped in there as well. "Have fun, boys. Be careful. Don't fall off those steps. Love you, Baxter," she said as she closed the door behind us. I thought I could hear Gramp laughing in the background.

We were careful going down those steps because our masks kept slipping so we couldn't see very well. And we were still a little scared of that witch mask.

"I have to go home now," Ant said in a hurry. "Your Gram really scared me and I just peed myself back there. See you tomorrow." And he ran off, heading for home. I didn't want to tell him that I had peed a little, too. And let out a fart.

5

NOW: If there was one area where Ant and I were definitively *not* simpatico it was scouting.

THEN: For some reason Ant didn't show any interest in joining the Cub Scouts with me. I thought he would enjoy all the activity, especially since Mom became a Den Mother. But, no. I couldn't persuade him to join. He said that wearing the uniform sort of scared him. Made him think of the military, which really scared him. With a lot of encouragement from Mom, Gram and Gramp, I advanced through the years from the very first badge, the Lion Badge, straight through to almost the highest level, the Arrow of Light. After that, the next step, when I would turn twelve, was becoming a Boy Scout. I was excited and looked forward to it. That's where us big boys went...

NOW...and where some of us big boys learned some things not in any scout manual.

THEN: A new world opened up for me on my tenth birthday. Gram and Gramp gave me a camera. It was a Kodak Signet 35. Wow! Not like that silly little boxy Brownie that my mom has been using for years. And it has a neat little chart kinda thing on the back that tells me about what shutter speeds to use in what kind of light conditions. And it lets me change the aperture for different exposures. Oh, the fun I'm going to have with this! That was the bestest present I had ever gotten.

Aside from all the comic books that Ant and I share, sometimes I look through the old National Geographic *magazines that Gram and Gramp had gotten delivered to their house. Maybe I could become a famous photographer, travel all over the world and see my pictures in this great magazine. Laddie lets me take his pictures out in the back yard. I pretend he's a wild beast and we are in deepest Africa or someplace like that. He doesn't really get in the poses that I'd like for a wild beast. He mostly just lies there, licking himself or scratching. And he sleeps a lot. Anyway, there are a lot of places around that look sort of wild. I walk down the path, through the woods, to our little school. Every once in a while I encounter a hobo or two, but they're nice and friendly. They let me take their pictures as they sit around their campfire and we talk. We talk about life. What it's like for them and what it's like for me. Some of them are pretty smart. One of the older guys, he said his name was Dumpster but I didn't believe him, gave me a good-luck charm. It was an acorn. He pronounced it a-kern. He told me acorns had special powers and could protect your health. "It's true," he said. "They bring you good luck, for sure. And they can protect you from all kinds of illnesses and aches and pains. Witches always carried them as good luck. I'm not kidding, I always carry one or two of them with me and I'm healthy as a horse. Poor as a church mouse, but healthy as a horse," and he laughed.*

I thanked him very much, put the acorn in my pocket and went back home. I put the acorn in a safe place, in a box on my dresser, but I always made sure it was back in my pocket again whenever I went out of the house.

NOW: I later found out that Dumpster's real name was Jake. I'm not really a superstitious guy but, believe it or not, I still have that damn acorn. I'm afraid to get rid of it! But, on the other hand, if acorns bring good luck, why was he still a hobo?

❧

THEN: *I had my twelfth birthday and transitioned from the Cubs into the Boy Scouts. Ant really didn't care for the uniform when he saw me in it. I had to admit, the brown uniform looked very military. I was able to earn several merit badges, but my dad mocked a few of them.*

"A merit badge for reading?" he laughed. "For Christ's sake, you do that every damn day any way. What's the big deal?" I ignored him. And continued reading.

Summer was approaching and, actually, it was Dad who made the suggestion that I go away to camp for two weeks. I wasn't sure if he thought it would be a good experience for me or that it would mean he'd have two weeks with me not being around. I was apprehensive. I had never been away from home before by myself. The place sounded okay, I guess. The camp was located somewhere in the Kittatinny Mountains and, sure, there'd be plenty of activity but could I stand something like that for two whole, long weeks? My heart and mind said "no", but Mom and Dad said "yes"...so off I went.

Gramp drove as Mom and Gram talked all the way there. I sat and silently looked out the window at the passing view as it got more and more country and more and more isolated. We followed the directions to get to the place for registration. The councilors all seemed nice and very friendly. None of my other friends in my troop were going to be here so everyone was a total stranger. A new experience for me all the way around. I was told that I'd be sharing a tent with a kid named Drake Zitron. After signing in, and Mom signing all kinds of insurance waivers and stuff, an older scout showed me to my tent. The two-man tents were set up on wooden platforms and contained two rickety metal cots with squeaking, rusting springs. There were two trunks where we could stow our gear. Aside from my sleeping bag, I carried my duffle bag filled with all the items required, based on the registration information we had read back home weeks ago. Didn't need a shave kit, though. I hadn't started to shave yet although certain parts of my body were beginning to change. Hair was growing in the most unexpected places.

"Here ya go, Janus," said Ebner, the older scout, as we got to my tent. "Get yourself situated and be back at the big main house by 4 o'clock sharp. Orientation starts on time." He gave me the scout's salute as he left.

We all walked around a little bit, looking the place over. I was getting a lump in my throat. I was going to left alone...in this wilderness...with strangers. And, maybe, bears. Gramp was the one to say they better get going. He could sense my apprehension. There were a lot of hugs and kisses. I could see other kids doing the same thing with their parents. Maybe I wouldn't really feel so alone after all. I watched as Mom, Gram and Gramp disappeared through the woods, heading back to his Buick…and the safety of home. And a nice comfortable warm bed. I sighed.

By the time I got back to my tent, another kid was unloading some of his stuff and unrolling his sleeping bag. I assumed this was my tent mate for two weeks. He looked to be about my age, maybe just a little older.

"Hey," he said, extending his hand. "I'm Drake. Drake Zitron."

He was a dark-haired Jewish kid from Hackensack.

"And I'm Baxter Janus, but you can call me Bax."

"Hey, Bax. Okay. Just don't call me Zit. All the other jerkoffs in my troop call me that. A bunch of them are here too."

He seems nice enough, so maybe I'd have a new friend. At least for two weeks. I soon found out that Drake Zitron from Hackensack could be very blunt.

"Oh, and ya know that blond kid, Ebner, who showed you to this tent? He's in my troop. He's a queer and he'll give you a blowjob for a quarter if you're interested."

"What?"

"I said, he'll give…"

"I heard what you said, but I have no idea what that is?"

Drake rolled back and laughed like a crazed person.

He told me what it was and I was fairly certain they don't give out ~~merit~~ badges for that! My education this week was going to head in a very different direction.

NOW: No pun intended.

THEN: *The first week went fairly smoothly. I already knew how to swim, but now I had become an even better swimmer, learning more strokes and developing more stamina. I already knew how to row a boat and paddle a canoe, but now I was kayaking across the lake and beating out others in races. I could now tie twelve different knots with my eyes closed. For what purpose, I'll* *never know. I still gagged every time I went to the latrine, however, and tried to make it a once a day thing. Hey, at least I can pee in the woods. Bears do it.*

The food was okay. Not bad but not real great either. I did like the "bug juice". That's what the kids called the fruity beverage served with the meals. It left some kind of sediment in the bottom of our drinking mugs; I guess that's where that name came from. My homesickness had lasted only the first day or so, and I was now getting accustomed to the ruggedness of the outdoors. Drake and I stuck together most of the times and we shared stories about our lives back home.

For the first part of the second week, the weather was good but extremely hot and humid. It didn't take too much effort to be dripping with sweat by noontime. After waking up to the daily Reveille, I stepped out of our tent on Thursday and the temperature had dropped. It was very comfortable and the humidity seemed to be gone. Drake was sitting on the edge of the tent's platform trying his shoes and he greeted me when I appeared. I took in a nice long breath of that fresh-smelling air.

"Mmm…it feels nice out," I said.

"Then leave it out," he responded and snickered.

It took me a few seconds to catch the meaning. I'll have a lot to tell Ant when I get back home.

NOW: The best (or worst) was yet to come.

THEN: *I didn't know what time it was but it was late. Long after Taps. You know…*Day is done, gone the sun. *Somebody poked his head into our tent and shined a flashlight into our then-sleeping faces.*

"Hey, Zit, come on, it's time. Wanna watch? Or join in? Gotta keep it down. Don't want to bring any of the leaders out here and catch us."

Drake sat up and rubbed his eyes, and then reached over to shake me awake. I was already awake.

"What's going on?" I asked. "Not one of those stupid old snipe hunt things, is it? I went through that crap in Cub Scouts."

"Nah, not that. That's kid stuff, Bax. There's gonna be a circle jerk down by the lake."

"A what?"

He let out a hoot and then filled me in.

"Some naked guys stand around pulling their putzes until somebody shoots their load. Sometimes the first guy who shoots is the winner. Tonight they're gonna see who can hold out the longest."

"Are you serious, or what?? That sounds really queer to me," I said with my mouth agape. "What for?"

"Nah, nothing queer about these guys. Really. Well, except for Ebner maybe. They just like showing off and proving what studs they are."

I pulled on my shorts and sneakers and grabbed our Coleman lantern. I didn't know what the leaders might do if they caught us roaming around after lights out. Following Drake through the woods, I wondered why I was even going to watch such a weird activity. The more I thought about it, the queerer it sounded. In the clearing, close to the lake was a bunch of naked guys prancing around and laughing like a pack of hyenas. Their lanterns cast long shadows up into the surrounding trees. Now, I've seen naked guys before. After all, we showered after our phys ed classes at school. But all these guys had huge raging, bobbing boners. I have never seen another guy with an erection.

NOW: Nor did I ever want to! Granted, most of these guys were a couple years older than I was and certainly far more developed, but I suddenly felt very inadequate and was glad that I was wearing shorts. For that matter, I seriously considered remaining fully clothed for the remainder of the week.

THEN: *Six of them formed a rough circle and passed around a tube of some kind of lubricant. Each of them squeezed a bit of it into their "dominant" hand.*

"Okay," said one the kids, "Let's see who has the best stamina here. The last guy to shoot his jizz is the winner. Once you start pumping your dick, you can't stop until you come. No cheating. Ready? Go!"

I couldn't believe I was actually watching this. Why was I watching this?

NOW: I was not unfamiliar with masturbation at this stage in my life. I just never considered it a team sport.

THEN: "Oh, fuck," said one little guy after about thirty seconds, "I can't hold back." All of a sudden I saw a weak stream of semen drip from his pecker as a few of the spectators laughed.

One by one, a minute or two apart, jets of hot maleness shot out into the center of the circle. The lone holdout, and still pumping away, was Ebner. He stood at least six or seven feet away from me and he looked right into my eyes. Why? What was he thinking? Suddenly there was a very slight buckle to his knees and he inhaled deeply through his teeth, squinting his eyes.

"Okay, guys, I can't hold on any longer. Fuck it. I'm coming...I'm coming....I'm...!"

Still pumping, he let loose. Accompanied by a low groan of ecstasy, his first squirt, followed very quickly by his second, arched up across the circle heading in my direction, actually landing on my leg. I felt his hot, sticky semen run down my calf and I let out a yell. Everybody else, including Drake, laughed and applauded.

"Fucking hell!" yelled one of the other guys, "that was some shot! Never saw anything go that far before!"

By that time I was down at the lake trying to wash off that stuff. For the remainder of the week I would make sure to keep my distance from Ebner. I also decided to drop out of Boy Scouts.

NOW: To this day, I have never mentioned that incident to anyone. Not even Ant. But by the time I got back home from camp, my repertoire of dirty jokes had increased by 200% and I caught myself swearing like a drunken sailor. Mom nearly fainted and Dad laughed until he choked when I uttered my first "fuck".

6

THEN: I dealt and passed. I wondered how many other 15-year-old kids play bridge. Gram and Gramp taught Mom and me how to play last year and just about every Sunday afternoon we play. Mom also passed. Gram, my partner bid one club. Could be a short club but she was telling me she had opening points. Gramp passed. Bid your longest and strongest suit. I looked at my hand again and made a choice.

"One spade?" I answered, almost a question. This is a fabulous game. It teaches strategy and concentration. Oh, and patience. Sometimes a lot of patience. Gram studied her hand again and I could tell she was concentrating. I, too, was concentrating. She hadn't opened with a bid of no trump, so she didn't have the point count for that. She was asking for a long suit and perhaps I had hit it right off. She knew I didn't have thirteen points, otherwise I would have opened. She looked up at me and smiled.

"Four spades," she responded. I nearly wet myself! The look on my face made Gram laugh. "You'll make it," she said confidently. I wasn't so sure.

Mom led with a meek two of diamonds. As the dummy, Gram then laid down her hand for all of us to see. She had five of my spades, Ace, Jack high. I, also, held five spades, King, Queen high. That meant that only three spades were out against us. I pulled a ten of diamonds from dummy to cover Mom's two. Gramp proudly laid down an Ace, which I, just as proudly, took with a two of spades. I had a void in diamonds.

"Well, shit!" Gramp exclaimed and we all laughed.

I went on to win that hand and win that game, but Gramp and Mom actually won with the highest score by the end of the afternoon. After downing the dregs in our glasses of ginger ale and hugs all around, we got ready to head for home.

"Next week, Mom, you and I will be partners and beat the old folks, okay?" I said as we walked along the sidewalk.

"Brave soul, Bax, brave soul. Sure, sure…whatever you say."

Ant met us halfway home. He was going to see if he could get more vegetables from Gramp's garden but he was too late.

"I'll go back and get some for you, Anthony," Mom said. "I should have gotten some for us as well. You go on home and I'll stop by to drop some off with your mother. I just know that Bax is craving some nice fresh beets for supper tonight." I could hear her chuckle as she headed back to her parents' house. I can't stand beets and she knows it. I made a horrible face and stuck out my tongue, pretending to gag.

"Three…two…one…go!" shouted Ant. We both laughed and started racing each other back home.

NOW: Ant and I were always trying to race each other wherever we went. He was still shorter than me but, man, he seemed to be getting faster and faster. Eventually, he joined the Track and Field team in high school and won event after event. He earned his letter in Cross-Country. I lettered in nothing. I was in the Photography Club.

At about that same time Ant discovered that he enjoyed cooking. His mother was a fabulous cook and started teaching him everything she had learned from *her* mother. All the fresh vegetables from Gramp's garden ended up in one great Italian concoction after the other. That's when I discovered that I actually like eggplant, especially a la Parmesan. Ant and his mom worked wonders in the kitchen. I spent more dinnertimes at his place than my own. Although I never, ever would have told her but my Mom was a mediocre cook. Blah and bland. Her spice rack consisted of salt, pepper, sugar and cinnamon. Period. Ant's girlfriend at the time, Sandy something or other, spent a lot of time with all of us at dinnertime as well. I was honing my photography skills photographing food…lots of it… and smiling, laughing faces with various sauces smeared around our lips.

THEN: It was two weeks before our high school senior prom, with graduation one month beyond that. Ant and I were sitting on my front porch steps talking about our proposed trip down the shore afterwards. I'd be taking my date, Donna Blakely. Ant and his girlfriend, Sandy Aletta, had been dating for several months and I hadn't seen much of him for quite a while. We were playing catch-up. There was something different about him this evening and I couldn't quite put my finger on it. I stared at him for a few minutes, hoping that he wouldn't notice.

He did.

"What?" he asked, throwing up his hands, "What?"

I shook my head. "Not sure," I responded. "You seem to be acting a bit weird or something tonight. You have a shit-eating grin on your face. What happened?"

He leaned forward, resting his elbows on his knees and looked down to the ground. When his head came up, he turned to me with the largest smile I had ever seen him give.

"Keep a secret?" he asked.

"Well, yeah. I'm good."

He looked down again.

"Sandy and I went all the way last night!"

"What? No way. I thought she was such a goody-goody. You always said she never went past the heavy kissing stage. Maybe a little fondling or something."

"Yeah, well…let me tell you, pal, she bangs like a bunny! Please don't let on that I spilled the beans, okay?"

"Yeah, yeah, no problem there. How and when did this happen? Details. But they stay with me, I promise."

Ant hesitated a moment, and then took a deep breath.

"As I said, it was last night. After dinner. We were taking a leisurely walk through the cemetery over there," he said, pointing to just beyond his own house. *"It was a nice night. The sun had gone down but there was still light in the sky. The stars were coming out and, all of a sudden, she just leaned in and kissed me. Kissed me hard. And I mean hard. And, damn, I got hard…fast. There was this big, flat grave marker and we just sorta fell down on it and started fumbling with each other. We never thought that anybody would be coming into the cemetery so late in the evening so…"*

"So….yeah, then what, damn it?" I asked.

"This is crazy. This is so fucking crazy. Before we knew what was happening we were both naked as jaybirds. Clothes all over the ground. Shit, Bax, I've never seen a real pussy in person, only in my Pop's girly magazines. She grabbed my dick like it was a…I don't know what it was like…but I thought I was going to explode. Next thing I knew we were screwing big time."

I just stared at him, my mouth agape.

"In the fucking cemetery?" was all I could say. *"Well, that sure as hell takes on a whole new meaning now, doesn't it?"*

We both laughed until we cried. Neither one of us said anything for a minute or two.

"And on top of an old grave marker?"

"Yeah," Ant sighed. *"I think I'll remember Franklin L. Lyman, 1892 – 1937 for the rest of my life."*

So, my best buddy went all the way. Gee whiz, I've barely made it half way to second base with any girl I've dated. Barely. Last night Ant broke new ground, hitting a home run, and Donna and I had gone to the movies.

"Whadya gonna see?" Mom asked as I was getting ready to go and she was finishing washing the dinner dishes.

"Oh, some silly dumb thing that's playing down at the Baker. Donna has been dying to see it. 'Pillow Talk' with Doris Day and Rock Hudson."

"Oooooh," cooed Mom, *"Rock Hudson. He's sooo dreamy. Now there's a real man's man."*

NOW: Oh, Lordy, if she only knew then what we know now.

7

When I received my acceptance letter from The New York Institute of Photography I was ecstatic. Mom hugged me so hard I thought my eyes would pop out. My daily commute into the city every day would be on the Lakeland Bus Line and would take a little over an hour, straight down Route 46. I was so looking forward to it. I loved going into Manhattan and had taken countless trips there to photograph the buildings and various neighborhoods. I envisioned a whole new world opening up for me.

NOW: And a whole new future opened up for me on that commute as well. I met the love of my life and my wife-to-be. Aberdeen Smith, the most beautiful girl I had ever seen, got on the bus at the Parsippany stop one morning two months after I had started school.

THEN: *During the summer following high school graduation and on weekends after starting photography school, I worked at To Die For Booksellers, just off of Blackwell Street in downtown Dover. They specialized in mysteries and thrillers. I started off as a stock boy and soon became a sales clerk. Actually, I had a lot of downtime while working there, so I was able to read a lot. So now my role model went from Flash Gordon to Lew Archer. I was hooked!*

Ant's uncle Salvatore, Sallie to all of his friends, owned a popular Italian restaurant, Sallie's Bella Luna Trattoria, just down the street from the bookstore. When he learned that Ant was becoming a terrific cook, he hired him. For some reason, after Ant started working there, business picked up. Mainly from young, giggly girls. They came in to flirt with this new guy who was just so damn good-looking. Of course, the food was great as well. True, Ant got a little cocky at times. He worked out with weights on occasion and loved to wear tight white T-shirts to show off his muscles. I teased him about it and he brushed it off, laughing. He had hopes of opening his own restaurant in the future, perhaps buying out Sallie when he got too old. And that's where he met the love of his life, soon to be fiancée, Valerie Panatone. Damn, she was gorgeous! They would certainly make beautiful babies together.

But another uncle, Uncle Sam, had other plans for Ant however. Not too long after starting at the restaurant, Ant was drafted.

NOW: Cliché, I know, but an inescapable fact of life: Reality can sneak in and bite your dreams right on the ass.

THEN: *I slowly came to observe, on my ride into NYC every morning, all of us "regular" passengers would sit in the exact same seat every day. It was a ritual, claiming a particular spot. If an interloper would happen to be in our "own" seat, our entire day would be thrown off kilter. I preferred sitting in the far back of the bus, so people getting on or off wouldn't be a distraction. Being that where I got on was early in the run, there were very few people where I sat. By the time we pulled into the Port Authority Terminal, however, the bus was standing room only. The commute, into and back out of the city, was a great way to breeze through book after book.*

The weather had changed and Thanksgiving was fast approaching. I happened to glance up from my book in time to see a very beautiful young woman get on the bus at the stop in Parsippany. Classy town, to say the least. Even though I hadn't seen her before, I assumed by the way she acknowledged a few of the regular riders that she must also be a regular on this particular ride every morning. I should have gotten my nose out of those books sooner. I watched her walk up the aisle and give a silent evil-eye stare at a person sitting in what was obviously "her" seat. She shrugged and moved on, coming to the back. There were two empty seats near me. One next to me, the other on the opposite side of the aisle. She didn't select the one next to me. Damn! I put my head down and continued reading The Wycherly Woman, *the latest Lew Archer mystery. I nonchalantly sneaked a look across the aisle, hoping that she wouldn't notice, and saw that she had pulled* The Doomsters *from her purse. Hot damn! I took another sly peek only to discover that she was peeking at me at the same time. We both shrugged and smiled. Was this flirting? And on whose part? I sighed.*

She stood up and carefully slid across the aisle to sit next to me. "Seems as though we share an interest in murder and mayhem," she laughed.

"Excellent reading material, for sure," I responded, nodding at her book. "I think by now one of us or both of us should certainly know how to commit the perfect crime."

"I won't tell if you won't," she coyly answered. Oh, be still my heart!

"I really enjoyed that one that you're reading now," I lied. I actually found it rather boring.

"Oh, really?" she responded with a slight wrinkling of her nose. "Perhaps it will pick up as it goes along because, at this point, I'm finding it rather boring."

Oops! Too late to backpedal.

"I haven't seen you on this bus before," I decided to try a different approach, "Are you just going into the city for the day?"

"Oh, no, I've been riding this bus for three years now."

Well, shit, how could I have not noticed her a couple months ago?

She chuckled. "I've seen you back there…well, back here now, but you've always been so engrossed in whatever book you were reading. You never looked up. Not even once. Until today."

"Obviously I've missed out," was my flirtatious response. "Do you work in the city or what?"

"I'm a student. I'm studying marketing at NYU. My father's an account exec at Doyle Dane. I hope to get a job there, too."

I must have had a puzzled look on my face. "Doyle Dane?"

She nodded. "Doyle Dane Bernbach. An ad agency. You know, Madison Avenue."

"Oh, nice," I said rather sheepishly, shrugging my shoulders. "I haven't heard about them."

"Oh, but I'm sure you'd recognize their work. They just did that "Think Small" campaign for Volkswagon. You've seen that all over the place, right?"

"Oh, shit…I mean, oh, hell…damn…I'm sorry, yes I have!" I stammered like a freaking idiot! "I love that campaign. It is so unique and not like all the other advertising shit…crap…damn, stuff. You know what I mean."

By this time she was laughing hysterically.

Shifting gears again I hastily asked, "Well, then, what year are you in? I'm a freshman this year. Just started a couple months ago. I'm studying photography."

"I'm a junior, " she answered.

NOW: A couple years older than me. At that time, the word "cougar" was still just referring to a large cat.

THEN: *I opened up my large camera case and took out several of the shots that I had recently taken. I had them in a small portfolio and I let her flip through the pages. All black and white shots. Several portraits, a few cityscapes, and some still lifes of fruits and vegetables. I thought she looked impressed.*

"My name is Baxter, by the way," I said as I outstretched my hand. "Baxter Janus. But you can call me Bax."

She turned to me with a huge smile and took my hand. Firm grip. "Aberdeen," she said, "Aberdeen Smith. But you can call me Abbie."

"Aberdeen. That's an unusual name, for sure."

"Well," she laughed, "with a last name of Smith I guess my parents figured they better try something a bit out of the ordinary. Actually, my maternal grandmother was from Aberdeen, Scotland, so it's not such a drastic stretch."

She turned back to my portfolio and switched back and forth between a couple of the pages.

"Who are these characters?" she asked, raising her eyebrows.

"Ha! Those guys are a couple of hobos who sometimes camp a short distance from our house. A few of them come through our area every once in a while and I enjoy chatting with them. During the summer months I bring them fresh veggies from my grandfather's garden."

"God, aren't you afraid of them? They look so ominous."

"Nah, they're harmless. I guess so, anyway. I think one of them might have saved me from a tough situation when I was a kid. Don't you have any such guys around where you live?"

"In Parsippany? Don't be funny, Baxter!"

We hadn't realized it, but the bus was emptying out at the Port Authority. We said our good-byes and hoped we'd see each other again in the morning. The ride back to Dover every day was at different times, depending upon my classes, so there were never the same passengers vying for their "designated" seats. Evidently my classes and Abbie's never matched up, time-wise, so we both rode home alone…alone with dozens of other passengers and Lew Archer, that is.

NOW: I had grown, at that point in my life, from a naïve, optimistic kid into a young man, still optimistic, but with convictions and opinions---lots of them---which irritated the hell out of my father for one reason or another. It seemed that every thought that I might have on any subject, he would negate it outright, just on general principles. The nightly news was filled with protests, violent or otherwise, The Civil Rights Movement (I was for it, Dad opposed it); the anti-Vietnam War Movement (I was a Dove, Dad was a Hawk); The Gay Rights Movement…(well, we were at an impasse here. Neither one of us knew too much about it). I was ambivalent and bounced back and forth, pro/con, regarding the Students for a Democratic Society, but the days where I was pro, Dad was con and vice versa. It was almost like a game for him, trying to see how soon he could piss me off every night at dinnertime. Mom never took sides in our disagreements. She remained mostly silent during these sometimes-heated arguments. Maybe she had no opinions at all. Maybe she had learned that arguing with her husband was futile.

8

THEN: *Classes were going better than I had even expected and I had very high expectations to begin with. By the Christmas break I was in the school's darkroom developing film. It was still just black and white and 35mm, but it opened up my creativity and my imagination. I converted a musty old room up in our musty old attic to a sort of studio. I set up some cheap floodlights and bought a couple rolls of seamless backdrop paper, one black, one white. I was ready to try my hand at some professional-looking portraits. Ant and his girlfriend, Val, were my first subjects. We tried all kinds of angles and lighting situations. He would be going into the army soon and they both wanted pictures to carry with them while he was away. I hadn't worked up the courage yet to invite Abbie here, but I was very eager to get her in front of my lens. Even Mom and Dad were willing to let me shoot them. Dad, as usual, seemed uncomfortable and fidgeted a lot. I really wanted Gram and Gramp to climb up the long, narrow staircase to my little studio. I was proud of it and wanted to capture their wonderful faces on film.*

They finally agreed. I had been so busy growing up that I hadn't noticed that, at the same time, they were growing older. Gram was winded by the time she got to the top of the stairs and had to sit to catch her breath. Gramp was a few steps behind her, red-faced, but not huffing or puffing. Ant came running up the stairs following them. They had gotten to our house just before

43

a cloudburst sent torrents of rain slamming on to the roof. Here in the attic we could hear it hit like hundreds of marbles. A ray of brilliant sunshine suddenly shot through one of the windows on the far side of the room.

"What the hell?" I blurted, turning to look at it. "It's pouring rain and yet the sun is shining."

"Aw, it's just a clear-up shower," Gramp said matter-of-factly.

"Really?" Ant asked.

"Yeah, clear up to your neck," Gramp said, with a hearty laugh. I just shook my head. I had heard that line…often…when I was a kid and I had set him up.

"Mr. Freemont," Ant said with his hands on his hips, "what are we going to do with you?"

Gramp shrugged, throwing up his hands, "What? What?"

I worked with my grandparents for over an hour, shot after shot, individually and as a loving couple. I used both of my backdrops, achieving different effects with each. I swelled with pride as I looked at each shot through the viewfinder. Beautiful. Elegant. Regal. A retired lawyer and his wonderful, loving wife of decades. I could hardly wait to process the film and make several prints. When we finished, Ant helped Gram down the steps and I made sure Gramp was able to manage without losing his balance and falling on top of them. They hugged my Mom, ignored my Dad, and headed for home. The rain had stopped. Ant came running back up stairs.

"Can I watch?" he asked.

"Sure. Come on down," I answered as we headed down three flights of stairs.

I certainly took advantage of my newfound knowledge and the size of our house. Our cavernous basement had just the right space for my private darkroom, complete with running water. Mom and Dad surprised me at Christmas with an enlarger and several other darkroom necessities. I was ready! I made a large sign that I hung on the basement door. DARKROOM IN USE. PLEASE DO NOT ENTER. I really didn't have to worry. I used the darkroom only after dark (there were tiny windows down there, which I blacked out anyway) and my Mom did the laundry only during the daylight hours.

We were in the basement and my red safelight was on, casting a warm glow. I had to get the film into its developing tank in total darkness, but that was for a quick moment or two and then I switched the safelight on again.

"Can I talk while you do this?" Ant asked, "or will that distract you?"

"No, no, you can talk. I'm very used to your chatter by now, my friend."

"Okay, good. You know I head out for basic training in a couple weeks. You've probably observed that Val and I have gotten very serious. We're holding off for now but we're gonna get hitched when I get out of the service. This shouldn't come as any surprise, but I want you to be my best man."

"I was wondering when you were going to get around to asking me. If you hadn't, I would have kicked you right in your nuts, you big oaf."

We both laughed. It was a nervous laugh. The timer for the film would be going off in two minutes.

NOW: To this day I still can remember the deathly silence that hung in the air at that moment.

THEN: *We both jumped when the timer went off.*

"This isn't the same as you going off to Boy Scout camp, you know. I'm scared, Bax. Really scared," he said, almost as a raspy whisper.

"Me, too, Ant. Me, too," I whispered back.

Ant stayed with me in the darkroom for another hour or so. I dried the negatives and he watched as I started to make some prints. No more words were spoken but I knew what was going on in his mind. He squeezed me tightly on the shoulder, uttered a barely audible goodnight and left to go back home. I suddenly felt empty.

A few days later I had made several 8 X 10 prints of Gram and Gramp. Damn, they were great portraits. All ego aside, I had done a fabulous job. They sure as hell looked like professional shots. I called to make sure they were home and then went running around the block to their house. When I went in I heard very soft opera music being played. Not a radio this time, but on their stereo. They were both sitting in their private seats at the Met and they were holding hands.

"I just couldn't wait to show you these shots. You both look so great! You made my work so easy with these portraits. Prizewinners, if I say so myself," and I laughed.

I handed them the stack of the prints and waited for their reaction.

It wasn't the reaction I was expecting.

Their faces dropped. Gramp almost frowned.
"But we look so old," was his only response.

I was devastated. That's when I first realized that mirrors may lie, but photographs do not.

NOW: But then, that was several decades before Photoshop.

9

THEN: *Efrem Goldschmitt was a well-known commercial photographer within the NYC Madison Avenue crowd. He also taught at the school. He gave us assignments and a deadline. Then a week or two later, we would all meet for a critique. After viewing my latest work, he thought for a moment and asked me to come out into the hall, away from the other students.*

"I didn't want the others to hear. I don't like to make anyone nervous or anxious, yes?" he said with a thick accent. He was in his late 40s, short, perhaps five-five or six, muscular and sported a graying handlebar moustache on his weathered face. His voice was so smooth you could spread it like soft butter on toast. When he'd first introduced himself to the class, I had assumed the accent was German. We then learned that he was Russian. But he spoke French and Italian aside from English, German and Russian so his accent was a conglomeration. "I've been paying special attention to your work…Baxter, is it? Yes. I see something here that I haven't seen in the other students this year. Don't let this go to your young head, but I'm impressed. Here is my card. Can you stop by my studio, say, after class tomorrow? I'd like to talk to you about being one of my assistants. You can learn a lot from actually working in a real studio. If you have some more work, a portfolio, say, bring it along too, yes?"

My mouth hung open in disbelief. "Ahh, yeah, sure, Mr. Goldschmitt. That would be fantastic. I get out tomorrow around 2:30 and…" I glanced at the address on his card, "oh, that's just a bit uptown and I could be there at 3 or 3:15 at the latest."

"I'll be there," he responded. "I'll be in the middle of a shoot but that's okay, yes? I can take a break and we can talk a little."

I didn't really need to take the bus back home that afternoon---I floated all the way.

I could hardly wait for Abbie to get on the bus in the morning. She could tell something was afoot as she approached my seat. It must have been that shit-eating grin on my face. I told her what was going on.

"Oh, he's great," she said, practically clapping her hands. "Doyle Dane uses him a lot. I've never met him but my father speaks very highly of him. Well, well, well…good luck!" And she pecked me on my cheek. Heaven. I was in Heaven.

The school was on Lexington Avenue and East 32nd Street and Goldschmitt's studio was on East 45th Street. A brisk, but easy walk. The studio was on the 4th floor and the elevator opened directly into his waiting area. There were huge blowups on all the walls. Gorgeous models, expansive landscapes, food of all kind. Color, black and white, duotones. Several sleek, prestigious, and very coveted CLIO awards stood, side-by-side, on a credenza, flanked by half a dozen Art Director's Club of New York medallions. I gaped. I could hear all kinds of activity toward the back of the studio, through other doors, which I figured led to where all the photography actually occurred. A shoot was in progress. There were voices, perhaps a laugh or two then the flash of a strobe and silence. Then more chatter.

"Hello?" I called out. "Mr. Goldschmitt?"

An attractive young woman came running toward me from the back. She was wearing faded bellbottom jeans, barefoot, a beaded headband kept her long, flowing blonde hair in place and a fringed vest…open…nothing else under it.

"I'm so sorry I didn't hear the elevator ding. We were having too much fun, I guess. You're Baxter, right? Efrem told us you'd be stopping by this afternoon. He'll be right out with you. Make yourself comfortable." And she pointed to the huge turquoise beanbag sofa next to a round glass-top table with a stack of fashion magazines. I sat down, making a squeaking sound on the slick surface. Off to the side of the sofa, slightly behind me, was a door that must have led to his office.

Five minutes later Efrem came sauntering out of the studio area, still laughing at something that must have been spoken a few moments before. He extended his hand. I stood up.

"Mr. Janus, welcome to paradise," and he laughed again. "Sit, sit. Let's talk. And then I shall show you around."

We sat side by side. He asked a few questions about my interest in photography, what I hoped to achieve and how long had I been taking photos, not just snapshots, but real, artistic shots. We chatted for five minutes or so, and then I extended my portfolio to him. It was a large leather case with a zipper closing. He unzipped it and started leafing through the pages. He stopped at the second or third page in and studied it, cocking his head to one side. There were three 5"X7" black and white prints on that particular page. I had printed them on matte stock as opposed to glossy. I thought it helped reflect the subject matter better.

"Oh, such sad, wonderful faces. They look so rugged. Who are they?"

"Those are some hobos who come through the area near our home from time to time."

"Hobos?" he asked, looking confused. "What are they? Like hippies?"

I chuckled. "No, they're not hippies, they're…"

"Liar!" screeched a raspy voice from his office. No reaction from Goldschmitt.

Pausing for a stunned moment, I looked at him but continued on. "Maybe you don't know that term, but hobos are, ummm, unemployed, homeless guys who ride the rails from town to …"

"Liar!" came the screech again. "Liar!"

Goldschmitt leaned forward, his right elbow leaning on his knee and put his hand to his mouth, stifling a laugh. With his finger he motioned for me to get up and follow him. We went into his office. Sitting on a perch in the far corner was a huge, colorful parrot. The bird scratched his beak with one of his claws and called out again. "Liar!…Liar!"

"Baxter, meet my rude friend Zoom," said Goldschmitt.

"Pants on fire," said the bird.

Gramp loved Buicks. He would never consider driving anything else, and bought a new one every three years without fail. When I got my drivers license, to keep it legal (he was a lawyer, after all), he sold me his soon-to-be-replaced

car for one dollar. He always kept his cars in exceptional condition. Needless to say, a Buick isn't the ideal car for a young guy but what the hell, the price was right. Perhaps it would impress the father of the girl I was now dating. Our morning bus rides into the city had progressed to meeting for lunches at times, chatting at length about my new part-time job with Efrem Goldschmitt, and perhaps catching an early dinner at Schrafft's before heading back out to New Jersey. Abbie was fun to be with, no matter the locale or situation. She had suggested that I come out to meet her parents before we headed off to the theater for a show. I had heard about the Papermill Playhouse in nearby Milburn but had never been there.

"The Threepenny Opera *is playing there," Abbie told me, "and I'm dying to see it. I read that Gypsy Rose Lee was supposed to be in it, but she's not. I wonder why?"*

I had heard about Gypsy Rose Lee from my father. He had seen her at someplace called Minsky's and that she was a stripper. Interesting. Is this going to be an opera where everybody takes his or her clothes off?

I tried to follow the directions that Abbie gave to me regarding getting to her house. The streets were unfamiliar to me being that I had never been to this area before. Parsippany-Troy Hills, the full name of the township, was very upscale and very confusing to me.

NOW: A little local trivia. Parsippany-Troy Hills has consistently appeared, for years, in *Money Magazine's* annual list as one of the top places to live in the United States.

THEN: *Yay, I finally found it! There were cars, fancy expensive cars, parked out front along the street and in her driveway. I located a place to park my Buick a few houses away and walked up their long, slopping driveway. Abbie must have been watching for me because she opened the door as soon as I got to the top step on their porch.*

"Somebody must be having a party!" I exclaimed as I swept my arm out indicating all the cars. Abbie laughed.

"My parents are great hosts. They love to entertain. This happens just about every week. This is just a small group of their closest friends tonight. Come on in and I'll introduce you."

I stepped into their expansive foyer and my ears immediately filled with the cacophony of adults having a good time. I looked into their large living room to the left of the foyer and saw a sea of people, each with a drink of some sort in his or her hand. Most of them were casually dressed, a few of the men wore sports jackets and all of the women were adorned with various strands of jewelry. One pale, blond guy in very animated conversation stood out for some particular reason.

I leaned into Abbie so she could hear me above all the chatter and laughter. "That guy over there," I nodded in his direction, "is sure doing a mean impression of Andy Warhol, isn't he?" I chuckled and she smiled.

She, in turn, leaned into me. "That is Andy Warhol," she calmly responded.

"Daddy, Daddy!" Abbie called out to a good-looking gentleman headed out to the back of the house, possibly to where the bar might be. He stopped and turned around, giving his daughter a huge smile. We caught up to him.

"Daddy, this is Baxter Janus, Bax, this is my father, Russell Smith."

He was holding a drink glass in his right hand and he switched it to his left so he could shake my hand. His hand was wet from the sweat on his glass but his grip was firm. Very firm.

"Very nice to meet you, Baxter," he said with a mellow voice and a warm smile. "Aberdeen speaks very highly of you. Cliché, isn't it?" and he laughed. "Time will tell."

I nodded and smiled, not knowing if he was teasing me or testing me.

A short, attractive woman came up behind Russell Smith, tapped him on the back and handed him an empty martini glass. "I need a refill. Oh, hello, dear," she said to Abbie, as she peered from behind her husband.

"Mother, this is Baxter Janus. Bax, this is my mother, Beatrice Smith."

"My, you are a tall one, aren't you," cooed Beatrice Smith, looking up into my face. She stood perhaps a couple inches over five feet. I was six-two.

Mr. Smith came up behind his wife and handed her a refreshed martini, two olives, and smiled at us both.

"You'd better run along, kids. Don't want to miss the opening number. It's a great show. We saw it last night."

We said our goodbyes, hurried out to the car and drove away. Abbie knew a short cut to take to get to the theater faster. We slid into our seats just as the house lights were dimming.

It was, indeed, a great show. I liked it a lot and I could tell that Abbie equally enjoyed it. We stopped at one of those all-night silver diners for a couple of burgers and conversation on the way home. By the time we got back to her house, there were just a couple remaining cars out front. I slowed the car to a stop, parked at the foot of their driveway and turned off the engine. She slid closer to me.

"Let's just stay out here," she said, looking into my eyes. "It's a nice night, isn't it?"

The Buick has a nice roomy front seat. Perfect for a couple of kids to get romantic. I was thinking baseball. She and I had already gotten to first base. I had never gotten all the way to second base with any girl I had dated before, but there was definitely a chance here tonight. I could tell. The car windows began to steam up and for good reason. My erection was pressing so hard against my pants that I thought they might tear open. As we kissed I carefully, slowly, cautiously put my hand on her left breast. Almost at the same time I felt her fingers brush against my pants. My pecker throbbed like crazy. Holy shit, made it to second base! If she dared to touch me there again I'd surely come in my pants. I'll be brazen, I thought. At this point what could it hurt? I started to unbutton her blouse. We heard a car door slam, then another and an engine starting up. A car backed down out of their driveway and turned in our direction. The driver flashed his lights and honked the horn as they drove past us. We had been spotted. Through the steamy car windows I saw Russell Smith standing at his open front door, looking down toward our car. Don't come down…don't come down! He didn't. He went back inside and closed the door. I decided, then, to see if there was any chance of sliding into third base. Abbie smiled and backed away.

"That's all for tonight," she laughed. "A good beginning, Bax, a great beginning."

"What?!" I was frustrated as hell. "You are a tease, Aberdeen Smith, a big tease!"

"See you on the bus Monday." She kissed me firmly, got out, slamming the door behind her, and ran up to her house.

I drove back home with the tune of Mack the Knife *rattling around in my head and with Pete the Pecker throbbing in my pants.*

10

THEN: *The day came for Ant to take that bus ride to Fort Dix for basic training. Depending upon his particular abilities, he may be headed to Vietnam in eight weeks, perhaps later if he received advanced training. It was cold and rainy but we all stood under the shelter at the bus depot. There were a few other recruits waiting there as well, a few of the guys I recognized from high school. We all nodded sadly at one another. I brought Abbie along with me and introduced her to my best friend and his fiancée. We stood back and watched as Valerie squeezed the life out of Ant, not wanting to let go. She was sobbing, my eyes were getting extremely moist and Ant was stoic. Abbie held my hand tightly. She had heard me tell of so many wonderful adventures with the young man who would soon be departing.*

"Hey, hey," Ant said, trying to calm his fiancée, "I'm only going to be a mere 85 miles away. An hour and a half."

"Bullshit!" she responded, as only a Jerseyite could. "And then what? Another ten thousand miles away in Viet- fuckin'- nam?"

She was gorgeous, but she did have a certain way with words.

"Well, after I graduate from basic training I'll get a short leave. Then we'll see what happens next."

We all knew what would happen next. The war was raging out of control with no end in sight. A frightening chapter was about to begin for Ant. And a long, wonderful chapter for me was about to come to an end. Where was

Johnny Mercer when we needed him? Ac-Cent-Tchu-Ate the Positive, my ass! Maybe I'd see him again after basic training, more than likely I wouldn't. I just felt that the last time I would see Ant before he was deployed would be the very last time that I would ever see Ant. Perhaps that day was today.

It was mid-February and I was hoping that there might be an early spring, but Mother Nature had other ideas. I had no classes today, but I had helped Efrem with a long shoot at the studio. Starting around 10 A.M., we finally wrapped things up at 4. We were exhausted and Efrem said for me to lock up when I finished with the few remaining cleaning up chores that I had. He was heading home. His apartment was way uptown somewhere on the west side. He left to get to the subway and face the rush hour crowds. When I got outside, I nearly fell on my ass. It was dark, it was sleeting, and the sidewalks were slick. Traffic was crawling and car horns were honking. I decided not to fight the chaos in the subway so I was going to hoof it. It took me forever to carefully walk my way to the Port Authority Bus Terminal. The place was mobbed and I could barely get into the door. What the hell?

"Busses aren't running," a guy in front of me turned to say. "The Lincoln Tunnel is closed. The ramp on the other side is a sheet of ice. I just heard somebody else say the George Washington Bridge is closed too. Not even sure about the trains. This is going to be a long night."

I thought about my plight for a moment, and then realized that I could go back to the studio and spend the night. So I turned around and bucked the incoming throngs through the doors and made it back out to the wet, slippery streets. I managed to slowly, carefully cross 8th Avenue again without landing on the pavement and worked my way up 41st Street heading back to the studio. I glanced across the street and just happened to see Abbie struggling on her way to the terminal.

"Hey, Abbie!" I called loudly, hoping she'd hear above all the traffic noise and confusion. She turned to look behind her. "Abbie! Over here!" And I wildly waved my hand. She saw me and tried to inch her way between the taxis that were moving nowhere. All of a sudden she disappeared and I saw some books fly into the air. She had slipped and fallen, unfortunately into a

mushy mess of slush and water. I ran over as quickly as I could, got to her, helped her up and collected her things that had scattered. I explained the dire situation and took her hand. "Are you okay? Didn't break anything did you? Come on back to the studio with me. Obviously we're not getting out of the city tonight. You can call your parents from there so they won't worry and I'll call mine as well. There's a shower in the dressing room there, so you can clean up if you want. Let's go." And off we went, still bucking the human traffic that was heading toward the bus terminal. We stopped off at a Chock Full O'Nuts lunch counter to pick up a couple very thin sandwiches, a cup of their famous, and my favorite, green pea soup, and some hot coffee. We made it back to the studio without further incident.

The elevator door opened and there was a small red lava lamp burning on a credenza casting a warm glow. I had forgotten to turn it off before I left a bit earlier. Everything else was pitch black. I switched on a few small lights and ushered her into the waiting room area. She looked around at all the photos on the wall. Hmm, *I thought,* this could be a very pleasant, fortuitous situation, indeed. *We took off our coats, hung them up and she sat on the squeaky vinyl beanbag sofa. It looked comfortable…and enticing. I switched on the stereo, flipped through some records in Efrem's collection and selected* Nice 'n' Easy *by Frank Sinatra. We opened the bags with our sandwiches and each of us took a long sip of our coffees.*

"Did you want to take a shower or something to get that city grime off of you?" I asked.

"No, not yet. I'm good. I'll call my parents in a while. After we…eat," she said coyly. I was wondering if she might be thinking the same thing I was. We could turn an annoying inconvenience into something memorable.

If I play my cards right, this could be a very enlightening event for me, for sure. Thank you, Mother Nature. By this time in our relationship we had made it to third base. I was hoping for a home run. Something tells me tonight is *the night. We chat a little, telling each other about our day's activities, as we finish our sandwiches.*

"Kinda romantic here, isn't it?" I ask. "Wanna dance?" We put our empty sandwich bags aside and stood up. I took her into my arms and drew her closer to me. Her hair smelled so good. So clean and fresh, despite the small bits of

street residue from her tumble. We kissed. I was wondering if she could feel my erection as I pressed into her.

"I've never spent the night with a beautiful woman before," I said softly, trying to be suave, sexy and innocent all at the same time.

"Liar!" screeched a raspy voice from behind the closed door to Efrem's office.

I was awakened the next morning by the ding of the elevator arriving. I had found a blanket in one of the studio's prop rooms the night before and I pulled it up around me. I was alone on the beanbag sofa.

"Well, well, what a surprise, Mr. Janus," said Efrem with a warm smile. "I'm glad to see that you're safe and sound. I heard on the television about the mess last night and was afraid for your safety. Evidently you must have spent the night here. Good for you. I have already cancelled the shoots for today and tomorrow so I came here just to feed poor Zoom."

"Love you," squawked the bird from behind the closed door.

"If I had known we wouldn't be here for a few days I would have taken him home with me last night. I'm glad you had the foresight to do what you did last night. I was concerned about you, my boy."

I was concerned too. While I was wearing a T-shirt; I was naked from the waist down. I had no idea where my underwear or pants were. I pulled the blanket closer around me.

Efrem fed Zoom, answered a few phone messages and then headed for the elevator.

"Stay as long as you like. Please be safe and don't be foolish and try to head back…uh, oh. Well, another surprise this morning," he said with a twinkle in his eye. I turned my head to follow his gaze.

Abbie had come out from the dressing room. She obviously had showered. Her hair was still wet but, fortunately, she was fully dressed.

"Oh, ah, Efrem, this is Abbie Smith. She and I take the same busses in and out of the city every day. I happened to run into her amongst all the chaos at the terminal last night. I figured you wouldn't mind if she stayed here too." I smiled weakly.

"Sure, sure, no problem of course," he shrugged. "That was very chivalrous of you, Baxter. Your momma raised you well. I am glad that you both are

safe. Very nice meeting you…Abbie, was it? Yes. Well, see you again sometime I hope."

Abbie nodded, gave him an embarrassed little wave and headed back to the dressing room. Hopefully to cautiously retrieve the remainder of my clothes. Efrem pushed the button for the elevator. When it dinged, he stepped in, turned and held the doors open for a moment.

"May I assume that you're not as intimate with all your other fellow passengers, yes?" he asked, winking at me and laughing loudly as the doors closed in front of him.

11

One year later I was working full-time for Efrem. He had suggested that I drop out of school considering the fact that, frankly, I could be doing the teaching. He was an amazing mentor and friend. I had become more than an assistant, really. My tasks varied, from loading the sheet film into the holders, running to the lab for processing following the shoots, to prop shopping, location scouting and model hiring. And the shoots varied as well. One day we might be shooting gorgeous fashions, the next day would be tabletop sessions for food packaging, followed by catalogue work. It was never dull, never boring. Without fail, following the final shot of every shoot, Efrem would say in his thick accent "Ahh, beautiful." Several of his clients relied on me as well as him to direct various shoots. I was getting a reputation, and a damn good one, with account executives, art directors, fashion coordinators and food stylists by the dozens. I thrived on the excitement. I loved working for Efrem but I was really craving a studio of my own.

Abbie and I were engaged and we rented a small apartment on 2ⁿᵈ Avenue, between East 6ᵗʰ Street and East 7ᵗʰ, in the East Village. We were New Yorkers now! She was working at a small, upstart ad agency on 57ᵗʰ Street, just west of Park Avenue, putting her marketing degree to good use. To avoid the expense of keeping a car in the city, my beloved old Buick remained at Mom and Dad's in Dover. If our life in Manhattan had a soundtrack it would be a lot of Miles Davis, with a little of Gershwin thrown in for good measure. Slowly but surely the Beatles were beginning to creep in, too...with a little help from my friends.

Regarding Dover, perhaps I had seen the subtle changes but they seemed to elude me. Mom, on the other hand, had been very *aware of them. It was a forgotten word here and there, or perhaps an unusual blank stare on occasion. Gram was slowly slipping into another world. Gramp was taking up the slack. Things that Gram had done routinely became his chores. He knew what was happening but he honestly didn't want to accept it. Not yet, anyway.*

He sold their big, beautiful house and most of its furnishings. I asked for and was given those two old seats from the Metropolitan Opera House and an old watercolor painting of a seascape that I had loved ever since I was a kid. They moved into a small apartment on the outskirts of Dover, which further seemed to confuse poor Gram.

We closed up the studio for a few hours one afternoon so Efrem and I could run over to Broadway and photograph an historic tickertape parade. A week or so earlier, John Glenn had become the first American to orbit the Earth and his achievement was being honored and rewarded with gusto. So many unsettling things going on around the globe…rising tensions with the Soviet Union, Vietnam still a roaring tinderbox…that it was refreshing having a happy event to celebrate. We both took several great shots and one, in particular, will remain in my portfolio for years to come. I laughed at the plight of the poor sanitation workers who then had to clean up the estimated 3,700 tons of ticker tape!

NOW: Trivia Time Again: That tickertape parade up Broadway would be repeated in November of 1998. John Glenn had returned from another space flight at the age of 77.

THEN: *So, by moving to the East Village, I exchanged my random encounters with hobos to daily encounters with hippies. Lots of them! We lived* *only a couple blocks from Washington Square and, good lord; the place was overrun with them. Constant activity. Love-Ins, Be-Ins, Sit-Ins, whatever the new "in" thing was it was happening there. They were there in the daylight hours, but when the sun went down their numbers doubled. Like roaches creeping out from their hiding places into the nighttime. The air in New York City was constantly filled with the aroma of car exhaust fumes. The air around Washington Square, however, was filled with something else entirely. Aside from the body odors, that is. One could get high just by walking from one side of that massive arch to the other. I did my part to fit in. I grew a moustache and had hair down to my shoulders, complete with long sideburns. I was in a creative profession, after all. Never wore love beads, however. I would go only so far. On Saturday nights we would often hang out in a place called Stanley's Bar, a few blocks further south of the apartment. To use a current term or two, Stanley's was hip. It was cool. It was where Harlem met Bohemia. We even ran into Allen Ginsberg a few times there.*

Our visits to New Jersey were far and few between, to the annoyance of my mother especially. Obviously my dad didn't give two shits one way or the other. Abbie had occasional lunches with her father, being that their offices were somewhat close together, and she phoned her mom like clockwork every Friday evening.

Another year went by and then the day came that I was long dreading. I knew it as soon as I awoke that morning. As soon as the phone rang at 4 A.M. Gram had had a stroke two weeks ago and I was hoping to get back out to New Jersey to see her on Saturday. Mom was calling from the hospital and told me to get there as soon as I could. One of most important influences in my life was nearing the end of hers. I showered, shaved, and dressed with little energy. I was feeling drained. My emotions were on the brink. Ignoring the expense, Abbie and I took a taxi out to Dover General. My Dad was waiting for us in the lobby. He took one look at me and said "Jeez-zus, you look like a fucking hippie!" Hi, Dad, nice to see you, too! We rode up in the elevator and rushed to her room. There were wires and tubes sticking into her everywhere. She had been in a semi-comatose state for days, getting weaker with each passing hour. No need to bring flowers. She wouldn't see them, nor would she care. She loved to see them growing, not cut and plopped into a vase. Gramp was standing by the side of her bed, head lowered almost in prayer. Mom was sitting in a chair with tears in her eyes. She acknowledged Abbie and me with a wan smile.

"Her blood pressure, Bax, is dropping quickly," Mom said softly. "Just before you got here the doctor told me it's just a matter of minutes now, not hours or days."

I tried to breathe without sounding like I was gasping for air. I was stifling the tears that I knew would soon be flowing. I slowly walked to the end of her bed and looked down at this once-beautiful woman, now shriveled and sunken, with skin so pale it looked translucent. There was a slight movement. At first I thought it was my imagination. It happened again. Her eyes slowly fluttered open…eyes, which once had been a vibrant, sparking blue were now dull and clouded. Eyes, which hadn't opened in weeks. It startled me and I nearly stopped breathing. She looked right up at me, smiled, and weakly pointed to the ceiling.

"Fledermaus," she whispered, "fledermaus." And then she expired.

The floodgates opened. I collapsed into the nearest chair and sobbed, loudly, like a baby.

Efrem told me to take as much time as I needed. He understood completely as he, too, had been a favored grandchild. Abbie and I stayed with my parents, sleeping in my old room. I missed having a big dog come running to greet me and lick my hand as I walked in through the front door. Laddie died several years ago and there had been no replacement. We felt welcomed in the house by both Mom and Dad. My father was actually very pleasant. He liked Abbie a lot and thought I had done very well.

The day before the funeral Abbie and I took a walk down through the town. Dover had changed. There seemed to be a lot more Hispanic-looking faces and places than I had remembered. The world is changing. Sallie's Bella Luna Trattoria was no longer there, being replaced with Marques de la Habana. Herboristeria replaced the bookstore where I had once worked. Pat the Barber was still there, though. I had had my very first haircut there when I was just a towheaded tyke, and went there for years afterwards. We walked in. Holy shit, Pat was still there! He looked like he was at least 90, but he was still cutting hair. I'll be damned. He didn't remember me, of course, but that didn't matter. I sat down in his big leather swivel chair and told him to remove my long locks and get rid of the moustache. Twenty minutes later I left his chair, hair looking neatly shorn and face cleanly shaven, smelling of Bay Rum.

The funeral the next afternoon was at the big Presbyterian Church on Blackwell Street. Internment followed at the cemetery just a few steps from our house. It was a beautiful day, not a cloud in the crisp blue sky and a gentle breeze was blowing. There was a larger crowd than I had anticipated. Gram and Gramp had a lot of friends and several of Gramp's former coworkers were there as well. I tried to stifle any tears or, worse, sobs that welled up in me during the graveside service. It was not easy. Abbie clutched my hand tightly. As the service ended and folks began to drift away, I released my hand from Abbie's. I nodded to her and slowly inched away. She understood and, with head down, I solemnly moved away from the dwindling crowd.

I meandered along the gravel roadways through the old cemetery. I needed to be alone and today, especially, I felt so alone. I thought that I couldn't possibly cry any more today. I was mistaken. Eventually I came upon the big flat grave marker on the ground. I kneeled down beside it. Someone had stuck a small American flag into the grass next to it and it fluttered in the breeze. I gently ran my fingers over the name, dipping into the recesses of every carved letter as my hand moved. ANTHONY JOSEPH BERTOLI. "A.J." to his army buddies; Ant to me. My emotions then turned very black. Despite the fact that the sun was shining brilliantly, I suddenly felt a cloud sweep over me. Gloom reached in and yanked out my heart.

(Fade-To-Black)

ACT TWO

HERE AND THERE

"It's good to be middle-aged. Things don't matter so much, you don't take it so hard when things happen to you that you don't like."

Eleanor Roosevelt

12

HERE: Fifty. Fifty! How the hell did I get here so damn fast? My favored fictional heroes have gone from Uncle Wiggily, to Flash Gordon, to Lew Archer, to Bond, James Bond, and then to Myron Bolitar in a heartbeat. Our beloved (and trés sarcastic) son called me "old man" on my last birthday. What, I wonder, will he call me twenty years hence? Assuming, that is, that this decrepit "old" body makes it that long. The little shit! But I love him anyway.

Fifty is the age when one crosses over that threshold from *Oh; I Can't Wait To Try That* to *What the* Hell *Was I Thinking?* It was the year I tried therapy. Sort of. Almost. Just barely. We were at one of those drink-filled, idle-gossip-filled neighborhood bridge playing nights when one of the players, an obnoxious jerk, Al Gottlieb, from around the corner cornered me for a chat. He was foul-mouthed and foul breathed and for some God-only-knows reason decided that we were, then and there, the best of friends. He leaned into me and rambled on about his job, his wife, the other wives at the card tables (including my own) and what pissed him off about President Jimmy Carter. Then he started in on me. Me? What the fuck?

"I've known you for, what…three or four years now?" he slurred. "You ever think of therapy?"

My head jerked back in astonishment. "Say what?" I was incredulous. Where the hell did *this* come from?

"Yeah, I mean it, Bax. You want to be everybody's best friend. I've observed. Ya know what I'm sayin'? You're a doormat. People walk all over you. Ya know what I'm sayin'? You are always Mr. Nice Guy. You want to please everybody all the time and you want everybody to like you, right?"

"Isn't that what everybody wants? To be liked?"

"Nah, not to the extent that you do. You take niceness to a whole new level. Ya know what I'm sayin'? I know that *I'm* not liked by everyone," he continued, "but everybody respects me, that's for damn sure. Ya know what I'm sayin'?"

I knew what he was saying and what was for damn sure was the fact that he was delusional. I knew, for *damn* sure, that he was mocked behind his back for his obnoxious behavior, his often wrong opinions about everything, and his dreadful taste in attire. Not to mention his horrible bridge playing. I was not alone in thinking that he was an asshole. Surprisingly, his wife agreed.

"Hey, give my shrink a call. Seriously. He's great. He's worked wonders with me, ya know what I'm sayin'? Dr. Langston. Timothy Langston. Here, I'll give you his card."

He carries his psychiatrist's card with him…to parties? Does he get a kickback for referrals or something? If he brings in five new patients will he get a toaster oven? And exactly what kind of wonders did the doctor work on Al? Ya know what I'm sayin'?

Walking back home arm-in-arm after leaving the party, I tell Abbie about the conversation with the jerk. I thought I would have to pick her up off the street she was laughing so hard.

"Well, honestly," she said after she finally calmed her laughing down to a mere giggle or two, "Al is *sort* of right, up to a point, I guess. Yes, he's a jerk like no other. Yes, he can't hold his tongue any better than he can hold his liquor. But. You knew a 'but' was coming, didn't you? Your niceness *can* be annoying at times. Calling you a doormat is a bit extreme, though. I really don't see that at all. I *do* see what he means about you always wanting to please everyone. Seriously, Bax, you simply cannot please everyone all the time…although, God knows, you certainly try."

We continued our walk home with my hands thrust deep into my pockets and my mind smoldering.

Oh, what the hell, I thought. I had been having some issues, mainly about growing older and losing some…hmmm…stamina, so maybe a session or two wouldn't hurt. Perhaps we could sneak in my "niceness addiction" somewhere along the line. It took a month to get an appointment. Dr. Timothy Langston was a mild-mannered, mousey little guy with an androgynous voice and who crossed his legs in a very peculiar manner when he sat down. His office was well appointed in ultra-modern furniture and smelled of teakwood. It was a pleasant enough session, with a few innocuous questions asked of me, and damn few answers given from him. Par for the course from what I've been told. I was neither overwhelmed nor disappointed in the hour spent with him, so we arranged another session one month hence.

I don't know if it was something I said, sheer coincidence or very poor timing on my part but the day after my initial meeting with Dr. Timothy Langston, he put a .38 five-shooter by Smith & Wesson into his mouth and blew his brains out. That's it! I'm cured! I'm done with this therapy crap. From this point onward, if anyone thinks that I'm too much of a Mr. Nice Guy…well, fuck 'em!

Three weeks later we had forgotten to get a loaf of rye bread for the sandwiches we had planned for lunch. Our favorite bakery was just a few short blocks away so I walked up and headed into the store. What were the chances? On the way out was Al Gottlieb. He spotted me, made a hasty detour, nearly sideswiping a little old lady using a walker, and came rushing up to me.

"Oh, my God, Bax, I am beyond devastated. I am distraught to say the least!"

He had launched right into it, almost out of breath. No *"Hey, how are ya? How's the family? Great weather, isn't it?"* Nope. Nothing.

He continued ranting and panting. "What the *hell* was that guy thinking? Look at me, I'm a wreck. Three fucking years of therapy down the crapper. He blows his brains out, so how can I believe anything he told me if *he* couldn't take life any better than *I* could? What the Hell, right? Holy fucking damn! Now what do I do?"

I held his gaze for perhaps fifteen seconds.

"I'm sorry," I said, pseudo sincerity dripping from every pore. "Please don't confuse me with somebody who really gives a fuck. Ya know what I'm sayin'?" And I continued on my quest for a perfect loaf of rye bread.

THERE: *I don't think I'll ever give in to therapy. Maybe I'm too young, too naïve or too stupid to believe all that mumbo-jumbo from shrinks. Several of our clients talk about it to both Efrem and me during the shoots sometimes. Years of therapy and pill popping for so many of them and they're all still nut cases as far as I'm concerned.*

"Ha," chuckled Efrem one day, "my sweet wife Annika tells me I should see a shrink because I talk to my rude parrot, Zoom, more than to her."

"And do you?"

"Yah, sure," he said, shrugging his shoulders, "and why not? Zoom is more interesting." And he laughed and laughed. "I was kidding, by the way. Oh, and by the way, a nutso art director from BBD and O will be directing a shoot here with us tomorrow. You've not met this one before. You're a very handsome young man, Baxter, just protect your goodies, if you know what I mean."

HERE: I'm not a great believer in coincidences, but what were the chances? Several years had passed; he had put on about twenty pounds and grown a beard. I didn't recognize him at first and he obviously didn't recognize me. Or if he did, he never said anything about it. The "nutso" art director from BBD and O was Allan Ebner, that straight shooter from Boy Scout camp.

13

THERE: *It has been six months since that very black day for me when we buried Gram. I still haven't gotten over it. Therapy might help, but then, it might hinder my healing process. I was surprised to get a phone call one evening from Gramp. He was coming into the city the next day and wondered if it was possible to join him for lunch. As it so happened, we didn't have a shoot scheduled so I had, basically, a free day. We arranged to meet at one of his and Gram's favorite restaurants in New York, on West 44th Street, in the heart of the theater district and practically right across the street from Shubert Alley.*

It was not Wednesday; matinee day, so there was not the theater crowd clamoring for tables. He was already there and seated when I arrived. All the waiters there knew him by name and one of them showed me to his table in a discreet, dark corner of one of the back rooms. He was drinking a Jack Rose, his favorite cocktail. He hadn't ordered it; it was just delivered to him by a knowledgeable waiter. He had started drinking them back in the late 1920s after reading about the concoction in Hemingway's classic The Sun Also Rises. *I ordered my favorite, a gin and tonic. The maître d' came over to the table and Gramp introduced us. He uttered a few somber words of condolence to both of us and went back to the front of the restaurant. My drink was delivered and we toasted each other. I looked at Gramp for the first time. I mean,* really *looked at him. He suddenly looked so old, so sad.*

"So what brings you into the city on this beautiful day," I asked.

He sighed and took a deep breath. "You, Baxter, you."

"Ah…and that means what, exactly?"

"Things happened too fast. Things went downhill way *too fast. It wasn't meant to be like this. We were hoping for a wedding, your Gram and me. We both like Abbie very, very much. Lillian and I had a wonderful wedding present planned. Something that would change your life. Well, it still will but, unfortunately, your grandmother never got to enjoy the surprise."*

I sat silent. Just staring at him, not knowing where this conversation was going. He was dressed, as always, like the lawyer he had been. A three-piece navy blue suit, starched white shirt and a deep maroon necktie with a perfect Windsor knot. He withdrew an envelope from his breast pocket and laid it gently beside him on the table. He put his elbows on the table, leaned forward a bit and steepled his fingers.

"This is all perfectly legal, Bax, as you might imagine. We opened an account in your name a month after you were born. We applied right at the hospital when you were born to get a Social Security number for you. You never questioned, did you, why you had one at such an early age?"

I nodded. I hadn't. Actually I didn't think anything about it.

"There is no tax liability. Lillian and I paid the required taxes every single year. It's up to date in that regard."

I gulped down my drink and signaled for another.

"Needless to say, it has grown nicely throughout the years, what with interest and reinvested dividends and the generous deposits that we made. By the way, neither one of your parents seem to remember that we had done this. It was long ago and they obviously forgot about it. Your mother has never mentioned this in all these years. Oh, I anticipate an uproar of some sort, but she will be nicely compensated when the time comes. As far as Corey is concerned, who the hell cares," and he chuckled.

"Okay," I started, " what the hell is this thing that you and Gram have with my dad? Ever since I can remember there has been…oh, I don't know… some kind of tension between the three of you. I couldn't figure it out."

"Well, that's neither here nor there," he shrugged. "Perhaps someday when you're a big boy I'll tell you," he winked at me and laughed a hearty laugh. "Sooner or later, I'm sure you'll find out."

My drink arrived and we toasted again.

"I will arrange, at your convenience, a meeting between you and my financial advisor to help you with what I am about to hand over to you. I know that you are eager to open your very own photo studio. Don't be too hasty. Take your time and play it cautious."

My heart was racing by now. There may even have been a few beads of sweat on my brow. I frowned as he slid the envelope across the table to me. I opened it, pulled out a stack of legal-sized forms and unfolded them. I flipped through them but they were all a blur to me. Until I hit the last page with a monetary figure. I quickly looked up into his face. His eyes were filled with tears as he smiled at me.

"This can't be happening," I said in bewilderment. "This isn't real. Things like this don't happen in real life. Only in some preposterous movies. What the hell? There will *be a wedding, you know. We're thinking about another year or so. Why now?"*

"I have my reasons," he answered with a slight shrug. "Your grandmother and I have loved you since the day you were born, Baxter. You have been so very special to us all these years and have given us more pleasure than you could ever imagine. You are my favorite grandson." We both laughed. He has kidded me about that since I was a kid. I am his only *grandson.*

He nodded to our waiter who was standing by. He came up to our table and smiled.

"Yes, Mr. Freemont, are we ready now?"

"We're hungry, Jimmy. What are you recommending today?"

I looked back at the paper in my hand and, now too, my eyes filled with tears. I tried to conceive what that number actually meant: two hundred and fifty thousand dollars.

I may have to reconsider that comment about therapy.

HERE: $250,000 in the year Gramp handed it over to me would have the equivalent in purchasing power today of approximately $1,939,378.74. It's a wonder I didn't have a fatal heart attack then and there at Sardi's.

However, six months later I discovered Gramp's "reasons". He had been diagnosed with prostate cancer. He had held off surgery as long as he could. He was afraid of it. Surgery was finally scheduled and he expected to be fully recovered in short time, but wanted to deliver my surprise just in case. Another very black day lay ahead for me. Gramp's very generous and loving heart gave out during surgery and he couldn't be revived.

14

THERE: *Abbie and I got married (big wedding...* **big!***). I have no doubt our guests will be talking about it for years to come. Even the local paparazzi showed up to catch a glimpse and snap some photos of a well-known star of the Pop Art crowd. How did they even know he'd be there? My bank must have thought we pulled off the heist of the century considering the deposits we made following the event. The friends of Abbie's parents were generous to a fault and even Mom and Dad gave us a wedding gift that stunned me beyond belief. Adding all this to Gram and Gramp's surprise gift kept my head swimming.*

The week after returning from our honeymoon in Europe, Abbie was called into her boss's office and offered a startling promotion. Not in their New York office, but in their soon-to-open offices in the new, exploding market in Atlanta, Georgia.

One hundred years after General William Tecumseh Sherman started his march to the sea with the frightening boast "I can make Georgia howl", a *sleepy Atlanta finally decided to blink its eyes, wake up, yawn, and start its recovery. It would soon become the fastest growing urban area in the nation. Once burned to the ground, the city grew, from the ground up, into what many people called the New York of the South...to the chagrin, I might add, of the true southerners who remain proud of their heritage. The city started out as Marthasville, in honor of the then-governor's daughter. It was at the end of the*

Western-Atlantic railroad line, so the name switched to Terminus, sounding somewhat funereal, in my honest opinion. Soon afterward it was finally called Atlanta, the feminine of Atlantic…as in the railroad, not the ocean.

HERE: Having lived in the south, now, decades longer than we lived in Damn Yankee-Land, neither one of us says *"y'all"* and grits still is the equivalent to eating beach sand. Despite the civil unrest that was shaking the nation when we made our move to Atlanta, the city's slogan at the time was *"The City Too Busy to Hate".*

THERE: *We had not told anyone, except our parents, about the major surprise that Gramp had dropped into my lap during that fateful luncheon. I wasn't going to be foolish and start a maniacal spending spree. Gramp's financial advisors set out a logical plan for me…I had so much to learn…and this possible move to Atlanta would certainly be less of a hassle, monetarily, than it would have been, say, last year. We started our research.*

HERE: Yes, we started our research. Good god, it was the Dark Ages! This was before the Internet, before Google. Before Facebook. Before Instagram. Hell, it was even before Prozac!

THERE: *Before we made our decision, I had a long discussion with Efrem. I explained about Abbie's potential promotion, and a move to the land of hooped skirts and Spanish moss. Okay, I was kidding about that part. It was now the land of mini-skirts and honeysuckle.*

"Efrem, I'm torn up about this," I sighed.

"Liar!" squawked Zoom from Efrem's office. He and I both laughed and shook our heads.

"Doesn't he know anything other than that?" I snickered.

"Love you," said the bird.

"Love you, too, Zoom," I replied. "Really, this is going to be a fabulous opportunity for Abbie, but we both love New York and I really, really love working here with you."

"Don't be foolish, my boy," answered Efrem. "You have an amazing talent and, seriously, how much longer would you have remained content to be working here with me? Without getting your own studio established, yes? I

know you surely must want that. I did when I was your age. I left my mentor behind…yes, to be sure with tears, but no regrets. And look what happened. I say, "go and rejoice", and I shall throw you both an enormous bon voyage party here. Will I miss you? Like my left leg if it should suddenly fall off. But you are ready. You are more than ready, my young friend."

"I don't know what to say, Efrem."

"Say good-bye! Simple, yes? You know, several of my clients have opened some new offices in the south. I'm sure Atlanta. Let's see what we can do to get you some work there."

HERE: I'm not sure the term "networking" was in use then, but that's exactly what Efrem did for me. A couple of Abbie's clients in the new Atlanta office opened a few more doors of opportunity.

THERE: *We were so accustomed, at this point, to living in the city with throngs of people night and day, the sounds and smells…some kind of music all around us, taxis honking their horns, exhaust fumes…all wonderful and exciting. What would we face in Atlanta? Should we live in the city? Should we check out the suburbs?*

Not only did we need to find a new residence, but also I had to locate a place for my studio. We felt suddenly overwhelmed. Fortunately, Abbie's ad agency hired a realtor in Atlanta to assist us in the transition from northerner to southerner. She was to pick us up from our hotel the same morning that we flew into Atlanta to begin our search.

Samantha Hollingsworth, our uber-friendly realtor, flaxen hair bouncing as she walked, stood no more than five feet tall, had obviously spent more time in a donut shop than she should have and spoke with an accent that would have put Scarlett O'Hara to shame. She carried a purse that looked as though she could hide a small child in it, and wore enough perfume that could, just possibly, anesthetize a horse.

"I know," she said, sounding like Ah *know, "y'all are city folk up north, but let me show you a few places out in the suburbs first. You'll just love 'em, I can tell." She brushed a little something off the front of her dress. It looked like powdered sugar.*

We followed her out to her car and off we went. Abbie and I had to sit in the back seat because the passenger side of the front was loaded with real estate books and brochures. And a crumpled up empty bag from Dunkin' Donuts. We were staying in a hotel with a big blue flying saucer type of thing on the top floor that we soon discovered was a revolving restaurant. Weird place, Atlanta. Samantha zipped through the streets and, before we knew it, we were in lush green countryside.

"Subdivisions are popping up out here like warts on a hoppy toad," giggled Samantha. "Some of them I wouldn't want my dog to live in, but I'll show you a couple newer ones that are simply gooooorgeous!" We discovered that she looooooved to drag out her words on occasion.

She turned her car into a subdivision called Mimosa Ridge. As we passed several street signs I glanced at the names: Jo Beth Court, Mary Sue Ellen Drive, Annabelle Lane.

Abbie looked at me. "Don't be judgmental," she admonished.

"What? I didn't say a word," I responded.

"Your eyebrows were judgmental," she replied with a snicker.

The car came a slow stop in front of a faux craftsman-style home that actually looked out of place among all the other houses in the neighborhood.

"This one just came on the market and I think it's wonnnnnnderful. Shall we take a look? Whaddya say?" asked Samantha.

"Sure, why not?" I shrugged.

We got out of the car…it was nice to stretch our legs and take a whiff of the fresh southern air, free of New York city fumes. The color scheme of the house was browns and beiges but when we stepped up onto the front porch something caught my eye right away. The beadboard ceiling on the porch was painted a soft, pale blue. Samantha noticed that I was staring up at it.

"Isn't that just darlin'?" she almost purred. "You don't know about that, do y'all? That's called haint blue. A lot of us folks down here do that. I have it on my front porch as well. Haints and boo hags are evil spirits. They are deathly afraid of water, supposedly, and they dare not cross it. Sometimes you might see houses here with their front door painted that blue as well. That blue color tricks them into thinking that's water, so the evil spirits can't enter your house. Descendants of the slaves down here in the south believed that, so the trend started years ago. Don't y'all just looooove it?"

Actually, I didn't.

15

So, shall we be the city mouse or the country mouse? Decisions, decisions. Thinking that we would soon like to start a family, the suburbs might be the safer bet. My studio could be in the city and I'd still get to smell those car exhaust fumes. For some reason I was remembering a little knickknack that had sat on Gram's and Gramp's coffee table when I was a kid. A very good friend and neighbor of theirs traveled to Beirut, Lebanon on business and brought back a thoughtful gift for them. It was a small wooden box with a hinged lid. The box was made of apricot wood and had inlays of ivory as decoration. On the lid, in Arabic, carved in ivory, was the phrase "Judge the neighbor before buying the house". *Easy to do, in a manner of speaking, when checking out these various subdivisions with Samantha. Simply judge the landscaping. If the people living in a well-cared for house, exterior-wise, and care enough to have manicured lawns and well-kept shrubbery surrounding the place, then they must be okay. That was my philosophy and I was sticking to it. But I was also beginning to rethink my thoughts about the suburbs. I had a feeling that Abbie would back me up here.*

By the end of day one our realtor had shown us eight different houses in six different subdivisions.

"Didn't blow your skirt up here either, eh?" sighed a visibly exhausted and exasperated Samantha as we exited the final house on today's tour.

"Frankly, no, Samantha. None of them," I said, trying to be patient. "I can speak for both of us here, we simply do not like the cookie cutter houses that you've shown us today. They all look alike. Side by side, they are the same boring design and all have the same exact colors. Every one of them. No individuality. You seem to stress the fact that most of what we've seen are new constructions. I'll cut to the chase. They look like crappy construction as far as I'm concerned. And crappy designs. My dad is an architect and trust me, I know good design. I've seen it for years. And what did they do to all the trees? It looks as though the builders decided that trees got in the way and took them all down. The lots are bare. Bare and boring. Where Abbie and I grew up, in our respective towns in New Jersey, the houses were well built and interesting. Yes, they were much older than what you're showing us here. Maybe that's what we need to see. Older homes. In older neighborhoods. Established neighborhoods. I thought we had made it clear what we were looking for. I guess I was wrong. Or not clear enough. And all the houses we've seen are so damn close to each other. I don't want to sneeze and have someone three houses away say gesundheit."

She stood looking at me for a moment. She took in a long breath through her nose and slowly let it out again. I could almost tell by the look in her eyes that she was silently calling me a damn Yankee, possibly even a fucking damn Yankee, but I could be mistaken.

We had already agreed to split up on day two. That is, Abbie and Samantha would continue to look at houses, now perhaps with better direction. Samantha didn't handle commercial real estate leasing; so she arranged to have an appropriate associate, Alex Little, meet me at the hotel first thing in the morning. The front desk called to alert me that he had arrived at ten minutes after nine. I was eager to see what Atlanta had to offer regarding studio space.

As soon as the elevator opened in the lobby I could tell who Alex Little was. And he was anything but little. Everyone else was pulling luggage behind them, heading to the checkout counters. Alex stood waiting for the elevator doors to open. He held a clipboard in his hands. We seemed to recognize each other right away. I repeat, he was anything but little. He outweighed me by at least seventy-five pounds and stood three inches taller. He was wearing khaki slacks that were about one size smaller, waist-wise, than they should be, and a red pullover polo shirt that couldn't possible stretch any tighter. He appeared *to be in his early 50s and, poor guy, tried like crazy for a stylish comb-over that didn't quite work.*

"Good morning...Mr. Janus?" he asked as he approached me.

"Yes, and I assume you're Alex Little?" I replied. We both extended our hands and shook. He had a very firm grip.

"How ya doin' tahday, guy?" he replied back

Oh. My. God. Not a southern accent but one I recognized. I didn't want to insult him or anything but I was sure he wasn't born and raised on a plantation.

"I'm going to take a gamble here," I said cautiously, "but you wouldn't be from New York or New Jersey by any chance, would you? And please call me Baxter."

He rolled his head back and gave out a raucous laugh.

"You're a card, you are, Baxter. Good ear, guy, good ear. Yeah, I been down here a good number of years but can't get the Jersey out, eh?"

"Where in Jersey did you call home?"

"Oh, some little dinky place you probably never heard of. Wharton."

"No shit!" I exclaimed quickly.

"I shit you not," he replied just as quickly.

I outstretched both arms. "Dover," I said.

Dover and Wharton are no more than two miles apart. What were the chances?

Alex Little had attended and graduated from the University of Georgia on a football scholarship. He had fallen in love and eventually married the Home Coming Queen, sired three sons and his first grandchild was on the way. For years, he worked as a salesman for a paperboard packaging company but he got tired of the pressure and the required travel so he quit and got into commercial real estate. He hasn't been back to New Jersey in at least twenty years. I liked this guy. Really liked him.

"Okay," he said, "getting down to business. Let's sit here for a minute and I can go over some things I want to show you today, but I really need to hear your musts and wants first."

We sat and talked for over an hour. Told him about the studio I was leaving behind in Manhattan and listed the things I wanted in my own studio here in Hotlanta. He took notes and nodded as he did so.

"Great," he said after I finished. "That's exactly the info I was hoping for. I have a few really good choices and I just crossed two more off the list as you were talking. I parked in the garage here, let's git goin' and we'll head out to West Peachtree Street first. Oh, just to warn you, there are about fifty Peachtree something or others around here. Street…Avenue, Boulevard, Alley. Well, you get the picture. Just don't get confused."

There were three different storefront-type spaces along a stretch of West Peachtree Street, almost in the heart of town. We took our time going through each one. They were nice spaces and any one of them could work well for my place, but no bells went off. No gong sounded. We looked at another small space on Piedmont Avenue. No skirt was blown up here either.

"Let's grab a bite, then I'll take you to someplace that's top on my list but I saved it to see what you'd say about the others first."

He pulled the car into the parking lot of someplace called the Varsity. The "famous" hot dogs were just okay as far as I was concerned. Nowhere nearly as good as the ones from Stewart's car hop place on Route 46 in Dover. But, when in Rome, etc., etc.…

After lunch he drove us to a part of town that wasn't as built up. In fact, it looked a tad run down. There were railroad tracks a block before we got to the building in question and his car tires rumbled as we drove over them. We came to a stop sign and then could turn only either right or left. After the traffic cleared, he drove straight ahead, into a weed-strewn, litter-filled parking lot that surrounded a rectangular cinder block building. Sitting as the only building in the middle of a very short block, it was narrow in width but long in depth. No windows in it at all. It was painted a stark white that had apparently yellowed a bit with age and had a very shiny black metal door. Some very colorful, if somewhat vulgar graffiti had been spray-painted all along the sides. It was, probably, the ugliest building I had ever seen. Something clicked. I loved it.

"Okay, Baxter," he said as he put the car in park and turned off the engine. "Let me tell you a bit about this one and why I said that I saved the best for last. Maybe you'll agree with me. Maybe you'll think I'm fulla shit," and he shrugged. "Who knows? Right? Anyway. This section of Atlanta, here, is called Cabbagetown. Not the best of neighborhoods, but far from the worst. It has potential. This place actually has *been a photographer's studio for years. The guy did great stuff, so I've been told. He broke his lease by having a heart attack and up and dyin'. Boo-hoo. Sad, huh? He was up in years…I don't know, sixty something I'd guess. Anyway, his widow didn't want anything to do with it. His kids were grown and gone. They didn't want to know nothing from nothing as well. They took a couple of his old 35mm cameras and sold all the other stuff that was in there. There might be some leftover crap in there, but I don't know what it is. Wanna have a look-see?"*

"Well, absolutely!" I said with glee. "I know it looks sort of dumpy but it sure has character, doesn't it?"

"Whatever you say, Baxter, whatever you say. You're in the driver's seat now."

He unlocked the front door and ushered me in. There was a small entryway that led into a larger sitting area. Off to one side of that was an office. Not overly large but a good enough size nonetheless. The actual studio space was beyond the sitting area. It was larger than I had expected based on what the outside of the building looked like. I walked in and flicked on some light switches. The place lit up. It was expansive, with a door at the rear of the building. High ceilings, painted a matte black. Good! I walked around and wandered down a short hallway that led to what had been the darkroom. There were several empty sheet film holders lying around on a counter and boxes of sheet film in various sizes. Most of it had expired or soon would. Bottles of chemicals that needed disposed of…and soon. There was a small bathroom next to the darkroom. Whoever had used it last hadn't had the courtesy to flush. I nearly gagged as I reached in to flush the toilet. I was grateful that it hadn't clogged. Next to the darkroom was a full kitchen. The appliances were old. Very old. Back in the main studio area, leaning up against a wall were large rolls of seamless backdrop paper in every color imaginable. They actually looked quite new, for some reason. No dust, no tears or rips. They looked unused. I went to the back door, opened it and looked out into the space behind the building. My nose was greeted by the stench of rotting garbage. A huge dumpster stood at the far end of the parking area. A scruffy-looking grey cat stopped in mid stride to stare at me, and then it scampered away. A long concrete wall, perhaps eight feet high, ran along the back of the parking lot. It had been spray-painted with some gorgeous, colorful, and very creative graffiti. Over the wall, through some trees, I could see the top of what looked like an old red brick mill or warehouse of some kind. I hadn't noticed until I walked to the back end of the studio area that there was a large, roll-up door that could accommodate a vehicle if I ever decided to do automotive shoots inside.

"You wouldn't happen to have a large tape measure with you, would you?" I asked.

"You want to know the sizes? How about these?" And Alex Little lifted his clipboard and provided me with a floor plan of the place with all the measurements I was seeking.

I walked all around the interior of the place. Through every room. Several times. I went into the office area. I closed the door. I opened the door. I went out the front door. I walked completely around the building. I came back in the front door.

"Alex, it's nearly five. Get me back to the hotel. I'd like to introduce you to my wife. Let's take a ride in that strange flying saucer on the top of the hotel. I'll buy you a drink and let's talk business. I've made a decision."

HERE: Aside from marrying Aberdeen Smith, it was the best damn decision in my life.

16

THERE: *"Lease or buy outright?" asked Alex Little as he hefted his Heineken.*

"Hmmm…I didn't realize the place might actually be for sale," I said as I gingerly lifted my gin and tonic. "I thought it would just be a lease deal. Interesting. Why didn't you mention that beforehand?"

I paused in thought, looking at the city buildings around the hotel change as the restaurant slowly rotated. Abbie had gotten back to the hotel a little later than we had and would soon be joining us. I ordered a glass of Chablis and it was waiting for her next to me at the table.

"Wasn't sure how'd you react to it. I didn't want to scare you away from it if you thought it was just a sell deal and not a lease deal. Personally, I believe it checks every box on your Must List. Now, it certainly can go either way, but it's really priced to sell," He paused and I thought about it.

Alex responded after a moment's silence. "The owner thinks the area has gotten a bit dicey, to be honest with you, but I don't agree. I see potential in that area. He's afraid of it and wants to get rid of it. Perhaps I'm telling something I shouldn't, you know?" He shrugged. "He's asking a hundred twenty-five thousand."

HERE: $125,000, at that time, would be the equivalent in today's dollars to $837,364.69.

THERE: I sat back in my chair, scratched my head and stared back out at the changing buildings slowly moving past the large windows. I downed my drink and signaled for a refill.

"I want a complete inspection of the place to make sure everything is up to code. If it passes with little or no reservations from the inspector I'll pay ninety-five thousand. Cash. Non-negotiable."

Now the fun part began. Abbie soon joined us at the table and eventually went through an entire bottle of Chablis. Alex and I were a little (no pun intended) on the tipsy side within the hour. He told me what the real estate taxes would be for the building, and an approximate cost for the utilities. All reasonable and doable. I would also have to apply for a business license. Of course, I knew that already. I excitedly told Abbie about this little, ugly, graffiti-strewn cinder block building in someplace called Cabbagetown.

Alex excused himself to use the restroom and nearly tripped when he had to step over from our very slowly moving platform to the stable center. He giggled.

"Too bad he isn't showing us some houses," I whispered to Abbie, "instead of darlin' Samantha."

"Now, now, don't be mean or too hasty with your opinions. No doubt that she was rattled by your critique yesterday and she confessed to me that you made her cry. But she most definitely came through today. I have a surprise for you and I think you will be very, very happy."

"Seriously?"

"Seriously. It's a lot closer into the city than all the crap she was showing us yesterday, but it's still very much like an old familiar neighborhood to both of us, the kind of areas we grew up in. It's in Atlanta, but it's a section called Druid Hills."

"Druid Hills. Druids? We won't have to wear long, scratchy robes and learn strange chants, will we?"

"Smartass!" and she playfully swatted me.

We were waiting for Samantha at 9 A.M. outside the hotel, in the guest drop-off area. She tapped her car horn as she swung in and came to a stop. She motioned for me to sit in the front seat, which was now clean and neat. Abbie jumped into the back seat and, again, we were off and running.

"How y'all doin' this fine mornin'?" she chirped. "Were y'all successful yesterday, Baxter?"

She nervously watched me out of the corner of her eye. I chuckled inwardly. I guess my verbal barrage yesterday had her on edge. I figured that if I should so much as raise my hand quickly she'e leap out of the moving car and make a mad dash. I told her all about the building, which she thought sounded "darlin'!"

Traffic was a little stop and go. It was rush hour, after all, but less than fifteen minutes later we slowed down and pulled into a long driveway. My mouth dropped open and Abbie gave me that "told you" look.

"Now, that is a house, Samantha. A real house." She smiled broadly and reached over to give a high-five. I moved cautiously, slowly, not wanting to scare the poor lady.

The house took my breath away. It was, what Samantha called, an historic Tudor Revival. It had been built in 1929. A bit larger than we were actually looking for…with four bedrooms, three baths and 3,280 square feet…but what the hell? We were planning on having a family and this would be ideal. The little amount of furniture that we had in our East Village apartment would probably just about fill up the foyer here. There were steps leading up to a beautiful carved wooden door. There was no front porch. No haint blue. Don'tcha love it?

17

THERE: Efrem lived up to his word and threw us a huge going away party, but it was at his apartment on the upper west side, not his studio. Annika, his stunningly beautiful wife was a gracious hostess. Her Russian accent mesmerized me. The building was unpretentious but his place was exquisite in design. Stark white walls were covered with photos, very large and very small, taken all around the globe. I recognized so many of the sites and just knew that sooner or later, Abbie and I would photograph them as well. Hanging over the old, well-used fireplace in their living room was an enormous oil painting of St. Basil's Cathedral, the centerpiece of Red Square in Moscow. It was on my long list of places to visit sometime in the future.

I'm sure the Goldschmitt's were violating every known fire code by the number of people crammed into the place. It was loud and filled with music, laughter and animated conversation. Efrem had an enormous client list and, I assumed, that most of them were here this evening. Even Zoom was in attendance, sitting on his perch in the living room observing the crowd. I knew most of the people here and introduced them, one right after the other, to Abbie. Even that sketchy, wacko art director from BBD and O was there. I protected my goodies. Everyone wished us well and the term "good luck" was repeated over and over by one client after the other. A majority of them came up to me as they were leaving the party, slipped an envelope into my hands and whispered things like "a little something to help with the expenses until your studio gets up to full speed." *Of course, I hadn't expected that. Nobody there, including Efrem, knew about the generous surprise that Gramp had given to me at that luncheon at Sardi's. By the end of the evening I had envelopes stuffed into every pants pocket, every pocket of my sports jacket and had slipped a few envelopes to Abbie to put in her purse.*

It was the party of the year as far as Abbie and I were concerned. We'd miss New York and we'd miss New Yorkers but we knew that the future wouldn't happen without us taking our first steps away from the past. We were the last to leave but before we actually said our goodbyes Efrem went to a shelf on the top of the bookcases in the living room. He came to me, holding out an old camera that I had been looking at earlier.

"This is a camera from the 1920s," he said as he handed it to me. "It is a Kodak Autographic 2-C. It still works. Take it, please, yes?"

"But this is beautiful. I can't take this. You must be very proud of it."

"This is not a gift, Baxter. This is a tradition. My mentor gave this to me when I opened my first studio. His mentor had given him a Number 5 Folding Kodak from the late 1890s. Unfortunately it was destroyed in a studio fire, so he continued the tradition with this one. And I pass this now along to you, my friend. Us photographers record history, so why not carry a little piece of history with us. When the time comes for you to retire or whatever your next step should be, give this camera to one who you have mentored. Carry on this tradition, yes?"

I was touched.

"I…I don't know what to say," I muttered.

"Liar!" shrieked Zoom.

When we got back to our apartment, we opened the envelopes that had been given to us by the elite of Madison Avenue. Most of it was cash but there were a few checks scattered in there as well. The grand total for everything came to a staggering twenty-five thousand dollars and change. We were flabbergasted, to say the least. Abbie held up one check in particular.

"What the hell does this mean?" she asked.

It was a check from Ebner, that nutso art director at BBD and O. I shook my head as I read it. The amount was for one thousand dollars and in the memo line he had scribbled Nice ass, Baxter, I'll miss it.

An ugly cinder block building in the town of cabbages was bought and paid for in cash. A beautiful house where the hills are alive with the sound of Druids was purchased, attached to a 30-year mortgage. Samantha Hollingsworth was happy. Alex Little was happy. We were happy...excited, and nervous as hell. What adventures lay ahead for us now? The big moving date was set. A reliable (we hoped) moving company would take care of getting our stuff from the East Village to Atlanta. I rented a U-Haul truck to get what little we both had remaining at our parents' places in Dover and Parsippany. Abbie would drive my old Buick, while I followed her down the highways and byways, closing out one chapter and opening another.

The day before the movers were to arrive at our apartment we received a surprise delivery from Bloomingdales. It was a going away gift from Efrem. One of the delivery guys handed me an envelope.

"He wanted to make sure yous guys got dis here envelope," he said, sounding straight out of Brooklyn.

Abbie and I shook our heads and laughed hysterically when we read the card inside the envelope: I hope you find as wonderful an assistant as I did with you. By the way, this one hasn't been christened yet.

His gift was a large turquoise beanbag sofa.

18

THERE: *The move couldn't have been better. Furniture, what little we actually had had in New Jersey and New York, arrived on time and without incident. Multiple tasks now lay ahead for the both of us. Trying to fill up a huge house with new furniture, and trying to set up a studio with new photographic equipment. The spending spree was both exciting and nerve-wracking. On top of that, Abbie started her new job at a rapidly growing ad agency. Yes, our nerves were frazzled. Yes, we argued at times. Maybe more times than I would have liked, but the makeup sex was fantastic. Maybe I should start more arguments.*

The exterior of the building was pressure washed to remove the graffiti, and painted a bright stark white. I decided to keep the graffiti that was on the wall behind the building. The eclectic boldness of it made a vivid, colorful backdrop for the whiteness of my place. The parking lot was resurfaced. Tall shrubs were planted along each side of the now fresh, crisp-looking building, and huge numerals, 641, for my street address, were painted in brilliant turquoise next to the shiny black metal front door. The numbers were stacked, vertically. There would be no signage indicating that it was a photo studio. Dicey or not dicey, I didn't want to entice any neighbors with not-quite-legal intentions to break into the place. I wanted no invitation to burglary. Photo equipment was expensive and easily pawned. I decided upon a black and white color scheme for the entryway/sitting area in my studio. Three white walls and one black wall, black furniture (black leather Barcelona Chairs)…except for a vivid turquoise beanbag sofa. I made a very sizeable enlargement of one of the photos I had taken at the John Glenn tickertape parade a few years before. It was by luck that I had photographed him as he was waving directly at the area in which I was standing. Sitting beside him in the open-top car was his wife and the then-Vice President Johnson. They all appeared to be waving right at me. So, when visitors and or clients entered my studio they'd be greeted by that piece of history waving at them and almost welcoming them in.

I was trying to think of an appropriate name for my new studio. Needless to say, my name was not a recognizable one, not yet anyway, so I wanted something memorable and unique. As I was getting ready for bed, I emptied my pockets before taking off my pants. All the coins clinked as I plopped them onto the dresser top. Along with the change was the one thing that had remained in every pocket, in every pair of pants I had worn for years. My good luck charm. It hit me like a lightning bolt. The next week I had my business cards printed. Acorn Studio – All Your Photographic Needs in a Nutshell. *I was ready. I was really ready.*

The centerpiece attraction in our new living room was a large framed, signed print by Andy Warhol. It had been a wedding present. From Andy. It was of a Campbell's soup can, Green Pea. Somehow Andy had discovered that that was my favorite flavor. The artwork generated comments, as expected, from our new friends and neighbors, both pro and con. I agreed with the pro and scoffed at the con.

HERE: In case you might want to know, the recent appraisal of this very rare, signed print was for $150,000.

THERE: *Two seats from the old Metropolitan Opera House were placed lovingly in my home office. Whenever I was feeling particularly nostalgic I sat in one or the other while listening to* Die Fledermaus *on the stereo. It really didn't matter that I was not an opera fan.*

19

THERE: *Three years went by in a flash.*

Efrem had come through with the recommendations, so my studio was flourishing. It was booked solid for three months out. Really enjoying the tabletop photography better than anything else…with the exception of shooting nature…I specialized in stuff for packaging or advertising. My portfolio grew rapidly. There were a couple part-time assistants that helped me out on the larger shoots but, honestly, neither one seemed very ambitious. Ah, the youth of today.

A new development. No pun intended. Abbie was pregnant! We were ecstatic. Our respective mothers were ecstatic. My father-in-law was ecstatic. My father was…well, I guess blasé would be the appropriate word.

Darin Ansel Janus. A wonderful name for a handsome baby. We couldn't believe that we were actually parents. Abbie took a prolonged leave of absence from her lucrative career to become a full-time Mom and I was resigned to the fact that a full night's sleep was something of the past. We were both grateful that Darin had been courteous enough to hang in there until five days after we were able to see Star Wars *on opening day. And a few days after his birth the Apple II, one of the first personal computers, went on sale. I can be such a geek at times.*

So, now the fear sets in. What kind of father will I be? Especially to a son. I don't care for sports all that much. I'm definitely not a handy man. I can replace a light bulb, but I haven't a clue how to replace the socket into which it was just screwed. I'm screwed! I want to be the type of father that my *father isn't. Can you love a son* too *much? Can I say that I love him too often? If I show too much affection will he turn to me some day and yell* "Jeez…enough is enough, already! I get it…I get it!" *If I'm too aloof will he feel neglected? I've read so many thrillers throughout my life that I should know how to commit the perfect crime. Where to hide the bodies. But I haven't cracked one book relating to advice for the nervous new father. Mother's don't have this problem. I have no doubt that Abbie will win every Mother-of-the-Year award available. I think women are programed from birth to handle situations such as motherhood. Was that a sexist statement? Am I worrying too much? But I'm* not *going to be the type of parent who constantly takes countless photos of my kid just because I'm a photographer.*

HERE: Who the hell was I kidding? Just because I *am* a photographer I went through rolls of film weekly, with portraits of Darin all over the damn place!

THERE: *By the time Darin was two years old, I amazed myself by what I had learned, handyman-wise. Of course, it had more to do with challenges at the studio than at home. I knew various types of screwdrivers and how to use them; knew one drill bit from the other, and I could wield a hammer as good as the next guy. As long as the next guy isn't a carpenter.*

A client for a soft drink company (no, not Coke, if that's what you're thinking) presented some layouts for an ad campaign that, at first glance, appeared simple enough. But soon proved otherwise. The Magic-Marker layouts pictured five different cans of fruit-flavored soda nestled in between rocks in a rapidly flowing stream.

"I haven't scouted any locations yet," said Bert Adams, the art director for their in-house advertising department. "I was hoping you might have some ideas. I know that north Georgia has tons of streams and brooks that could work."

He was optimistic. And naïve.

"Oh, I've been to several of those babbling brooks, Bert," I responded. "I've forged many of them with my son in a carrier on my back. However. And this is a big however, mind you. That's a daunting challenge of finding just the right stream, with just the right rocks in just the right positions with just the right amount of water flowing over and around them in just the right way." I paused after that to catch my breath. "And, on top of that, getting my equipment in or close enough to the stream and getting the appropriate lighting that would show off your product in just the right way. I am impressed, by the way, with the packaging designs. Those cans are gorgeous and extremely appealing. We need just the right shots to capture that feeling." I paused again. And thought about this for a silent minute or two. "We'll do it in-house."

"Excuse me?" he asked incredulously.

"Here," I answered, "We'll do it here in the studio."

He stared at me as though my head had just spun completely around in The Exorcist style. I picked up a large note pad and sketched out my idea. I altered his layout from a horizontal format to a vertical one, which would be so much better for a flowing water image.

"I'll build a long, narrow box like this," as I pointed out my layout. "I'll line it with plastic sheeting for waterproofing. I…or you and me, if you'd like to accompany me…will go to a place not too far from here that sells riprap. You know what that is?"

Again, I got the deer-in-the-headlights stare.

"Okay, riprap is large, sometimes beautiful chunks of stone, mostly granite, that's used for all kinds of things, mostly erosion control and landscaping. We can select just the right sizes and shapes that will work best for this layout. I can position those rocks in the box that will look very natural and convincing. We can play with it as much as we need to make the cans fit and to show off the graphics effectively. Here comes my brilliant idea…well, the conclusion of it, anyway. The grand finale. Darin, my son, has a little kiddie wading pool. I'll bring it here to the studio. We'll prop the box up at a slight angle back, with the lower end in the pool. Then my assistant will pour a bucket of water down over the rocks and cans to make it look like a cool, babbling mountain stream. What do think?"

"Hmmm…" said Bert. "Hmmm…" he repeated. "Well, I like your layout better than mine. I'll have to run it by the product manager first to get her

approval. She can be a bitch but I can handle it." He shook his head. "I don't know. You think it could work? Look convincing?"

"Shit, I don't know. I'm making this up as I go along. Never did this before but it's worth a shot. No pun intended."

I built the box and bought the rocks. It took a while to find just the right pieces of riprap to resemble a rocky, roaring brook. When I got them back to the studio, I played for hours getting them assembled in the box to look natural and not a faked set…which, of course, they actually were. Several test "pours" were done so I could see how the water would flow. Mother Nature might strike me dead next time I stepped outdoors but, damn, my little babbling brook was looking good!

The day of the shoot arrived. When Bert Adams got to the studio he informed me that the product manager was going to be there as well. She was very apprehensive about our concept and would pull the plug immediately if things didn't look perfect. Sammy, the latest in my long list of assistants, was primed for an adventurous day that might include a temper tantrum or two. He had graduated from high school two years ago, had no discernable career path, loved photography, had an aptitude for following directions implicitly but, frankly, wasn't the sharpest knife in the drawer. I wasn't sure that he was even in *the drawer.*

I helped Bert carry several cases of Mountain Creek canned soda into the studio. Five flavors and he brought two cases of thirty-six cans of each. That was overkill in my humble opinion, being that we were going to use a total of five cans in the shot: one each of orange, grape, strawberry, lime, and lemon. The colors and the graphics were vibrant and would stand out beautifully against my rocky brook. No sooner had I put down the last case, than the back door to the studio opened and in walked a tall, very skinny woman with a severe haircut to her black locks and with a face that looked as though she had just sucked on a very sour pickle.

"My God, what a frightening place to select for your studio. What kind of neighborhood is this, anyway?" she asked nervously. "How many times have you been mugged down here?"

"Oh, about once every other day, but I've grown fond of it," I responded. "Hi, I'm Baxter Janus and you're…?"

She extended her bony hand to me. "I'm Pricilla Thewliss. I'm the product manager on this account and I assume Albert mentioned that I was going to be here today. I want this done right or I'm pulling the plug."

Nice to meet you, too, *I thought.* I'm sure the broom you flew in on will be perfectly safe out there in my parking lot. *Her hand was cold as ice. She looked around the place, as if scouting out safe shelter should the neighborhood ruffians attack. I figured that if I would suddenly jump and say* "Boo!" *she'd wet herself.*

The coffee was perking and smelling heavenly and I had my stereo system playing some bluegrass, which I thought was appropriate for my faux-bucolic set.

"Point me to your restroom," *Pricilla said abruptly,* "and then let's get started. Do we really need that god-awful music playing?"

Bert and I exchanged glances as she headed down the hallway.

"I really should have warned you," *Bert whispered with an apologetic tone.* "She micro-manages everything. I'm sure she even tells her husband how he can best wipe his ass."

"She's married?" *I asked with widened eyes. I was incredulous.*

"Yeah, to our top salesman. It's a match made in heaven. He's a dick and she's a bitch. And she has a bigger set than he does." *He looked around to make sure she hadn't reentered the room.* "We all call her Pricilla Thoughtless behind her back. She's been known to make grown men cry."

Oh, fuck, *I thought.* This is going to be a long day!

It took hours just to set the cans in among the rocks just perfectly before we even got to pour the water. Pricilla didn't like the color placement.

"We can't have the strawberry next to the lime. It looks too Christmas. We can't have the lemon and the orange close together, there's not enough contrast."

I took Polaroid shots of every placement so she could approve or disapprove until we finally reached a placement that she liked.

"There's a glare on strawberry's logo," *Pricilla said, while scrutinizing a Polaroid.*

I had already seen it and made the appropriate adjustment.

During that time, I had adjusted and readjusted my lights to get the right "outdoorsy" *feeling to the shot. It was looking good. We'd be shooting with 8"*

X 10" sheet film and my cases were all loaded ready to go live. Sammy had several buckets of water standing by. I held my breath.

On all-day shoots, with the client present, I usually order lunch brought in from one of the local restaurants. Pricilla wanted to work straight through. No lunch break. She rummaged through her purse, found a protein bar, unwrapped it and took one little bite before throwing it into the trash. I observed that she had been drinking bottled water all day and not once did she pop open a can of the soda. We had plenty to go around. I'll probably end up handing them out to our friendly neighborhood muggers. Just to be perfectly clear, I have not ever experienced any form of crime in my vicinity.

"Are we ready?" I finally asked.

"Yes," answered Bert, nervously looking toward Pricilla.

"Yes, " answered the thoughtless one. "But if this doesn't work we'll just get a large ice chest filled with ice and shoot that."

"Well, that requires a lot more than that," I said, almost gritting my teeth. "An ice chest shot is so cliché and every beer label does that over and over. Besides, we wouldn't use real ice cubes anyway. I have fake ones but not enough, at this point, to fill a chest. Trust me, this will work." I said that more to convince myself. And Bert has to report to this harridan every single day? I'd be suicidal.

She folded her arms across her chest and looked at me as though I had just squeezed her right tit. I got behind the camera.

"Sammy, get ready. When I say pour, let 'er rip."

"Wait," said Pricilla, "can't we do a test pour first to see how the cans react to the rushing water? It might not work."

Actually, I agreed with her. I should have suggested it. I nodded to Sammy and he poured. One of the cans shifted when hit with the water and disturbed the layout.

"Okay, good call, Pricilla," I said. "I'll get my glue gun and make sure those cans are all immoveable."

With all the cans finally glued to the rocks, I nodded to Sammy for another bucket to be poured. We all stared and I secretly crossed my fingers. Wow! It looked great. It really looked great. It actually did look like a mountainside creek, with water tumbling over the cans. Pricilla exhaled. I figured she probably did that only every ten minutes or so.

"Okay, folks," I said after a large sigh of relief. "Let's make magic."

Sammy poured, I clicked. The strobes went off and Pricilla jumped. I flipped my film holder and Sammy poured again and I clicked again…and again…and yet again. I took a total of fifteen shots. I gathered up all the sheet film holders and handed them to Sammy.

Faking the best Russian accent I could muster, I said "Ahh, beautiful." Pricilla stood momentarily expressionless. "Sammy, take care of these and get the film to the lab pronto. Ask for an express turnaround."

I thought that Bert had tears in his eyes. I hoped from happiness. Happy that the shots looked so great, at least they did through the camera anyway… and happy that it was over. Pricilla had a weird look on her face. I wasn't sure if it was the beginning of a smile or that she had just passed gas.

Magic had, indeed, happened that afternoon. Several months later the resulting ad campaign, with my babbling, flowing brook tumbling over ice-cold cans of Mountain Creek Soda, won a Gold Medal of Distinction at the Art Directors Club of Atlanta annual competition. That brought my gold medal collection to an even dozen.

HERE: Throughout the years, I eventually ended up with several more awards, including six of the prestigious CLIOS.

20

THERE: Although it was January, it still was unseasonably cold for Atlanta. Sub-zero temperatures may have been the norm in New Jersey while I was growing up, but I found it very uncomfortable here and now. The studio heater was working overtime but still there was a distinct chill inside. The late morning shoot was, fortunately, a short and sweet one. Pun intended. It was a simple plate full of pre-wrapped mini chocolate donuts that would be inserted into a catalogue. No food stylist was necessary for this one and no client was in attendance either. The art director supplied the easy-to-follow layout and click, click, click. It was a done deal. Plus I now had six cases of these god-awful donuts left unopened in my studio. Jason, the latest in my constantly changing lineup of assistants, went out the back door to take the trash out to the dumpster. By this time it was shortly after three in the afternoon and I thought that we both would be out of here and on our respective ways home shortly.

"Jesus Christ!" announced Jason as the back door slammed following his return. "It's snowin' out there like a motherfucker!"

He has such a way with words.

"Seriously?" I asked. "No mention of snow in the forecast, was there?"

"Nah, one guy on the TV this morning even said that it was too cold to snow…or that it wouldn't stick because the ground was too cold, or something. The snow would just blow off and swirl around. That's what he said. I think."

"Wait. What?" I asked, shaking my head. "What did he mean too cold

to snow? What the hell is all that white stuff at the north and south poles? It's colder there than a stepmother's kiss. What an idiotic statement."

I poked my head out the back door and was greeted by a blinding sight of white. Everywhere. I haven't seen snow like this in years. It was, indeed, sticking to the ground and was adding up quickly. The studio phone rang as I slammed the door shut.

"Hey, Pop!" exclaimed an excited six-year-old. "It's snowing, it's snowing. Did you see it?"

"I sure did, Darin, I just now saw it outside. If I get home in time, let's build a snowman. Is your mom, there?"

I chatted with Abbie for a couple of minutes and I motioned for Jason to head for home before the storm got any worse. He didn't hesitate.

I had a few remaining chores to do to get ready for tomorrow's shoot. An hour later, making sure the front door was locked, the coffee pot turned off, I grabbed my car keys and headed out to the parking lot in back. My feet crunched through the accumulation as I walked to my car. Snow had to be cleared off of the windshield and front side windows so I could see where I was going. Brought back memories of New Jersey. As a kid, of course, I loved snow. Always looked forward to it. As an adult, not so much. The car didn't seem to like driving around the side of the building. The tires spun in the deepening snow and it didn't come to a complete stop without skidding off to one side. I wasn't in the street yet, so I wasn't in the way of any oncoming traffic. That's when I noticed it. There wasn't any oncoming traffic. I flicked on the car radio.

"This is rapidly becoming a commuter's nightmare," announced a voice that was two octaves lower than God's, but still had a tone of near panic. "Please, folks, stay off the roads. Do not, I repeat, do not go out if you can avoid it. The Perimeter, Two-Eighty-five, has become a parking lot. The interstates are getting even worse. Cars are being abandoned and all the side streets are impassable. If you are sitting in your cars right now and all you see in your rearview mirrors are headlights and all you can see out your front windshield are brake lights, God love ya and good luck. Our thoughts and prayers are with you."

Wasn't that comforting?

I put the car into reverse. The tires spun until I could smell burning rubber, but at least I got the car far enough back into my property to avoid any calamities. Hopefully. I locked the car and went back into the studio.

"Guess what?" I asked as Abbie picked up the phone.

"Please don't tell me you've been in an accident!" she exclaimed with trepidation in her voice. "I've been watching the news and it's a freakin' zoo out there."

"Nope, no accident. I could hardly get out of my parking lot before I realized what was going on. Us Yankees might be used to this shit, but down here? Not so much. Are you guys okay?"

"Yes, we're fine. Hopefully we won't lose power. We're just concerned about you, Bax."

"Well, I'm fine too. Guess I'll be spending the night at the studio. I have plenty of coffee to keep me warm and a shitload of chocolate donuts. So, come the dawn, I'll be on both a sugar high and a caffeine high. I'll be able to bounce home. Kiss Darin goodnight for me…oh, and kiss yourself goodnight for me as well. I'll call you and let you know what the situation is in the morning. If you need me, call me. If need be, I'll walk home!"

I made a fresh pot of coffee and ate half dozen of those mini chocolate donuts. Actually, it was probably a dozen. I put a Dave Brubeck album on my stereo, found a blanket in my prop room and wrapped it around me. I drifted off to sleep on my big turquoise beanbag sofa. Brought back memories. Only this time I was alone.

HERE: And so, that night made history in Atlanta. By the morning of January 13, January 12 was dubbed *Snow Jam '82*. What brought Atlanta and its suburbs to a standstill was a mere 5.8 inches of snow. Not much by us northerners' standards by any stretch of the imagination. But this storm was the birthplace of stories that would surely be passed down through the generations.

~

THERE: *March 10, 1982. Today is the day that the world is supposed to come to an end. According to some doomsday handwringers, anyway. And why? Because of something called Syzygy. Pronounce it correctly and it sounds like you're roaring drunk and slurring your words. Pronounce it incorrectly* *and it sounds like you're roaring drunk and slurring your words. And what the hell is it? Today all nine planets will be in perfect alignment on the same side of the sun. The crackpots fear that the intense gravitational pull, as a result of this alignment, will cause global disasters such as earthquakes, tidal waves, violent storms, little old ladies will be pulled away from their walkers, buildings will tumble, heads will explode. Okay, the last few there were slight exaggerations on my part. Never mind that this has happened every 179 years and will, obviously, continue to do so every 179 years in the future.*

I scheduled my shoots as normal, waiting all day for the earth to move. It didn't. Perhaps Abbie and I can make the Earth move later tonight.

HERE: Obviously there were no catastrophic occurrences on that day, but the publicity that it generated *did* have an affect on six-year-old Darin. It awakened an awareness of nature and our globe in a way that changed the trajectory of his life. One never knows when influences will sneak up behind you and silently work their way into your very being.

21

THERE: *Halloween. One of my favorite nights. Candy, candy and more candy! Well, the candy I can pilfer from Darin's stash after his trick or treating, that is. He's now eight years old and it's no longer easy to grab a candy bar or two after he's gone to bed. Especially those peanut butter cups. I honestly think that he counts each and every piece in the pile before he leaves it alone or leaves me alone with it. And counts it again afterwards. The little twit!*

It was a perfect night for all the ghosts and goblins, princes and princesses, super heroes and villains to run from house to house, sure to end up with sugar highs that will last for days. I had bought a few bags of bite-sized candy bars to distribute at the studio should any kids venture to knock on my door. A couple had, but by the time I was ready to head for home I still had dozens of chocolate delights remaining. I was torn. Keep them here at the studio and devour them myself over the next week or bring them home to Darin? What the hell...I took them home. Abbie greeted me when I walked through the kitchen, in from the garage. She put her finger to her lips, indicating that I should keep quiet. She leaned in close and whispered in my ear.

"Darin hasn't gone out yet. He's been waiting patiently for you to get home. He wants to scare you. He'll be hiding down the hall somewhere. Act scared." And she giggled.

I started to walk down the long dark hallway leading into the living room and dining room. All the lights had been turned off, but there was still some faint light coming through the front windows on the porch. I actually had difficulty seeing anything as I slowly, ever so slowly walked forward. I didn't hear a sound. Was Darin really hiding here somewhere? I stopped to listen. Still not a sound. I could hear some kids calling "Trick or Treat?" far off in the distance, maybe across the street, but not a sound from inside the house. I took a cautious step. Then another.

"GAAARRRGH!" screamed Darin right up close behind me. Somehow he had hidden so well that I hadn't seen him as I passed his secret place. Actually I jumped and my heart started racing before I laughed and laughed. He was laughing so hard he almost fell down. I turned on the hall light and he spread his wings. He was dressed as a big black bat. And it was an awesome costume, at that. He headed back to the kitchen, laughing with glee, bouncing up and down, flapping his elegant bat wings.

"Fledermaus, fledermaus," I quietly whispered to myself. Gram would have been in tears by now. I was close to it.

HERE: I think I may have peed myself just a little when Darin scared me that night. At least I didn't fart.

~

THERE: *Old traditions can come crumbling, tumbling down like the walls of Jericho, not with the blaring bleating of rams' horns but with the pleading voice of an innocent eight-year-old child.*

Case in point: the Christmas tree.

When I was a young kid, our Christmas tree was always put up the day before Christmas. Santa would decorate it on his visit later that night. As a parent now, however, I can see how horrendously frustrating and tiring that must have been for our parents. Of course, at that time most of the toys were already preassembled. No hair-pulling and swearing to discover almost at the crack of dawn that there were two parts missing from one thing or another. Aside from books, my favorites gifts were Lincoln Logs and Erector Sets. No assembly required except by me! And, of course, the magnificent Lionel train set.

Back to the Christmas tree. I don't know if it's just a southern thing or if the times they are a-changin' all over. It seems to me these days that Christmas trees start appearing in houses before the last of the Halloween candy has been devoured. This did not go unnoticed by our ever-observant Darin.

We were barely finished stuffing ourselves with Thanksgiving dinner when he stated: "Carson has a Christmas tree up already. Decorated and everything. So does Bobby Matolla. And Greg Frazier. Why can't we put ours up?"

Is he at that point, now, when the magic of Christmas has dissipated? It's too soon. I hope it's too soon.

"Well," I started slowly after glancing at Abbie. "That's usually Santa's job. You know, decorating it and everything."

He stared at me and arched an eyebrow. Where did he get that *trait?*

"Pop, but we can help him out, you know. Make his night a little easier. I'm sure he'd really appreciate it and not feel slighted." Where did he learn that *word? "We can leave him a few extra cookies so we won't hurt his feelings. Please?"*

I sighed and looked into Abbie's tear-filled eyes.

Two days later we drove out to a tree farm in the country and picked out a beautiful Fraser fir, perfectly shaped. It was set up in our living room and decorated by all of us, with Bing Crosby and the Andrews Sisters caroling to us in the background. It looked gorgeous and the aroma was simply amazing. Christmas had started early for the first time at the Janus household.

HERE: And two days after that, Darin confessed to us that he had known we were Santa for the past year. Damn that Bobby Matolla!

22

THERE: *The first indication that something was afoot was a seemingly innocuous one.*

"If you weren't going to finish that apple," Abbie said to me one morning as she poured herself a cup of coffee, "the least you could have done was put it in the garbage."

"Excuse me?"

She pointed to a half-eaten apple, with its flesh a disturbing brown, resting on the kitchen counter. She continued getting breakfast ready for Darin.

"I didn't eat that apple," I replied. "I didn't leave it there."

"Well, I was the last one to go up to bed last night and Darin hasn't come down yet," she said with a stern, almost reprimanding tone. "And, speaking of Darin, he'd better get his ass down here pronto or he'll be late for school," she continued.

If I didn't know better, I'd say she wasn't in the best of moods.

"Please, Baxter, go up and get him moving. I've got to get to the agency earlier this morning. We have a major pitch this afternoon to a prospective client and I want to make sure my guys have their shit together."

Nope. Not a good mood.

I knocked on Darin's door. "Get a move on, kiddo. Time's wasting." Not a peep from inside. I slowly opened his door and he was still wrapped around the blankets, sound asleep. What the hell? "Darin, get your ass outta bed, dammit! You should be heading to school in fifteen minutes."

He groaned a groggy groan and slowly opened his eyes. "What? Isn't today Saturday?"

"No, it sure as hell isn't Saturday. It's Tuesday. Get your butt in gear and get ready."

He made it to school on time, but just barely.

The next morning I discovered a limp brown banana peel lying on the top shelf of the refrigerator when I opened it to get cream for my coffee. Without giving it a second thought, I tossed it into the garbage and headed out the door to the studio. Early shoot. By the time I had reached the car I had forgotten about the peel. Not only did I have an early shoot, but also it was going to be a late night tonight. I was invited to give a presentation about commercial photography and the new trends in marketing at the Art Directors Club of Atlanta. I was eager to see many of my current clients, schmooze some new ones and chat with some of my fellow photographers. All ego aside, I can be such a ham in front of an audience.

The morning after the night before, the wonderful aroma of coffee lured me down the stairs and into the kitchen. I bounced into the room with a dopey smile on my face and yawned, perhaps a bit too loudly. When Abbie heard me enter the room, she turned, leaned up against the counter, folded her arms across her chest and glowered at me.

Oh, Christ! Another bad mood morning.

"Were you drunk when you came home last night?"

"What? No! What the hell?" I lost that dopey smile.

"Are you sure?" Still glowering, now with one arched eyebrow.

I shook my head in confusion and shrugged my shoulders.

"A couple of us stopped off at Manuel's Tavern but, after a very long day, I had just one beer, thanked them all for a great meeting and left. I came straight home. Sober as a judge, as the cliché goes. What's got a hair up your ass this morning?"

She lowered her arms but still glowered. I may never use that term again.

"Did you happen to pee in the wastebasket when you came in?"

She pointed to the wastebasket she kept near her small workstation in the kitchen.

"What the fuck? Of course I didn't!"

"Are you sure?" she repeated.

"I did not pee in that fucking wastebasket. Are you insane?"

Oh, shit. Don't ever say that to an angry woman!

She took a step away from the counter, coming in my direction. My breathing may have halted for a moment but I didn't flinch.

"Well, somebody did," she said, pointing again to the wastebasket in question. "It certainly wasn't me. Darin had gone up to bed hours before I did. And you came into bed hours later. We have neither cat nor dog to blame it on."

I had to stop and think. One beer wouldn't render me with amnesia. All the doors had been locked when I got home, so no vagrant could wander in, take a piss, and vanish back into the night. Besides, we don't have vagrants in Druid Hills. They're not allowed. I heard Darin coming down the stairs and he came into the kitchen swinging his backpack.

"Did you pee in the wastebasket?" I asked him, pointing to the receptacle with a soggy bottom. He stopped, looked at me, and then looked at the wastebasket.

"Somebody peed in the wastebasket?" He giggled. " Eeww, gross," was all he could say.

The conversation regarding the dastardly act proceeded no further from there at the moment, but the case wasn't at all closed. Abbie was pissed (no pun intended), still certain that I had done the deed. I was confused, certain that I hadn't. Darin, on the other hand, nonchalantly gulped down his cereal, drank his milk, grabbed his backpack and cheerfully headed out the door with a wave and a "love you, guys!" Abbie continued to glo…stare, it was stare, at me as she went about her preparation for work.

Two nights later, after Abbie and Darin had long since gone to bed, I sat in the living room very eager to finish the latest thriller we had gotten from the library. The only light in the house shone down over my shoulder as I read. I was really concentrating and nearly had the final twist figured out when I heard a slight noise. It came from the kitchen.

I put the book down, marking my place, and slowly, quietly got up. I went to the hallway and started tiptoeing my way. Fortunately I was in stocking feet, so I didn't make a sound. I stepped on a floorboard that creaked and I held my breath. I reached the doorway and peeked in. The only light was coming from the refrigerator, the door of which was standing wide open. The silhouette in front of the fridge was small. It was Darin. He simply stood there, in his pajamas, staring into it.

"Darin?" I barely whispered. I didn't want to scare him. Well, shit! He had scared me. He didn't move. No indication that he had heard me. He slowly turned and looked right at me. No, actually, it seemed as though he was looking right through me. His eyes were wide open but vacant.

"Take everything out of here but the airplane," he said. And he slowly walked toward the hallway. He walked, blindly, right past me. I had to step aside so he wouldn't walk right into me.

"Holy shit," I muttered.

Darin was sleepwalking. Our son is a freakin' somnambulist! But since when? Certainly explains a lot of things and opens the door for more questions.

Sheer coincidence, but not really, the next day Abbie received a call from Darin's teacher. Abbie relayed this to me when I got home.

"Don't be alarmed, Mrs. Janus," said the sweet voice, Abbie related. "He didn't hurt himself, but I think Darin fell asleep at his desk and plopped out of his seat and onto the floor. Everybody thought he was playing a joke, but he looked just as surprised as the rest of us."

Abbie stopped telling me the rest of the conversation at that point. Now we were worried. We did a lot of research on the subject. Sleepwalking was, evidently, quite common especially among children. They can do strange things, including eating, (and peeing in wastebaskets), but usually outgrow it around eight or nine years old. It is often caused by trauma, stress or lack of sleep. There had been no trauma in Darin's young life. None that we were aware of, anyway. Stress? Are you kidding? He's so stress-free it's sickening. But lack of a proper amount of sleep? We know when he goes up to bed every night. He has to turn off the TV in his room by 9:30 and lights-out shortly thereafter. Lately, though, we practically have to drag him out of bed in the morning. That hadn't always been the case. So what was it? I had a plan.

Darin went up to bed at his usual time, kissing us both good night and taking the stairs two at a time. An hour later Abbie called it a night after falling asleep in front of the television. Evidently Magnum, P.I. *wasn't exciting enough for her. I told her that I'd be up there shortly, but I knew she'd be asleep before her head hit the pillow and wouldn't have a clue about when I actually came upstairs. Fortunately I didn't have a shoot in the morning, so no need to get to the studio. I fixed a cup of coffee to keep me alert. I started reading another book. I can zip through them in a heartbeat at times.*

It was almost 12:45 and I decided it was time. No pun intended. I turned out the lights, took off my shoes and crept up the stairs like a panther waiting to pounce. I looked down the long, dark hallway. Past our bedroom door, on the other side of the hall, was Darin's room. I wasn't sure but I could almost see a very faint light coming from under his door. I slinked up to it and pressed my ear gently against it. There was, indeed, a muffled sound. I took hold of the doorknob and slowly started to turn it. When the latch was free, I thrust the door open swiftly. Darin was seated on his bed. He jumped and let out a little shriek.

"Shit, Pop, why'd you do that?" he said sheepishly, dropping what he had in his hand. "Jeez, you nearly gave me an attack." Then I thought he started to cry. Just a little. Not a baby cry.

"Okay, kiddo, what's up?" I asked, with my hands on my hips. I could have done the Abbie thing with arms folded across my chest, but thought this was more masculine. I knew, now, exactly what was up. That damn Nintendo thing that we got him for Christmas has become an addiction. "Is this what you've been doing every fucking night?" I don't usually swear with him or at him, but we had been alarmed, to say the least. "This is why you fell outta your goddamn seat at school? Why you've been sleepwalking and scaring the holy crap out of us?" He buried his head. It could have been worse. It could have been far worse. It could have been drugs. He could have found my stash of Playboys. He's too young for either of those. Isn't he? Sleep deprivation is a serious thing. Abbie and I should know only too well. We've both had to pull all-nighters in the past.

With careful monitoring to make sure that Darin did, actually, go to bed and stay there every night, and with the Nintendo on restriction for the time being, his sleepwalking vanished within the week. He still giggles, from time to time, when he passes that wastebasket. It's a new one now.

HERE: Although Darin was given an allotted, much shortened, amount of daily Nintendo use at that time, video games increased in fascination and creativity as the years progressed. In fact, I was just reading a study conducted by researchers at Oxford University stating that the time spent playing video games could be good for mental health. Imagine that! Who knew, eh? Darin's abilities and skill at them enthralled us. So much so that we became major players as well. I have to admit that the graphics are simply breathtaking. Abbie still stays up long after I've gone to bed to play them on the computer. Addictions take on many forms.

23

THERE: We did manage to take time for ourselves every year and travel abroad. My childhood collection of thirty flags of as many nations served as our goal. Some years we managed to hit two or three of those countries in one trip. We were in awe of our magnificent globe and its many wonders. Poor Abbie got tired of hearing my camera clicking constantly on our travels. We were collecting memories as fast as frequent flier points. Sailing in a felucca down the Nile, kissing like young lovers on top of the Eiffel Tower, snuggling under an umbrella and sharing a large Cadbury chocolate bar while waiting for Big Ben to strike midnight, taking a horse trek in Australia, marveling at the architecture of Machu Picchu in Peru, walking hand-in-hand along the Great Wall of China. And almost getting thrown out of the theater at the Peking Opera. The Chinese seem to have a problem with translations and quite often transpose letters when converting Chinese to English; "carvings" became "cravings", for example. Such was the case at the opera house. Traditionally, all performers are male, meaning that beautiful maidens are actually guys. That was funny enough for my taste. But when two "lovers" are strolling through a beautiful blossom-laden garden on stage and stare lovingly into a pond and sing the line that should have been (I assumed, anyway) "See the golden carp floating in the pond", but the supertitles projected above the stage transposed two inappropriate letters to become "See the golden crap floating in the pond" I lost it. Loudly. Abbie grabbed me by the arm and we left the theater. Quickly.

HERE: Our trips weren't as frequent as every year the older we got. We spaced them out because of other priorities. Raising and educating Darin, for example. But after the fall of the Soviet Union, my dream had been to travel to Russia. Annika, Efrem's beautiful wife, had been born in Saint Petersburg. So, following her suggestions via long telephone conversations and emails, off we went. Magnificent country with incredible history. Strolling along Nevsky Prospect, sort of the main street of the city, we came across a huge bookstore, Dom Knigi. I can't resist bookstores. I made a few purchases just for the fun of it. They were thrillers that I had already read, the difference being that they were in Russian. Did I speak Russian? Hell, no, but they would be fun to have anyway. Upstairs, above the bookstore, was the Café Singer where we enjoyed a delicious, leisurely late luncheon of Russian dumplings, watching life go by down on the street below through large windows. The beautiful art nouveau building was originally constructed in 1904 for, surprise, surprise, the Singer Sewing Machine Company. During World War One it served as the U.S. Embassy.

We eventually made our way to a surprising Moscow by way of the bullet train, Sapsan, named after a fast, high-flying bird. Remembering that beautiful oil painting hanging in the Goldschmitt's living room, I finally got my chance to photograph the colorful architectural beauty of St. Basil's Cathedral in Red Square. It was worth the wait. I stood back and watched with fascination as fashion models, makeup artists, and a photographer preceded with a photo shoot outside of GUM Department store a few steps away.

24

THERE: *A few more years zipped by…*

I was just finishing up a photo shoot, a nice lucrative one, for one of my favorite clients. Marty Howce was a fairly new art director at the Compton Paperboard Packaging Company and he always managed to create some beautiful challenges for me. I had hired one of the best food stylists in town for the shoot, Maxine Gaffney, and she could work magic with even the most mundane products. This was the first time that Marty was going to work with Max. The shoot today involved frozen breaded fish sticks and filets. Marty had designed some interesting layouts involving beautiful folded napkins, colorful plates and a little dish of coleslaw to accompany each item. The setup was to look like the plates had been placed on rough-hewn wooden planks, such as on a weathered seaside dock. I watched in admiration as Max built each dish of coleslaw like a bird building a nest; one piece at a time, making sure it would be photogenic. Details like this simply amaze me every time. My former assistant had recently moved out of state, so I was handling this assignment totally on my own…meaning that I had to adjust the lights, and reload the sheet film…stuff like that, slowing things down a bit.

Marty and Max were chatting as they checked the set up and he adjusted the elements by looking in the back of the camera.

"Funny, but you're the second Max I know in this town," Marty said, as

he squinted and assessed the layout. "A coworker of mine is the art director for the corrugated division of my company. Max Holliday."

"Oh, yeah," answered Max as she fiddled with one of the napkins, trying to get it to look just right. "I know him and his crazy wife Camellia. The lady with all those big hats. I catered desserts for one of their big New Year's parties a couple years ago."

"Well, I'll be damned," Marty answered, "Small world, isn't it?"

"Ha!" Max responded, "sounds like a song from that show 'Gypsy', doesn't it?"

"I guess," Marty shrugged. "If you say so. I wouldn't know."

The shoot went well. It had been a long day, with six different setups, and we were all tired.

"I know you're looking for a new assistant," Max blurted out as we were wrapping things up and she was cleaning all the dishes. "A friend of mine is going to stop by. Actually, I thought he would have been here by now. He has aspirations of becoming a photographer as well…oh, and he's really good… but he's young and he needs to learn the ropes. He's great with fashion and fantastic with architecture, but he's never none any real food shoots, you know, tabletop stuff, like what we're doing today. And what you're the best at. You'd be great for him, I just know. I think you'll like him a lot. I told him where to park around back."

"Sure," I responded as I was slowly changing out the lenses in my camera. "I do need a helper around here, especially if…"

As if on cue, the back door to my studio opened and there stood a huge silhouette blocking out the daylight. The door shut behind him and he seemed to disappear in the darkness. He was the tallest black man I had ever seen. He was also the most handsome black man I had ever seen. His head was as smooth and shiny as one of those magic 8-balls.

"Hey, Liam," shouted Max, "Glad you could make it," and she laughed, almost snorting.

I stood and walked over to greet this giant. "Hi," I said, extending my hand," I'm Bax Janus."

"Nice to meet you," he responded in deep booming voice and with an accent that was very thick and, I thought, most distinctly Jamaican. "I'm Liam Thordycroft."

Because of his accent I misunderstood his last name. "Thundercloud?" I asked. Both he and Max laughed raucously.

"Thorndycroft," he corrected, still sounding like Thundercloud to me, "but, you know what, mon? I love that. Thundercloud. You can call me that if you'd like." And he chuckled again.

"Hell, no! Excuse the bluntness, but there's no way I'm going to call a big black guy Thundercloud! Thunder, maybe, but definitely not Thundercloud." And everybody laughed and laughed.

HERE: And from that day on, Liam Thorndycroft was known as Thunder. Just plain Thunder.

THERE: *Max got up and gave Liam…now Thunder…a big hug. Marty came over with his hand outstretched too.*

"You are certainly a tall guy!" Marty said as he looked up into the young man's face. "I'm six-four and I have to look way up. How tall are you?"

Thunder smiled. "A little over six-ten, I guess."

"Oh, for shit's sake!" gasped Marty.

"No shit," laughed Thunder.

"Okay, kids," I said. "Marty. Max. Out. Go home. Go to a bar. Whatever. Liam and I need to talk for a while and then I need to get this film to the lab before they close. I'll have the shots back by late tomorrow afternoon, Marty. Can you swing by then to go over them?"

"Nope, I'll be trapped in an all-day sales meeting at the office. I've been given an hour on the program. Courier them out to me and I'll let you know what's what day after tomorrow. Everything looked spectacular through the lens, though. Glad my client wasn't here today. He would have really slowed the process. He's an asshole, but his company pays well. I'm happy that he trusts me as well as he does. Just what the unsuspecting public needs, right? More frozen fish crap. At least the packaging will be gorgeous. All ego aside, of course."

I shook my head and rolled my eyes. I liked Marty a lot. A little high on himself at times, but justifiably so. He had a way with words and I could picture him winning over client after client with his talent and suave approach. Abbie thought he was gorgeous. She had stopped by the studio once recently when Marty and I were going over some proofs.

"He can put his shoes under my bed any time," she cooed later that evening.

"Oh, stop with that tired old cliché," I scolded. "He's married already."

"Well, he's hot," she said, pouting. "And that voice of his could melt the polar ice caps."

I sighed. "Jesus, take a cold shower, will ya?"

⟡

HERE: Thunder developed into far more than my trusted assistant. Aside from being the absolute best of my long line of sometimes good, sometimes fair, often times disappointing and lazy assistants, his photography style, more often than not, blew me away. He had a great eye for imaginative composition, not only with our tabletop setups, but also with his personal stuff including landscapes and portraits. He was a voracious reader of anything to do with photography. Our conversations throughout our days working together grew more fascinating as the months went by. I allowed him to take on projects of his own and to use the studio's facilities. All I asked in return was for him to pay the cost of his material. This relationship paid off eventually.

⟡

THERE: *Thunder came into the studio with a new camera under his arm.*

"It's a new digital thing, mon," he announced. "Thought I'd give it a try and see what happens. You know, they say this in the new wave in photography. Film is on the way out."

"I know, I know, " I responded. "I've been doing a lot of reading up on it. Not sold yet. Guess I'm still old school, you know? And I still prefer good old vinyl records to those CDs. I like the sound better. I still think that film is better than digital. But, we'll see."

Aside from the new camera, I could tell that there was something else different about Thunder this morning. He had an added spring to his step and I caught him smiling throughout the day for no apparent reason.

"What's up with you, Thunder?" I finally asked. By mid-day, curiosity was killing me.

"Say what, mon?"

"You've had a silly smile on your face for most of the day. So…what's up?"

"Oh, mon, don' want to put the goat mouth on it. You know, you say jinx."

I have gotten accustomed to his use of Jamaican slang and have even caught myself using it from time to time.

"A couple years ago doctors tol' my dear wife that we couldn't have kids, you know. Poor Constanse was heartbroken. My own fadder teased me about maybe I was a chi chi man…you know, gay…because we had no kids. We kept trying anyway. We tried a lot. But we tink she might be pregnant. Maybe, we keep our fingers and toes crossed. If it is so, it is truly a blessing."

Seven and a half months later, Constanse gave birth. Thunder was now the father to a healthy, handsome boy. A handsome boy named Blessing.

25

THERE: *It was a shoot that I was actually dreading. When I heard the name Pricilla Thewliss, my sphincter clamped shut. Although the shots for Mountain Creek Sodas that I had taken a few years ago had won all kinds of awards, dealing with that witchy woman was far from pleasant. Bert Adams, the old art director on the account, had moved on to greener (and friendlier) pastures. His replacement called to introduce himself and wanted to schedule a shoot for a new campaign. At first I thought he was being funny and simply pulling my leg. I soon realized that his parents must have played a very cruel, life-long joke on him. Seriously. His name was Justin Thyme. Seriously.*

He faxed over some layouts to me so I could get him an estimate. Being that the lovely Pricilla would be attending the shoot I was tempted to give him an outrageous number. But I acquiesced and was fair about it. Unlike the tumbling, splashing water of the last challenge, this was a picnic setting. Checkered tablecloth…cliché…picnic basket…cliché…cans of soda in an ice chest…cliché…and a smattering of the requisite food, such as fried chicken, chips, sliced veggies and what have you. This shoot would require a food stylist and a lot of props. The average consumer has no idea what goes into taking these "simple" shots. This one would be an all-day situation and then some.

I called Max Gaffney, my favorite food stylist, described the shot and faxed her the layout. She was also my prop shopper. Actually, she and Thunder went out together to gather all the stuff we needed. I look forward to food shoots. I already anticipated the wonderful aroma of frying chicken wafting throughout the studio.

The shoot was scheduled to start early, considering it elaborateness. Thunder and I got to the studio to start setting up at 7. And at 9, just in time, Justin Thyme came through the doors. I can't believe I really said that. He was a very good-looking young man. Probably in his late twenties, he stood a bit over six feet, had deep green eyes and very blond wavy hair. I wondered if his eyes were colored contacts, they were that brilliant. He was wearing jeans and a tight navy blue pullover polo shirt showing off a well- muscled torso. I was jealous. I tried to pull in my slight paunch.

Max arrived shortly after and headed right into the studio's kitchen. Justin carried in cases of the sodas from his car…three cases of each of the five flavors. I was positive that hidden somewhere in the recesses of my studio I must have dozens more cans from the previous shoot. I sent Thunder out to help him carry in the remaining cases. I thought I caught a strange look on Justin's face, but it might have been just my imagination.

"I'm sorry to have been so rude," I said to Justin. "I should have introduced the two of you a moment ago. Justin, this is my wonderful assistant Thunder." They shook hands and Justin had a weird little smirk on his face.

"What is it?" I asked.

Justin shook his head. "Nothing. Don't worry about it." But the smirk didn't disappear.

Thunder and I set up the scene. Fake grass with the tablecloth spread open. We placed the basket, still empty, and then arranged the ice chest. We filled it with acrylic ice cubes; so real you thought that they would surely melt. Once we placed the canned soda amongst the cubes I would spray them with glycerin to fake the frosty, glistening wet, enticing drinks. I heard Max slicing the veggies in the kitchen and began to smell the amazing aroma of frying chicken. I knew that she would prepare enough for our lunches when the time came. No need to order out today!

Justin was doing a good job of making sure the rough layouts were being followed in real life. He wasn't a novice. He got behind the camera to look through the lens and didn't question the fact that the image was upside down. I was impressed.

The back door to the studio opened and, once again, my sphincter reacted. If Pricilla Thewliss had a theme song, it would be similar to that of the Wicked Witch of the West, for sure. Although her skin wasn't green, she was dressed completely in black. A black pants suit and a long purple scarf around her neck. She carried a large purple purse to match the scarf.

"I see your neighborhood hasn't improved any since I was here last," were her very first words. "Find any bodies in that dumpster out back lately?"

Oh, dear God. That scarf around her neck was so tempting. Just one quick yank…

"Occasionally," I responded, "If they're fresh enough, we cook them and serve them as luncheon to clients here at our shoots." I caught Justin smirking again.

Thunder came back into the room from the kitchen and I saw a strange look come over Pricilla's face. Well, stranger than normal. Is it possible for a dour expression to become even dourer? I introduced the two of them but Pricilla didn't reach for Thunder's outstretched hand.

"I need to use your restroom," she announced in a hurry, clutching her purse to her chest as she went. I noticed that Justin had closed his eyes and was shaking his head. Uh, oh…this was not going to end well.

When Pricilla came back in to the room, she approached me and whispered into my ear.

"Do you have a place where I can lock this up?" she said, indicating her purse, and with quick glance toward Thunder.

"It's perfectly safe here," I said, indicating a nearby chair. "I haven't had any robberies in, oh, seven or eight hours now." She wasn't amused. But then, neither was I.

Thunder and I worked at setting the lights and then moving them accordingly as needed. We started taking light readings and placing the props. Max came in from the kitchen with the slices of fresh veggies, a couple bowls of chips (the chips, all perfectly shaped and strategically placed) and started arranging them according to Justin's layout. Pricilla watched. And kept an eye on her purse. The cans of soda were being placed in the faux ice cubes, all rotated so the flavors and logo appeared prominently. I had several film holders loaded and ready to go. Justin and Max worked, side by side, arranging and rearranging the various elements. It was beginning to look like a real picnic setting.

Pricilla kept poking her head under the black cloth I had placed over the camera. It keeps the ambient light out of the viewfinder and makes it a lot easier to see exactly what we're shooting. If Justin made any little adjustments to the layout, Pricilla would readjust. Simple little minor readjustments, and I mean minor. Turning a can a fraction of an inch in one direction or another. Moving a folded napkin further under a plate. And the color placement of the five flavors had to be just right. I remembered from the last shoot. But, what the hell. She was the client. She was paying the bills. It's a wonder that my tongue hadn't started bleeding from all the biting of it that I was doing.

Magic was about to happen again. It couldn't happen soon enough.

"You know, " I said to Justin as I played a bit with the focus, "Max has told me in the past that fried chicken is a major challenge, right, Max?"

"Oh, yeah," she answered as she continued to fidget with the props. "If you don't do it right, it all looks like batches of blotchy batter and mystery meat. You have to be able to separate the pieces so they photograph perfectly and look appetizing."

Before she brought out the chicken, I took some Polaroids to make sure the placement and lighting looked perfect. I attached a couple small branches with leaves on them in front of a light to cast some summery shadows on the set. Justin liked that idea. Pricilla did not. Scrap the leaves.

After a couple more hours of careful arranging, it was time for some clicking of the shutter. Out came the chicken. Needless to say, it was cold now, but who cares? It didn't matter and looked just perfect. Each piece was defined beautifully. Each piece was photogenic. I spritzed the soda cans with glycerin and they looked wet and refreshingly cold. The studio lights were turned off and the strobes flashed with each press of my cable release. I took half a dozen shots and they looked great through the camera back.

"Let's take a quick lunch break before we shoot a few more," I suggested. "I

might want to fritz around a little with the layout, if you have no objections, Justin...Pricilla?"

They agreed and Max went back into the kitchen to get some freshly cut veggies, more chips and some freshly fried chicken. What a feast! She wheeled everything out on a little cart, along with a stack of paper plates and lots of napkins. Obviously we had enough sodas for our beverages. I could have invited in half the neighborhood, for that matter.

Ever the true gentleman, Thunder asked Pricilla "Can I fix you a plate, ma'am?"

"NO!" was a too quick and too harsh of a reply. "No. Thank you. I'm a fussy eater and I'll take care of myself, thank you."

I glanced at Justin and he very slightly, quietly shook his head while pursing his lips.

"Justin," I said, "I want to show you something in the kitchen. Perhaps we can use it in a couple shots later."

He followed me.

"Okay, what the hell is happening out there?" I asked, hands placed firmly on my hips and staring right into his deep green eyes.

"Oh, Baxter. I am truly so sorry," he responded in a low whisper, visibly shaken. "I know you've dealt with Pricilla before but I'm sure under different circumstances, right? I didn't know if I should've warned you, but never thought you might have an assistant like Thunder. Look, I think he's great, for what it's worth, and I am thrilled by his attentiveness. I have absolutely no problem whatsoever. You have no idea what we all contend with at the office. This is not the segregated south anymore but Pricilla can't get over it. Hell, I think she's still fighting the fucking Civil War. I honestly refuse to believe that HR lets her get away with this shit, believe me. They simply look the other way. She's run off two previous art directors before me because of her rotten, strident behavior and abhorrent racist views. I'm about to give my two weeks notice. Before you ask, yes, I have another job all lined up. I can't wait to leave. Actually, I think I'd love to see her face if she ever found out that my significant other is black. And a man. She's never even bothered with asking about my personal life. She just doesn't care. You've probably heard that we call her Pricilla Thoughtless behind her back. Heartless would be more like it.

Baxter, you're a prince. The patience you've shown today has been remarkable. I sincerely hope I get to work with you again."

I shrugged my shoulders, sighed and slowly shook my head.

"Hey," I said, "let's go eat some chicken and get this shoot wound up. It's looking great. You're doing a fantastic job, Justin, I'm impressed." We shook hands and headed back into the studio.

Max and Thunder had cleaned up the area, but there were a few pieces of fried chicken left. Justin and I polished them off, licking our fingers and winking at each other. Max prepared some freshly sliced vegetable sticks, arranged some more chips in a bowl and fried a couple more pieces of chicken. The shoot proceeded, with me trying a couple of different angles and lighting arrangements.

Three more hours went by and then I finally said, with my faux Russian accent, "Ahhh...beautiful!" Justin laughed. Pricilla glowered.

We started cleaning up, breaking down the set, as I handed all the film holders to Thunder. "Off you go, my good man, get thee to the lab pronto, pronto. Can't wait to see them."

Pricilla watched as he left, and then looked around, putting her purse down in the chair I had indicated earlier.

"Fried chicken must have been right up his alley. Too bad we didn't throw in some watermelon for good measure. Have you not had any problems with him as an assistant?" she asked. Now it was my *turn to glower.*

"What do you mean?" I asked, folding my arms across my chest. This was going to be anything but clever, friendly repartee.

"Well, I think you know what I mean. Don't be coy. Can he be trusted? Anything of value suddenly disappearing?"

Justin suddenly disappeared into the rest room. Max stopped what she was doing and stared at Pricilla. I cleared my throat. And cleared it once more.

"Liam Thorndycroft, AKA Thunder, is one of the most honest, trustworthy, conscientious gentlemen I know. He is bright, friendly, cooperative and will make an exceptional photographer in his own right one of these days. I consider him a loyal friend. He is not naïve, nor was he oblivious to your rude behavior with him today."

She pulled herself up and huffed.

"I, quite frankly, was offended by it, Pricilla. Here's the deal. We took

some great shots here today. Your guy, Justin, did very well and I'm impressed. He is very talented. You, on the other hand, really pissed me off."

She started to speak but I put up my hand to cut her off.

"I'll get these shots to you sometime tomorrow. I have no doubt they will be award winners, just like the last time. They're freebies. I won't charge you a plug nickel for them. I've never done this nor said this to any other client. I may be biting off my nose to spite my face but, please, I implore you, don't ever ask to use my services again. The only thing I hate worse than a truly snobby, bitchy, control freak of a woman is a truly bigoted *snobby, bitchy, control freak of a woman. You, dear lady, hit it outta the fucking ballpark."*

Max dropped the bowl she was holding and I heard Justin flush in the restroom.

Fast-forward four months. Justin Thyme called me from his new job to set up a shoot. He eventually became a valued client and a good friend.

The new ad campaign for Mountain Creek Sodas broke, with some interesting picnic table shots. None of which were mine.

HERE: That incident was decades before laws were passed meant to prevent prejudicial behavior such as Pricilla's, blatant or otherwise, in the workplace. Alas, prejudice still exists, although less visible…less vocal.

I had used 8 X 10 sheet film for that shoot, which was expensive in itself, to say nothing of the fee for the food stylist, the cost of the food and props, the film processing, and then Thunder's hourly wage. I swallowed a shitload of money that day, but at least I hadn't swallowed my pride.

26

THERE: *I hate it when the phone rings at 3 A.M. As optimistic as I am as a rule, I knew this wasn't going to be a happy call.*

"Baxter," Mom sobbed into the phone, "I need you to get here as quickly as you can. I'm sorry to call at this hour but something horrible just happened and…" she paused to catch her breath and collect her thoughts. "The police just came to the house and, oh, shit, I can't believe this is happening!"

"Mom, take a breath, slow down for a second and tell me what the hell is going on." I could hear her breathing on the other end.

"Your father was working late, trying to finish up the plans for a new development. He's been working really late for weeks on end. He's looked so tired and haggard. He's getting too old for the pressure. I've told him for months to retire. I've been so afraid for his health. Oh, Baxter, just please get here. Your father's been shot."

HERE: That's a phrase you don't hear often.

THERE: *"Wait. What did you just say?"*

"The police just told me he's at some hospital in Denville, near where his offices are. It's been on the news that there's been a lot of crime in that area lately and that had me concerned, too. I'm waiting on a taxi to take me there now. The police think he was the victim of a robbery. Evidently

he was shot in the office parking lot. He must have been going out to his car to come home. Taxi's here. Gotta go. Please get here fast!"

How the hell does one get to New Jersey from Atlanta fast? First I had to leave a long, detailed message on Thunder's answering machine. The studio was booked solid for the next three weeks. Obviously schedules needed to be shuffled accordingly. Not knowing how long I would be gone made rescheduling tricky. Delta wasn't ready when I was. The first flight I could get to Newark was at 9:30.

"Go," Abbie said after I had related Mom's call. "I'll take care of all the stuff that I can around here. I'll help out with Thunder rearranging schedules if he needs me and Darin needs to not miss any more school than he has to, should a serious end come to this situation. Go. Just go. Don't worry about us here. If you need me, call, and I'll be there. If it comes down to that."

It came down to that. Dad was dead hours before I arrived at the hospital. He had survived the ambulance ride to the hospital but not the ride on the gurney into the emergency OR. Mom had waited there for me and collapsed into my arms when she saw me. I couldn't believe it. He wasn't the most loving of fathers and he and I had had our tense moments throughout the years but I, too, cried in my mother's embrace. His body was still in the hospital morgue. Mom said I could see him if I wanted to but she advised against it. Dad had been shot in the face and it wasn't a pretty sight. I had rented a car at the airport and asked my mom if there was anything else we needed to do here.

"Not that I know of," she answered meekly. "I'll have to make arrangements, I guess, today. I think the hospital might have a bag or something that has your father's clothes and whatever else he may have had on him."

I wasn't sure if the police might need any of his personal stuff considering that it may have been a robbery of sorts. Evidently they didn't because Mom was handed a large plastic zip-locked bag with his personal effects. Not pretty. Bloodstained clothing was very evident. Did we even want to deal with it?

"We'd better wait until we get you back home, Mom," I said. "I'd suggest getting rid of those damn clothes soon, but take a look at what else he had in his pockets and wallet. You don't want to just dispose of his cash or credit cards or whatever else might be there."

We got back to their house in Dover and I helped her in. She seemed frail and beyond distraught. I called Abbie and relayed as much information as I had at the moment. Obviously I was going to be here for a while. Mom went to lie down. I decided to go through that plastic bag and get rid of Dad's soiled clothing. I made note of the fact that there was no wristwatch in the bag. That was odd. His beloved old Rolex was not there. I knew that he constantly wore it. Well, it was a robbery, after all. His wallet was there but it contained no cash. Dad didn't like credit cards and used them only for emergency, relying on cash almost all the time. The wallet was dirt-encrusted. It must have been found on the ground near where he fell after being robbed and shot. I hated to do this part, but I started going through his pants pockets to find what else might be there. One folded handkerchief. Two quarters, three dimes and six pennies. And a couple ragged pieces of torn paper that looked like it had been crumpled up. It had been part of some pink stationery. On one piece, and only on one piece, there was writing in a very feminine cursive "so so sorry but we". The beginning and ending to a sentence cut off. Torn off. That was it. And no punctuation.

I read far too many thrillers and murder mysteries but something didn't ring true here. A red flag had just been thrown. I needed to keep this little slip of paper. Where was the rest of the note? Was it a clue? Was it nothing at all? Time would tell.

Abbie and Darin flew up to New Jersey for the funeral. Another one in that fucking cemetery a stone's throw from our house. The house was filled with bouquets of all shapes and sizes. The sympathy cards had been flowing in almost since the day the world had been notified about Dad's death. This is what I had been waiting for. I scrutinized each one. Carefully. Sherlock Holmes would have been proud. And, suddenly, there it was. The familiar, feminine cursive. I read the note. "So so sorry for your loss he was a great boss." *No punctuation. Signed Lisa Ray.*

I asked Mom if she happened to know who Lisa Ray was.

"Yes, she's one of the draftsmen, well, draftswomen I guess, who reports to your dad. Reported to your dad. I've met her a couple times at office parties. She's very sweet."

"Please point her out to me if she's at the funeral, okay?"

"Alright," Mom answered with a confused look on her face. *"Why?"*

"Oh, I really like her handwriting," I lied, holding up the sympathy card, *"and beautiful cursive like that seems to be rare these days. She must be very old school. I just want to compliment her on it, that's all."*

Lisa Ray was at the church, along with dozens of Dad's coworkers and few other friends. Dad was not very sociable so this surprised me somewhat. Mom nodded to me as we were filing out after the service.

"That's her," she said sotto voce, *"In the hunter green suit."*

She was very pretty, young…possibly early 40s…beautiful red hair that was set off nicely by her stylish green suit. Nice legs. I'm a leg man.

I caught up with her as she was approaching her car in the parking lot.

"Miss Ray?" I called to her.

"Mrs. Ray," she corrected. *"Hi, Baxter. I recognized you immediately. No mistaking the resemblance. Again, I am so, so sorry for your terrible loss. He was a wonderful man."* This time, I assume, with punctuation. *"He always spoke so highly of you."*

I was sure that was a blatant lie and said only out of condolence and comfort.

"You have very beautiful handwriting," I started. *"One doesn't see such beautiful cursive used so much these days."*

She looked at me quizzically. *"Well, thank you. I guess."* And she gave a gentle little shrug.

"Mrs. Ray, after my father was killed I found a torn note in his pants pocket."

She suddenly gasped, put her hand to her mouth and started to move away from me.

"Wait, please," I continued. *"Please. Please. I need to know. I can let my imagination run away with me at times. Then, at other times, alarm bells go off."*

We stood there in the parking lot of the church and spoke for fifteen minutes. She did. Nonstop. Were she and Dad having an affair? Yes. Sort of. It was the stupid stuff you hear about all the time. Older guy flirts with younger woman. Or vice versa. Yes, there had been some sexual fumbling and tumbling late nights, alone at the office. But Lisa Ray loved her husband…

and her three kids…and guilt had set in. Her husband must have suspected something and had asked a few questions. She had played innocent and did some fancy dancing around his suspicions. She was breaking things off. She saw Dad crumble up the note but didn't know he had torn it or how any of it ended up in his pocket. At first she had assumed that the entire note was in his pocket, not just one tiny piece. But what had happened to the rest of the note? I guess we'll never know that one.

HERE: Okay, so was this the old cliché murder mystery of the husband finding out and gunning down the perpetrator late at night? Alone in the parking lot? Nothing that nefarious. Not by a long shot. No pun intended. It actually *was* a robbery by an unknown (to my dad) assailant. Apparently there were some bruises on my dad's knuckles. He must have tried to fight back. An incredibly stupid robber who barely spoke English, and with a recently broken nose, tried to pawn Dad's Rolex, which was engraved. He also had in his possession my dad's black onyx ring, which I had totally missed while doing my inventory of the bag from the hospital. Surveillance cameras caught the transaction. The cops had been told about the missing Rolex so they were on the lookout.

THERE: *Lisa Ray and I finished our conversation. I thanked her for her candor and apologized for ambushing her like that in the parking lot. Poor choice of words there. We shook hands but she barely looked me in the eye. She started to walk away, and then stopped. She came up to me and gave me a gentle hug.*

"Thanks, Baxter. I thought that I would faint when you mentioned the note. You're a true gentleman. I never intended any of this to happen and I certainly did not anticipate the tragic conclusion. I apologize. I can do no more." Again, she headed back to her car.

"This will be just between us, Mrs. Ray. Forever. My mom will never know of this."

And, indeed, my mother never found out about my father's infidelity. His guilt was buried with him.

HERE: Or so I thought.

27

THERE: *Six months later I was back in New Jersey again to help Mom move out of her big house. So many good memories here, along with a few unhappy ones. The house sold quickly, to a young dentist and his family. He intended to build an extension in the back for his offices. Mom's friend from Lake Hopatcong, "Aunt" Sophie, had recently sold her big house as well. The two ladies made out very well with their respective sales. Mom, along with her inheritance from Gram and Gramp and some exemplary advice from their financial advisors, was sitting pretty monetarily. She and Sophie bought a condo in a senior-friendly complex and planned to travel the world together. It was like a breath of fresh air. Something awakened in Mom that must have been dormant for decades.*

Keeping only the furniture to help furnish the condo, she sold the rest at bargain prices. Even still, she raked in a couple thousand dollars more. She was in heaven. An antique dealer was due to arrive later one afternoon to check out Dad's very old walnut double pedestal roll-top desk. He had been very proud of it and kept it well polished and in excellent condition. After she and I moved it from Dad's home office to the hallway, we decided to let it stay there for the dealer to see. If he liked it and wanted it, we'd help him carry it out. It was very heavy.

"I haven't even taken the time to clean it out," Mom said after we had moved it. *"Corey paid all the bills and stuff, so it just has a lot of his old paperwork, I guess. I'll shred anything that shouldn't be seen by busybodies going through our trash. You take that side,"* she said indicating the right side of all the drawers, *"and I'll do this side."*

The cubicles under the roll top had a few loose papers and a couple ledgers. I flipped through the pages and there wasn't anything of importance. There was an old glass paperweight that I recognized as the one I had bought for him when I visited the glassworks in Flemington years before. The drawers below the desktop were filled with files…old taxes, bills, receipts, etc., and dozens of ballpoint pens. Under the pens was another old ledger. I held the book upside down and flipped through the pages. A tiny photograph fell out onto the floor. It was a black and white photograph and it appeared to be very old. It was a snapshot of a very young boy, perhaps two or three years old. He was wearing a little sailor suit. At first, I thought it must have been me in the picture but then I looked more closely.

"Mom, is this me in this photo? I don't remember seeing this one before."

She looked at it and scrunched up her face. She held it close to her face, and then moved it further away again. Maybe she just might need some new glasses. She flipped it over to see if anything was written on the back. Nope, nothing.

"My goodness," she said, adjusting her glasses more. "I can't tell. I don't think so, but it's so old. It could be you but I don't think you had an outfit like that. Obviously this was ages ago. Maybe your Gram took that one. Who can remember, right? Don't know what your father was doing with it, though. Oh, well. My photo albums are all packed and ready to move. I'll take this and stick it in one of them when I get the chance."

We finished cleaning out the desk and awaited the dealer. Ralph Josephson, selected from the Yellow Pages, parked his large van in Mom's driveway. A stocky guy, he was somewhere in his late fifties and had a full head of pure white hair. He threw a stub of a cigar out into the street and waddled up to the door. She greeted him before he could ring the bell and showed him the desk now sitting in the front hallway. His eyes widened when he saw it, but he quickly recovered. But I had seen his initial reaction. I knew what was coming. He rolled up the top and rolled it back down again. Pulled open a couple drawers and walked all the way around it.

"Hmmm," he said, cocking his head from side to side. "Yeah, this one is pretty old. Not in the best of conditions, I can tell. That roll top is wobbly and needs some serious repair. And a couple of those drawers look iffy. Might be ready to fall apart. Best I can do is a couple hundred bucks." .

"Okay, thanks," I said as I started to usher him out. "We have another dealer coming in later this afternoon. He's already shown interest in it from the photo that I showed to him at his shop, and he *thought it looked like it was in excellent condition. He was intrigued by the fact that it dated back at least to the 1940s, if not earlier. So, who knows? He made a tentative offer but wanted to see the desk in person."*

"How much did he offer?" asked the dealer, jerking his head in my direction. "I might could do better."

There was a nibble on the line and I started to reel it in slowly.

"Wellll…not sure if I should say. Don't want to sway you in any way. But it was certainly way higher than your *offer. I suppose that could change once he sees it, however. He could go higher still…or lower even but I'd like to give him the opportunity, that's only fair, right? Thanks, again, for stopping by Mister Josephson"*

He hesitated. He licked his lips.

"Was it Stevens? This other guy. It was Mike Stevens, wasn't it?"

I shrugged my shoulders, being noncommittal.

"Was it more than a grand?"

I shrugged again, arched my eyebrows, made a funny little look with my mouth and slowly nodded.

"Okay, fifteen hundred. Best I can do."

I wrinkled my nose and shook my head.

"Eighteen hundred, cash. Now," he said, looking flushed.

I sighed. "The other dealer will be pissed if it's gone before he even has a chance to see it. I… I don't know."

"Two thousand and he'll never know what he's missed," said Mister Josephson, the crook.

"Well…I suppose. You did get first dibs by seeing it here and now. Okay, two thousand…cash, you said?"

I helped him get the old desk out to his van. Damn, that thing was heavy! From a wad of cash in his pocket, he peeled two thousand in hundreds and handed it to me. Mom and I waved as he drove away.

"I didn't know you had shown photos of that desk to another dealer. Who was it? When did you do that?" Mom asked.

"There was no other dealer, Mom, I just lied. I played him like a fiddle. Haven't got the foggiest clue who that Mike Stevens guy might be. I was toying with him just to see how far he would go. I guess we got lucky, eh?"

28

THERE: *The sun had long since gone down behind the trees along side our house, no longer casting long shadows across the back yard. Dusk had settled in for a while before giving way to nighttime darkness. Summer would be coming to an end soon and Darin would be starting as a freshman in high school. He and I were playing catch when I just happened to glace up.*

"Fledermaus, fledermaus!" I exclaimed, as Gram flashed into my memories. Something I hadn't thought about in years. Darin looked up.

"Oh, yeah. Bats. Cool, aren't they, Pop?"

"Did you know that word, fledermaus, Darin?"

"My friend Carson's father is German. He told us one day when we saw them in the sky at their house."

"Carson? I don't believe you've mentioned him before. Does he live around here somewhere?"

"She, Pop. Carson's a girl. Carson Wagner."

"Oh," was my only response.

"Did you know," continued Darin, "that the fastest bat can fly as fast as 100 miles per hour?"

How did he know that?

"How did you know that?" I asked.

"Mr. Wagner told us, He works at Fernbank and knows lots of cool stuff."

"Cool," was my only response.

Kids are smarter now than when I was their age. I thought I was a pretty smart kid but I may have been mistaken. Fernbank Museum of Natural History was just a couple blocks from our house. We have taken Darin there several times when he was growing up and one exhibition or another has always fascinated him. Smart kid. Smarter than me. Well, maybe.

Thanks to Darin and his friendship with Carson, we were introduced to the Wagners. They were around our ages, both dark-haired and each one was probably tens pounds overweight. An extremely friendly couple, Axel and Mila, were very competitive bridge players we soon discovered. We were invited to their place one Saturday evening for an early dinner and some card playing. As it turned out, there was a lot *of card playing. Three tables of bridge, twelve players. Our neighborhood bridge club was formed that evening. The Wagners were gracious hosts, but Axel was ruthless when it came to bidding. I have never experienced such an aggressive player.*

Changing partners after several games played, he eventually became my partner. The player to my left dealt and passed. Axel arranged his hand, studied it, and opened with two no trump, telling me that he had an outstanding hand with a high count of at least twenty points. The player to my right sighed loudly and passed. I had a fairly good hand with spades being my longest and strongest suit. I responded accordingly.

"Three spades," I answered.

Axel looked back at his hand. I could almost see the gears spinning. He folded his thirteen cards into a single stack, laying it face down on the table. He steepled his fingers and looked straight at me. "Okay. Seven spades," he said without hesitation. "And you will *make it."*

I do believe my heart may have stopped. Seven spades. That meant, of course, that I had to take every single trick, not losing even one. The player to my right looked at me.

"Double!" she exclaimed loudly. Meaning that every trick I might lose would give my opponents double the points as a reward and a penalty for Axel and me. I gulped and passed and my opponent to my left also passed.

"No guts, no glory," responded Axel as he looked right at me again, shaking his head. "Redouble!"

Meaning that should we make our bid we'd be rewarded with four times the normal score. This was a first for me. The aggressive bidding war generated a lot of interest from the other tables; consequently we had several curious bystanders watching the playing. My playing. It was my spades. Axel was the dummy. The player to my left, with a wry smile on his face, confidently led with the ace of hearts. Possibly the only card in his hand with a point value. A sure winner. Or so he thought. But I was void in hearts, so I would soon trump his smartass ace. Axel laid out his cards on the table. I scanned the arrangement carefully, inhaled deeply and let out an audible "Hmmmmm." I closed my eyes and quickly strategized.

The bloodbath was soon over. It was nerve-wracking. Even though I was very cautious, I easily took every trick and we were rewarded with the highest score I have ever had at the card tables. The applause from all the other players who had been watching us was overwhelming. Abbie came up behind me and kissed me on the top of my head.

"I was afraid to watch," she said, "I had to go out of the house while you played."

Axel and I stood and shook hands. The player who had been the opponent to my right, the one who doubled us, just shook her head.

"I'm not playing with you any more," she said laughing and then stuck out her tongue at me.

HERE: Many new friendships were started that evening. Once a month, for the next few years, we all took turns being the host house. But nothing could ever top that seven-spade grand slam heart stopper.

THERE: *Our bridge playing friends were a diverse group. Their ages varied but they were all pretty much around our age, with similarly aged children. Aside from much business chatter as the games progressed, the raising of teenagers became a popular topic. Not that we complained about it by any stretch of the imagination, but we soon discovered that we were in the minority regarding problem kids. Drugs were mentioned, as was alcohol, shoplifting, and sexuality. Where had we gone wrong? Or right? Unless we were totally oblivious, Darin presented us with none of these situations. He was a*

damn good guy. Well-groomed, handsome, and always neat. A great student, excelling in all the science subjects. He appeared to show no interest in adult beverages of any kind. True, he had given us a jolt a few years earlier with his stunt of sleepwalking. But, dammit, that was it.

We got home late from one Saturday night of bridge playing. Carson was just leaving our house as we arrived. She waved to us and went on her way. Hmm, what had been going on? Any hanky-panky, as Abbie would say? When we went in, we found Darin, books scattered across the dining room table, and he was scribbling notes like crazy. Another classmate of theirs was packing up his backpack. He nodded politely to us and bade us a goodnight as he left. It appeared that they had actually been doing a lot of homework together. I sighed.

"What the hell's wrong with you?" I asked, with my hands on my hips. Abbie stopped short, coming up behind me almost bumping into me.

"Excuse me?" answered Darin. He put down his pen. A look of puzzlement crossed his face.

"I mean, what's going on with you? Why aren't you giving your mother and me any problems?"

His eyes shot wide open. Then he squinted and cocked his head.

"Pop, are you drunk?"

"Well, maybe a little."

Abbie laughed and went up behind Darin, hugging him around the shoulders. She explained about the dilemmas of so many of our bridge-playing friends and their offspring. Darin buried his face in his hands and shook his head.

"Hey, okay, if it'll make you feel any better, before your next bridge night I'll set fire to my hair, rip off all my clothes and sit naked in your car in the church parking lot on Sunday morning. Jeez, sometimes you people freak me out!"

By the time he was halfway through his senior year, Darin had been accepted to four colleges, including his favorite choice. As hard as he studied, though, he could make only salutatorian of his class. Carson was valedictorian. Here's a bit of trivia: the term valedictorian comes from the Latin vale dicere *meaning "to say farewell".*

HERE: As inadequate as we felt, what with a too-decent, no-catastrophe teenager and all, we continued our bridge playing, commiserating with the other parents who shared their woes with us. Lo and behold, something on the night of Darin's high school graduation party pushed him over the brink. We allowed him to have a few beers…it was at our house and he wasn't going to be going out anywhere anyway…but perhaps he had a few too many. He threw up in the bushes in our back yard. I was so proud!

29

THERE: *It came as no surprise to us that Darin would major in Environmental Studies in college. And what better place to further one's education than at Harvard? Even with his scholarship the annual tuition was enough to give a parent's heart a jolt or two. Fortunately we were in the position to afford it, no matter how unnerving it may have been to write those damn tuition checks. We managed to take a couple short trips up to Boston every year and walk with him through the bustling streets of Harvard Square. The hotel we always stayed in was only a few blocks away and there was always some form of activity going on there, reminding me greatly of our years living in the East Village in New York. That seemed so long ago, yet seemed just like yesterday at times. In the middle of his sophomore year he mentioned something to us on the phone about joining some sort of social club. Our conversations always seemed to be one-sided, with him chattering away like a magpie. That kid sure could talk. He seemed very enthused about it but I guess we really didn't pay that much attention to it. Obviously a fraternity of some sort and we hoped it was a good one. For some reason, it just never seemed to come up in any further conversations.*

After being in a traditional dorm for his freshman year, now that he was a junior he was living in one of Harvard's twelve residential houses. Each visit to Cambridge would bring another surprise regarding Darin's appearance. We never knew if he might be bearded or clean-shaven. Long, shoulder-length hair or cropped closely. We were extremely proud of our very handsome son, no matter what. His grades were exceptional, that's what really mattered. He surprised us further, on one of our visits during his junior year. He requested that our visit be scheduled around a particular date but he didn't say why. He was beardless when we saw him as he ushered us up to his room. We asked about his roommate, a nice young man from Wisconsin.

"Last I saw him, a couple hours ago, he and his girlfriend were headed out to the Harvard Coop. He needed a couple books. That guy studies even more than I do!"

Their room was a mess. Dirty clothes all over the place and it had the aroma of…well, men.

"Well, talking about studies, Darin," I asked, "How are things going? Any classes giving you headaches or are they all a snap? We haven't been having many of our usual phone chats lately"

"Oh…well…no, I guess we haven't," he answered with a hint of a slight grin. "Regarding my classes, my favorite right now, for obvious reasons, is Sustainability of Southern Cities. *I can relate, for sure. The one that's giving me the most fits is* Introduction to International Relations. *But that one intrigues me. I really want to delve further into it. But I've been sorta slammed. That's why I haven't called in a while.*"

And he had that silly little grin on his face again. All of a sudden he popped up out of his chair.

"Okay. Sit there on my bed and wait until I come out of the bathroom," he told us. "But don't jump to any conclusions. Especially you, Pop."

What now?

A few minutes later he opened the bathroom door and struck a pose. With his bare, hairy chest above and his hairy legs below, he was wearing a short hot pink miniskirt in between.

Stunned silence from both Abbie and me for ten seconds.

"What in the holy fuck has happened to you?" I spouted suddenly, my eyes as wide as they could possibly go. Abbie put a hand to her mouth.

"Don't you guys remember me telling you about that social club I joined? Surely you must know about the Hasty Pudding Club, Pop? Don't you?" Darin asked, holding back the laughter. "It's a great club here that, among other things, puts on an original musical every year and tradition dictates that all the female characters are played by guys. Yeah, yeah, I guess a drag show of sorts, but not really…and it's totally satirical in nature. And certainly not gay. Although I think that half the audience might be! Jack Lemmon was once a member decades ago. So was JFK. A bunch of my friends here dared me to try out. And, guess what? I got one of the leads! It's a political spoof. My character's name is Polly-Ester Pantsafyre. She's a hooker trying to seduce both presidential candidates running for office. The show's hilarious. I didn't want to tell you before you came up here and ruin this surprise. I got the best seats in the house for you for tonight's show.

After Abbie regained her composure and stopped laughing she shook her head and said, "I didn't know you could sing. Since when? This is a musical?"

"Oh, hell, I can't sing worth a crap," laughed Darin. "That's half the fun. Most of the cast can't sing either but that makes it even funnier. We could barely get through the rehearsals because we were cracking up so much."

HERE: My handsome son couldn't have gotten the male lead at least? What the hell?

THERE: *We left Darin later that afternoon so he could get ready for his show. After stopping off for a couple beers and some munchies at Grendel's Den, we made our way to the building housing the club's theatricals. Obviously we had absolutely no idea what to expect. The shock of seeing Darin in a mini skirt hadn't totally worn off, but we began to relax as the house lights dimmed and the overture began. And it was a damn catchy overture, at that! I was actually tapping my feet. The audience was abuzz and I figured we just might be in for a treat. Or an embarrassment.*

The show, irreverent to the core and funny as hell, was a total delight. Darin's first entrance, in blazing hot pink short shorts, a cropped white top exposing his bare, hairy midriff, and a big blonde wig of teased hair got rousing applause and riotous laughter from the audience. Our boy was a hit! The very clever political satire, titled "Haute Pursuits", had a large, talented cast and a slew of the most bizarre and inane characters imaginable. A drug-crazed Venezuelan terrorist named Roberto San Clemente El Nino; an outrageous, volatile radio talk show host named Howard Sternum; a loopy Peter Deadwood, a presidential candidate with erectile dysfunction, and William T. Flickoff, the incumbent presidential candidate. His initials, W.T.F, were used for some gut-busting funny campaign posters and banners in the show. They even managed to work a cloned sheep named Dolly into the proceedings. It turned out to be the most entertaining evening we had had in years. What a shocker! Our son was brilliant. His big number, "Doin' The Raucous Caucus", filled with racy double entendres and backed by a chorus line of high-kicking congressmen, brought down the house. But honestly, because of, or in spite of, all that makeup including garish blue eye shadow and deep red lipstick, Darin was the ugliest hooker I've ever seen!

HERE: Not that I know from personal experience, mind you!

THERE: *"Don't worry, guys," Darin assured us after the show. "This is my one and only theatrical endeavor. We run for a couple more weeks, and then I'll never don makeup and short shorts again. Promise!"*

We all laughed and hugged him, congratulating him once again for the incredible performance. That god-awful wig of piled-high teased blonde hair would surely give me nightmares for months to come, though.

HERE: As we would find out in the years ahead, Darin *did* hit the stage again. Often. But in a totally different capacity.

30

THERE: A couple times a year I do what I call a customer appreciation night. Abbie and I will host one or two of our favored clients, and their significant other, at a local restaurant for drinks and dinner. I select the ones who I think will be most compatible for a get-together or ones who might even know each other. On this particular evening, Justin Thyme and his companion Ryle Madries would be joining us, along with Marty Howce and his wife Jessica. Both of the art directors, Justin and Marty, had new jobs and both had used my services extensively (and successfully) over the past couple of years. Although I had met Marty's wife a couple times, I have never met Justin's friend. I had the feeling that Abbie would probably spend the night mooning over "dreamy" Marty. I wasn't wrong.

Abbie selected one of the newest, trendiest restaurants in the Buckhead area of Atlanta. Buckhead is often referred to as the Beverly Hills of the south. Marty and Jessica pulled up behind our car as I was handing my keys to the valet. We waited for them, and then went inside. The most appealing aromas greeted us. I know that the olfactory senses can trigger memories, both good and bad. I had not been to an Italian restaurant in years, decades perhaps. The immediate thought that flashed, just for the briefest second, through my mind was of Ant and his mom working side by side in their kitchen in Dover. I closed my eyes and inhaled.

The hostess approached us and acknowledged our reservations. Abbie had requested a table in the quietest part of the restaurant, even though she knew from past experience that we would, more than likely, end up the most raucous table in the place. There would be no delay; our table was ready and waiting for us. As she was about to lead us to our seats, Justin and his friend came through the revolving door. Introductions were made, hands were shaken and hugs were given. I wasn't surprised to discover that Marty and Justin had met once before at an Art Directors Club of Atlanta meeting. When we were all introduced to Ryle Madries he spoke with the most wonderful, mellifluous accent. As tall, blond-haired and fair as Justin was, Ryle was a bit taller, a bit more slender, had close-cropped black hair and skin the color of coffee with just a splash of cream.

After we were all seated and our drink orders taken, the conversation began and continued for hours, stopping only momentarily while we chewed our respective entrees. What a congenial group I had assembled!

"Ryle," I said after taking my first sip of my first gin and tonic of the evening, "your beautiful accent is intriguing."

"Is it Australian?" asked Jessica.

He threw back his head and laughed.

"People often make that mistake for some reason," he answered. "No, ma'am, I am from South Africa. Originally from a small town called Empangeni, in the province of Zwa-Zulu-Natal. But my family and I lived most of my young life in Joburg. Oh, sorry. Johannesburg."

"So, what brought you to Atlanta?" asked Marty.

"An airplane, sir," answered Ryle, his brown eyes sparkling through his thin wire-rimmed glasses. And he chuckled, shaking his head. "Sorry, I couldn't resist, Marty. My family moved here about ten years ago. My father now heads up the phys. ed. department at Morehouse. In a roundabout way, that's how Justin and I met."

"Isn't Morehouse a black college?" Abbie asked.

Justin and Ryle both laughed.

"Well, yes, of course," answered Justin, "but we were on competing tennis teams a couple years ago. His dad was coaching their team. I was going to Georgia Tech and was the captain on ours."

"I thought he had great legs," laughed Ryle, winking.

"And I thought he had a great ass," chuckled Justin.

"This might be more info than we need to hear," snickered Jessica.

There were laughs all around the table and we toasted to great legs...great asses...and great tits. Oh, and to tennis. Marty and Jessica played. Abbie and I did not.

"Ah, sports," I sighed. *"I'm not a sports enthusiast and I worried about that regarding our son when he was growing up. I wondered how he might think about that when..."*

"But," Justin interrupted, *" you are always talking so lovingly about him when we have our shoots. You certainly seem to have a great relationship despite your...ummm...shortcomings in the sports area"*

I took a second sip from my second gin and tonic. I sighed.

"You know, that's just what I'm afraid of. Maybe I talk too lovingly about him. Perhaps I show a bit too much affection toward him. I don't want to alienate him by overwhelming him with too much of...well, too much of me! I certainly don't want him to have daddy issues in the years ahead."

"In one respect, Baxter," said Jessica, *"you're lucky. You have only one child to contend with at this point. We have two and, believe me, sibling rivalry is alive and well at the Howce house. I'm hoping they outgrow it, but I have my doubts."*

"Ha!" blurted Marty, *" I can't see how loving your kid too much will create a problem. Now, let me enlighten you about daddy issues!"*

Marty kept us in stitches for the next several minutes telling us about his father's outrageous stories and outlandish behavior while Marty and his brother were growing up. His phobias, as a result, continue to this day.

And then it was Justin's turn.

"I never got any support from my dad while I was growing up, or even now, for that matter. Let's just say that he's not a fan of my lifestyle. He's an automotive mechanic. He owns his own place and it's a pretty successful one. I remember vividly his comment to me when I mentioned years ago that I wanted to go into the art field in some way. We were at the dinner table and he simply blared 'One day you'll wish to Christ that you learned how to do something with your hands.' *It made me cry and has stuck with me all these years. Ironic, isn't it? I actually ended up doing something with my hands. I create. He merely repairs. That sounds too snarky, doesn't it? Don't get me wrong, there. He has a great talent for repairing things and, God knows, we all need that at some time or another. But I honestly think he failed to catch that irony."*

HERE: The irony wasn't lost on me. My father created, being an architect. He never belittled my choice of profession, also in the creative field, but somehow we still had issues.

THERE: *"Here's to Daddy Issues!" I said, raising my glass. "And here's to you mothers, as well," turning to Abbie and Jessica.*

"Seriously, Bax," said Marty, "you shouldn't worry about that sports situation at all. If your son has any interest in sports, he'll get involved one way or the other. Through his friends and classmates probably. If he does so, maybe you'll get to learn a thing or two. Just sit back and enjoy the ride. Keep telling him you love him and cheer him on. Case closed!"

"I totally agree with you, Marty," Ryle responded. "Look, Baxter, I have none of those daddy issues that you are so concerned about. My father and I have had a very loving relationship from the very beginning. My entire family is loving and supportive, for that matter. Stop worrying about it. If he feels as though he's loved too much…which I really find difficult to believe…he just might turn to you one day and say 'hey, old man, fuck off!' But I sincerely doubt that that will happen."

I suddenly came to the realization that my fear of instilling daddy issues in Darin was pointless. First of all, he really didn't show too much interest in organized sports anyway. Oh, an occasional game of catch, or backyard badminton, but that was all. By the time he entered college, sports had never played a role in his life. A short foray into musical comedy last year gave us a momentary shock, but that was it. That little fucker better damn well be near perfect by the time he reaches full adulthood!

Throughout the remainder of the dinner and straight through our decadent desserts we all spoke of lighter topics. Eschewing politics entirely, we ventured into the latest books and movies, travels abroad and every once in a while an off-color joke set us giggling like school kids. I ordered a bottle of limoncello for our table. Justin let out a loud laugh when I did so.

"That is so funny," he said, "reminds me of the time I first heard someone order that. I thought they asked for lemon Jell-O. I just had a minor déjà vu moment there, Baxter!"

We all laughed at that.

"I love things about déjà vu," chimed in Marty. "Shit like that intrigues me. I've experienced it several times. Anybody else? You know, strange things happen that you can't explain or, well, déjà vu that blows your mind?"

"Well, yes," I responded, "regarding unexplained occurrences I have, indeed, experienced it and it rattled me, to say the least. I have always been fascinated by stuff like that. Déjà vu, you know, and time travel, too. I know, I know, weird shit, right? Somebody right out of The Twilight Zone, that's me. Anyway, this one time really had me scratching my head. I still can't figure it out to this day. But I can't really define it as déjà vu, though."

I paused for a moment to collect my thoughts. Abbie knew exactly where I was going with this story.

"It was on our third trip to Europe. We were in Spain for the very first time, driving along the Costa del Sol. We stayed in a nice little villa in Marbella, but we took a day trip east to a little fishing village named Nerja. It was around dinnertime on a gorgeous afternoon. We wanted to find a little restaurant, far from the touristy places, where the locals ate. Strolling around some narrow back streets we found such a place. It was that obvious. Neither Abbie nor I know Spanish…well, no more beyond 'mas café, por favor' or 'gracias'…but the little menu taped to the front door was in English as well. The place was packed but the beautiful young hostess smiled and led us to a table for two in one of the little side rooms. There were, maybe, a dozen people laughing, eating, and yammering away in Spanish around the tiny room. An older man, in a tuxedo, either the maître d' or the owner of the place was going from table to table greeting all the diners. They laughed and chatted, again all in Spanish. He finally made his way to our table. He stopped abruptly and stared at me for a second. A huge smile came across his face as he extended his hand to shake mine.

'Good evening, senor,' he said in perfect English. 'How nice to see you back here again. It's been some time, hasn't it?'"

I paused to take a sip of my limoncello.

"I was thunderstruck. All I could do was nod. Cue the soundtrack. That wonderful old song "Where or When?" should be playing now. I have no idea who he thought I was, but to top things off and make things even more bizarre, he sent a bottle of wine to our table with his compliments. It was Bodegas Mauro, and it had been my favorite wine for years."

"Wow," said Justin, "Just wow! That would have freaked me out. But, ya know, I just read somewhere that there are at least six people in the world who look exactly like each of us. Doppelgangers, I guess."

"I find that very difficult to believe, don't you? Come on. Really? Genetics has to play a factor in how we all look. No offense, but I think that theory, quote-unquote, is a lot of bunk."

"You just mentioned that word theory,*" Marty said with a pensive look in his eyes. "Yeah, I love all that crap about time travel, déjà vu, and weird shit like that. But I was watching something on one of those science channels a couple nights ago. Whoever the guy was, he was talking about our planet and life on it. It made me really think about our time here. He said that if the timeline of the universe was condensed into one year starting on New Year's Day, homo sapiens would appear at 11:54 on December 31ˢᵗ. Doesn't that just fuck with your brain, or what?"*

We all sat silent for a minute, I guess just letting that deep thought work its way through our woozy heads.

"Seriously?" I suddenly thought. "You know, going along with that mind bender, I honestly think that a couple of my clients haven't made it to 11:55 yet."

Silence once again. Well, I *thought it was funny anyway!*

By the time we had polished off the bottle of limoncello and I had paid the bill, tipping the wait staff generously, we all sort of stumbled laughingly out to fetch our respective cars from the awaiting valets. We acted like long-time friends, hugging, shaking hands, slapping backs, whatever. Our car was the last to be brought around and we waved as each of our guests drove off into the star-filled night. Well, early morning by this time. Our valet held the car door for Abbie as she settled into her seat and then rushed around to open my door. I tipped him probably more than I should have but what the hell. As I drove away I suddenly had a craving for lemon Jell-O.

31

HERE: We knew it was bound to happen sooner or later.

THERE: *"Hey, guys, guess what?" Darin blurted into the phone, excitement oozing from his voice. "Looks like I might be staying up here in Massachusetts after graduation. I am beyond elated and can't believe it yet. I think I'm going to be working with NOAA!"*

"Who's Noah?" I asked, after Abbie and I exchanged confused glances. "Should we know who he is?"

Darin laughed.

"No, no, not a who, a what. NOAA is the National Oceanic Atmospheric Administration. They're headquartered in D.C. but they have offices here in Boston, too. I've applied to several different environmental corporations, you know, like the EPA and the U.S. Geological Survey but these guys responded first, two months ago. I didn't want to jinx anything by telling anyone, but I'm just so excited right now that I wanted to share it with you. You can't believe the interview processes I've been through. Three different people have already interviewed me and today I'm going back a fourth time. Today, though, it will be a whole roomful of people."

There was a sharp crack of thunder in the background that turned into a slow rumble as it drifted away.

"Did ya hear that?" Darin asked. "Yeah, a nor'easter is moving in on us.

It's raining like hell out there. Traffic is going to be a bitch. I gotta hit the shower and get going. I'll call you guys after I find out what's what. Oh, and I'll be sure tell Noah hello from you next time I see him!"

"Smartass!" I laughed.

We both wished him good luck.

HERE: Just like with me, good luck has always seemed to follow Darin in all his endeavors. I often wonder if he still has that acorn in his pocket that I picked up and gave to him when he was seven years old.

THERE: *Darin called us a week later. The storm had caused traffic delays and he was a nervous wreck by the time he arrived, late, at NOAA's offices. As luck would have it, the power had been knocked out in the area so it really hadn't mattered.*

Cut to the chase: he must have impressed the hell outta that roomful of people. He got the job.

32

THERE Abbie and I were so accustomed, at this point, to living in an in-town neighborhood. Not really city, but not really country either. But it had gotten boring. The people all began to look the same. Young executives got transferred to the Atlanta area and just as many got transferred back out again. The neighborhood faces and families changed so many times over the years we lost track. Our next-door neighbors changed so often that I seriously couldn't remember their names. Our neighborhood bridge club had started out as a monthly thing, with three tables of players. In time it dwindled to two tables, then one. Then none. As soon as we had befriended one group, out they went again to parts unknown. Well, to parts back up north...or further out west. Wherever. Darin was soon to graduate from college and, from what we learned during a few phone conversations, not returning to live at home after graduation. We began to think about buying a quiet piece of property in the middle of the woods somewhere but yet close enough to the city so my commute to the studio wouldn't be a burden.

We had to make a decision. After too many years of living surrounded by other homes, no matter how beautiful, we were finally going to move into a more private area. More property. Smaller house. I hunted around for a realtor who handled stuff like that, away from the hustle and bustle of the city. I still needed to be in easy commuting distance but far enough away so we couldn't hear cars honking and smell exhaust fumes. We had really gotten rid of our big city attitudes.

We were shown a half dozen promising parcels of land and then something clicked. Six acres of wooded land in a little town called Between. Great name. I guess it was so named because it was midway between Atlanta and Athens. It was a cute, quiet little place. Abbie and I felt this was the right place for us, in the right town with an appropriate name. After all, we were somewhere between fifty and death.

Now the fun part began. Abbie and I began sourcing the area for good, reputable and creative builders. Obviously we'd be downsizing and we wanted to keep as many trees around the house-to-be as possible. Most of the homes we saw while driving around Between were older and small. We wanted ours to be modern and small. The price, per acre, was perfect and well below our means. The real estate taxes in the area were so minimal they were almost ridiculous.

HERE: Yes, a new chapter was starting for us. We bought the property, hired an extremely talented contractor, and started getting ready for our next move, leaving Druid Hills behind.

THERE: *We knew that Darin and Carson had kept in touch over the years. They had both dated others while at college but their friendship was growing closer and stronger by the hour. We could feel it. And we encouraged it. Carson, a journalism major in college, had grown into an intelligent and strikingly beautiful young lady. Almost as tall and as slender as Darin, her auburn hair and sparking green eyes were captivating. They made an extremely good-looking couple.*

So it came as no surprise to us upon learning that she had gotten a job at the Boston Globe *that she and Darin were moving in together into a small apartment in Somerville, a stone's throw from the city.*

HERE: Coming from the generation where morals and mores were totally different than those of our son's generation, Abbie had some reservations about that *living together* arrangement. But she voiced them only to me. How quickly one forgets. She obviously didn't remember that we had lived together in that little apartment in the East Village many moons ago. I, on the other hand, kept an open mind and figured that marriage would soon follow.

Two years later, after purchasing a house in Lunenburg, fifty miles to the west of Boston, and with a child on the way, I then figured that marriage for Darin and Carson had gotten lost somewhere along Route 2.

33

THERE: So now we each had homes in the middle of the woods. Ours, three years old by now, was a contemporary one-story just perfect for a couple ready for retirement. Darin's house was a sprawling split-level just perfect for a young, growing family. I had a one-hour commute to my studio. Well, certain traffic conditions made it worse at times. And Darin had a fifty-mile commute to his office near the Boston harbor. The times for his commute would depend greatly upon the season. Winter, for obvious reasons, made his travels longer and more hazardous.

I was getting tired of the commute. Darin didn't let his bother him at all. Of course, he traveled a lot for his job. He was racking up frequent flier points like crazy. We never knew which part of the globe he might be in from week to week. We also didn't know if it was because of his good looks and commanding voice or, primarily, his developed expertise, but he had become a very popular lecturer for various organizations and schools. I was exceptionally proud to let everyone know that he was our son when we attended a lecture he gave at Fernbank.

HERE: Another two years went by and grandson Greyson was joined by grandson Hayden. Handsome and bright, both of them. Isn't that what all grandparents say? The subject of marriage never came up, so I assumed that "living in sin", as Abbie used to say, was a satisfactory situation for Darin and Carson. What the hell, eh?

THERE: *Gram would have been devastated to hear about the dying of the bats. Millions of them. A fungus causing white-nose syndrome was attacking them while they hibernated in their caves. Ever since Gram had first taught me about those fascinating creatures, decades ago, I have often looked up at dusk hoping to see some on their nightly hunt. I was always delighted when I saw five or six of them diving and swooping far above my head. It happened almost without me being aware of it…that bat-killing disease. I hadn't realized that the five or six became three or four. Then one or two. And, eventually, none. No more fledermaus. So many changes going on around the globe and most of them horrendous. And now the poor little bats were decimated. Darin explained the situation to me, based on what he had learned and observed. Humans were actually unknowingly exacerbating the dire fungus by carrying it into caves with them on their clothing. Caves were being closed to exploration around the country to help ease the transmittal but it would take years for this to be resolved. In the meantime, millions of bats would die. But, I'm an optimist. Ac-Cent-Tchu-Ate the Positive! Maybe someday all will be right with the world again. At least for the bats. I might be an optimist but I'm certainly not hopelessly naïve. All will* never *be right with the world. But I long for the day—well, evenings—when I can look skyward and see those little creatures fluttering around, diving and swooping once again.*

34

THERE: "I'll Be Home For Christmas"…*That song always made Mom cry when she heard it on the radio decades ago. Dad was overseas fighting in the war. It was our turn to cry when hearing it this year. Darin was overseeing a major study of some sort way down in the south Pacific. For some reason Mary Martin came to mind when he told us about it. Carson and the boys, now aged four and six, flew over to be with him during the holiday time. Those two little twits had just about as many stamps in their respective passports as we did! They were getting the experiences afforded to very few kids their age.*

I hate it when the phone rings at 5 A.M.

"This can't be good," I said to Abbie as I got out of bed reaching for the damn phone, nearly falling on my ass doing so.

Before I could even say "hello" I heard loud explosions or gunshots. It sounded like people yelling or screaming in the background.

"Pop? Mom? Can you hear me?" yelled Darin.

"What the hell, Darin, what's wrong?" I shouted, my heart racing. "Dear, God, are you in the middle of a revolution or what? Are you under attack? Jesus Christ, did your plane crash?""

"It's New Years, Pop. Happy New Year!" he exclaimed loudly.

"What the fuck do you mean by that?" I asked, my nerves more than a bit

rattled by now. I ran my fingers through my hair. "It's…what time? Where the hell are you?"

"Pop, we're on the other side of the international date line. If you guys had listened to me and downloaded Facetime we could be looking at each other right now. And you could be seeing what's going on all around here. Damn, I've never seen such outrageous fireworks! The boys are ecstatic and jumping up and down like little monkeys. Can you hear those church bells? The place is going crazy. It's weird, isn't it? Look at it this way. You're talking to someone in the future right now. It's next year here."

My heart rate was slowly coming down to normal as I punched the speaker mode on our phone. I had a sneaky suspicion that that guy I was talking to in the future had been enjoying a few adult beverages before he called.

"Darin!" exclaimed Abbie a bit louder than I thought she should have. "You nearly gave us heart attacks, you big shit!" But then her laughter turned into tears. "I miss you, son. Hell, I miss all of you not being home for the holidays. But Happy New Year. And thanks for giving us a celebration we'll never, ever forget, even if we can't see it."

Later that morning, after our long conversation with Darin, Carson and the boys ended, I downloaded Facetime and Skype, as well, just to cover all bases. At midnight, on our New Year's Eve, we called Darin. I didn't give a shit what time it might be wherever the hell he was!

HERE: It was a few months into the new year and my thoughts had begun to drift more and more into a strange new, unfamiliar direction. I assume there comes a time in everyone's life that, no matter how much they might love their jobs, one just knows when it's time to hang it up. To pull the plug. To turn out the lights.

THERE: *Abbie came up behind me as I was sitting in front of the computer in our home office. I was on my Acorn Studio website, slowly scrolling through my portfolio. Mostly the table-top stuff, but a smattering of fashion and architectural shoots as well.*

"What are you doing? Reminiscing?"

"Kinda," I responded.

She picked up on the wistful tone in my one-word answer.

"You're ready, aren't you?" she asked.

She knew. We had talked about this, a lot more so recently than we had in the past. I still loved photography. That aspect would never leave me. But my daily routine had become…well, routine. Perhaps a bit too routine.

"Kinda." I repeated.

She pulled up a chair and sat down beside me, leaning her head into my shoulder.

"So what's the plan," she asked.

I sighed.

"Although we haven't seen each other in several years, Thunder and I have kept in touch. He's been the in-house photographer for a small agency over in Decatur. He's done well enough but he's longing to expand and get his own place. He does video stuff. Something I could never get into. Nor did I want to. He and I spoke on the phone for about an hour this afternoon."

"And?"

"And…we're meeting for lunch at Manuel's Tavern tomorrow."

HERE: Retirement isn't for sissies. Well, perhaps if you're a lazy, indolent son of a bitch you can sit on your fat ass all day, watch TV, munch Cheetos, lick your orange fingers, and guzzle beer. That was definitely *not* in my game plan. A large piece of property seems to grow in size through the years, with projects of one sort or another continually keeping one busy. Sometimes to the point of exhaustion.

THERE: *It had been a long, tiring day. Running errands and making several purchases at our local gardening shop. I always looked forward to working in the yard, trying to make our place a small paradise. Retirement was within my grasp and I'd soon have all the time in the world to do anything I wanted. Well, realistically? Just about anything Abbie wanted as well. Across from our driveway, in that large open field, I stopped and watched as several hot air balloons lifted off and sailed into the sky. I had seen this group here before. It is obviously a local club of enthusiasts. By the time I pulled down our driveway and had unloaded the truck, I was exhausted and decided that a nice drink out on the deck would be the best way to wind things down.*

"Abbie, want to join me?" I called as I squeezed the lime and poured the tonic into my glass. "Let's go out on the deck. Bring that book you're reading, it's beautiful out there now."

It was a cloudless afternoon and the sun had moved slightly behind the tall trees growing all around our back yard. The air was warm and still had a bit of the late spring aroma to it. This was my favorite place in the entire world. My decompression chamber. I plopped down into my chair and took a long swig of my drink. The ice sparkled like tiny diamonds as the cubes caught the bright sun. I leaned back as Abbie came out, holding her bottle of Coke and a book she was intent on finishing before dinner. The only thing breaking the silence was the loud chattering of the birds. I watched for a while as they flew about the two bird feeders we had positioned in the garden on the far side of our back lawn. I took another sip, set my glass down on the small table by my side, leaned my head back and closed my eyes.

A moment or two passed, then I could feel the temperature drop on my face as though a cloud had quickly covered the sun, then moved away bringing the warmth back again. I heard the crunching sound of branches breaking. I opened my eyes in time to see something fall through the trees and land, with a horrible sound, in our yard. Fluttering leaves followed the object and swirled about until they, too, landed on the grass. I leaped up, knocking over my drink and the glass fell to the deck floor.

"What in the holy fucking hell?" I screeched, hanging onto the deck railing for support. "Jesus fucking Christ, Abbie…Jesus, what the fuck?"

Abbie just stared up at me in confusion. She didn't see it. Yet.

"It's a body, Abbie! A woman just fell out of the sky and landed in our fucking yard!" I heard Abbie's book fall to the deck. She had fainted.

Through the tops of the trees on the far side of our property I caught sight of a strange shape, slowly drifting away. "What the hell?" I thought until I realized that it was a hot air balloon.

HERE: Going to the beach every summer is what I looked forward to the most. We went to a quiet little town called Normandy Beach along a narrow strip of land on the New Jersey shore. The big ocean was on one side of the town and a bay was on the other side. I loved to lie on the blanket and watch the big silver blimps float through the sky, way out over the ocean. Sometimes they would come close enough for us to hear their motors and they would cast a shadow that would drift over us. My dad said the blimps came from someplace called Lakehurst. Several years ago a huge blimp called the Hindenburg blew up over there as it was trying to dock and people were falling and jumping and ----

THERE: *"Bax,...Baxter!"*

I snapped awake with a jolt, letting out a loud gasp! Abbie was looking at me and slowly closed her book.

"Dreaming?" she asked as she chuckled softly. "You must be getting really old to fall asleep so easily without even downing one whole drink. At first I thought you were having an attack of some sort, you were making some muffled grunts."

I read too many thrillers. Far too many! I picked up my half empty glass from the table. Obviously I had not dropped it. I turned and slowly glanced out into the yard, making sure there really wasn't a dead lady lying out there amongst the gardenias and headed back into the house to refresh my drink. Abbie was still chuckling.

Old forgotten memories can resurface, unexpectedly, from time to time to influence us in the strangest of ways. I may switch my reading material for a while. Murder and mayhem do horrible things to this aging brain. Or is it the gin?

35

HERE: This was the end of one more chapter in my life. A passion, which had become a profession, was reverting to being a pastime. It had been a long time coming but the timing was just right. I knew it. Abbie knew it. The papers had been signed, the deal had been done. As of tomorrow the studio would be called Thundercloud Productions. Thunder and his equally talented son, Blessing, were ready to go. A sunset in one place is a sunrise in another. I couldn't be happier…and yet, I couldn't be sadder. My career had come to a close. It had been an incredible ride.

Thunder understood that I wanted to say "goodbye" to my studio—now *his* studio—alone. He and Blessing waited for me out in the parking lot so we could go and have a celebratory dinner together. I walked slowly, quietly through every room one last time. I turned out the lights as I walked from the back of the studio to the front. The remaining light was in the entryway. Several new photos were already hanging on the wall, welcoming clients. No matter who would come through the front door; no matter what language they might speak, photography is the only language that can be understood anywhere in the world. I had read that somewhere and it stuck with me. So true. The furniture was different. The feeling was different. It was no longer mine. Sitting inside a locked display cabinet was an old Kodak Autographic 2-C. It was the camera from the 1920s that my beloved mentor, Efrem Goldschmitt, had given to me decades ago. I passed it on to Thunder with the same request that he continue the tradition and give it on to a valued mentee sometime in the future.

I reached for the front door handle. Before I opened the door to let in the bright glow of sunset, I turned for one last look. And then I flicked off the last light switch.

(Blackout)

ACT THREE

SOONER OR LATER

"The closing years in life are like the end of a masquerade party, when the masks are dropped."

Anonymous

36

SOONER: Perhaps I've given people the impression throughout the years that I'm an optimist. Basically, I've *tried* to remain optimistic, but I've noticed more and more cynicism slipping in uninvited from time to time. Although I kiddingly claim to eschew reality and act jovial, sometimes I'm just faking it. Somewhere along the line that *Ac-Cent-Tuate the Positive* attitude and behavior may have gotten derailed. Temporarily, I hope. Maybe it's just because I'm getting old. Well, have *gotten* older. Old. I'm feeling old. And, perhaps, a tad useless. Time is speeding up. It seems as though all my remaining tomorrows are rushing toward me at warp speed. Another day, another week, another month, another year. Another day, another week, another month, another year! Too fast, too fucking fast. I've gone from 0 to 70 in a freakin' heartbeat! I've come to that age when, I guess, there are no more surprises. No more goals or aspirations. What do us old folks do now; just sit around waiting for winter, metaphorically speaking? Life has become the same, somewhat dull routine every day.

I have to admit (to myself only) that perhaps I shouldn't have retired yet. There are many nights when I dream that I'm still at the studio. Still doing incredible shoots, with incredible clients. Winning accolades. Even that bigoted bossy bitch Pricilla Thewliss…Thoughtless…Clueless…came strutting through a dream one night. I awoke with a jolt and in a cold sweat with that one! I have the feeling that I'm slipping sloppily into boring old age. Abbie and I have had some wonderful adventures together. Traveled all around the world and have seen so many astounding sites. Our son has given us great pleasure throughout the years and bestowed upon us two exceptionally gifted grandchildren. What's left for us to do now? I suppose I could write a book. About what? A thriller? I love to read them but I don't really have the imagination to conjure up nefarious characters and intricate, twist-laden plots. A travelogue? Been done to death. A memoire? Hah! Who cares? Nothing in my past would interest a reader. I may as well admit it, a quiet, reserved, albeit boring life is all that remains ahead for us now. I fear that I'm fast approaching that part of my life where one morning I just might wake up dead.

But then, there is the unpredictability of things.

I went out to collect the mail, such as it was. Probably more political ads and junk mail. We've gotten (and thrown away) so many "invitations" from a local assisted-living facility that they must think we are both non-ambulatory by now. But today it was not the usual. That's when the solid floor on which I was standing opened up and I fell through the trap door.

The envelope was hand-addressed, using a beautiful cursive. You certainly don't see much of that anymore these days. It almost looked like it was a greeting card. There was a return address for a town in Vermont and a person's name: Thackeray Brecklyn. *"What kind of name is that?"* I thought. *"Sounds like something out of a Dickens novel."* Definitely not an ad or junk mail. A letter was enclosed, also in that same beautiful cursive. I walked into the kitchen as I read it and looked at Abbie with shock and confusion in my eyes.

"What is it?" she asked with a twinkle in her eye and sarcasm in her voice. "Did you just win a lottery or something? Will Publisher's Clearing House be knocking on our front door?" and she laughed.

"I have a brother," I blurted out, and stood stock-still staring at her.

"Say what?"

I handed her the letter. "I have a brother…apparently," I repeated.

Both of my parents are long gone, Gram and Gramp preceding them. I have no one to ask about this situation. My first thought was a scam-alert. Those infamous emails about transferring huge sums of money from distant places, such as Nigeria or East Bumblefuck, into one's bank account instantly came to my mind. Horribly naïve and gullible people obviously fell for those scams because they continued for years…decades, even. But this letter was different. No request for banking information. Just a request for a response. Was I naïve? Would I fall into a trap of some sort? Would I be gullible enough to actually respond? According to the letter, Thackeray Brecklyn was just as astonished as I was to learn that he had a sibling. There was an email address and a telephone number. Were these legit? I put Google to work. The town in Vermont was Pittsford and I discovered, via the fabulous Internet, that it was not too far from Rutland and that the very first U.S. patent was issued there in 1790, signed by George Washington. Useless information. Obviously a sleepy, remote little town, but was it the epicenter for the latest scam? A reverse-telephone number search came up blank. More than likely a cell phone number. Googled his name and the only Brecklyn that came up was a stainless steel kitchen faucet made by MOEN. I can't imagine that a household fixture is claiming to be a relative.

Okay, so what's my next move? Email him? Call him? If I emailed him would I open up my computer to be easily hacked and all my personal information be violated and my bank account drained? If I called him would my every word be recorded and edited into me agreeing to purchase some useless piece of junk costing thousands of dollars?

I emailed him.

I was cautious. I made sure that nothing I wrote could be interpreted or rewritten in a compromising way. I read it and reread it before I hit the SEND button. I asked for a few details and divulged none of my own. I did state, however, that I was very apprehensive about this being a scam of some sort and if my fears proved correct, my email address would be changed. Big damn deal…he had my home address. I couldn't change that! I didn't expect to get an instant reply or, for that matter, to get a reply at all. But ten minutes later he responded. He claimed that he, too, had been very apprehensive about contacting me. Good ploy there. Trying to lull me into a more comfortable mode. A false sense of security, so to speak. He had been born and raised in England, and had recently come to the United States from his home in London. Aha! That Dickensian name! He urged me to call him so we could discuss this turn of events more easily rather than through back and forth emails. He attached a photo of himself. I was afraid to click on the attachment, fearing that it might be one of those stupid things that folks post on Facebook that seem beautiful and innocuous but then all of a sudden it turns into some horrible screaming ghoul that makes you wet yourself as you back away from the screen. You know that old cliché about cats and curiosity? I clicked. And I backed away from the screen. I was staring at a face that most definitely had familiar characteristics. Same eyes and bone structure. Same distinctive shape of his ears. My father…our father…had very strong genes. Although there *were* differences, I was staring at a face that could have been mine five years ago. Was it a Photoshop trick?

It was a Saturday morning around 11, one of those rare early August days when it was actually raining in Between. I couldn't mow the lawn, a task I had been lazily avoiding for the last week or so…so why not see if he's home. See if this is real. See what trouble I could get myself into. The phone rang five times before he picked up.

"Yes, hello?" was the terse answer with a touch of a British accent.

"Mr. Brecklyn," I responded with trepidation. "This is Baxter Janus." There was a pause. And then it sounded like a gasp.

"Oh, right! Oh, my god! Yes, hello. And please, just call me Tack. I couldn't pronounce my name when I was a wee bit of a thing. Came out *Tackeray*. So the nickname Tack just stuck. No pun intended. So sorry, I didn't recognize this number and was hesitant to answer. So many bloody scam calls these days, even on the cell. Hang on a sec, I'm out in the yard and I'll head back in so we can talk in peace and quiet. I'm supervising some work done on the house and the hammering out here is driving me batty."

I waited for several seconds and I could, indeed, hear hammering and some words being spoken in the distance but couldn't make out any of them. I could hear footsteps sounding like they were running up stairs (a front or back porch perhaps) and the slamming of a door. Obviously it wasn't raining in Pittsford, Vermont.

"Right then, I'm back again. Sorry about that. I am so glad that you called. I wasn't sure what would happen after I sent off that letter. Not sure what *I* might have done considering the contents. But I was hoping for a decent chin-wag."

As I soon discovered (aside from the meaning of chin-wag), the more we chatted, the more certain aspects of my life began to click into view and the focus sharpened.

"I only recently discovered about you, Baxter," he continued. "And to say that I was flummoxed is a gross understatement. My mother never told me anything about my father aside from the fact that they met during the war, and that he had died shortly after I was born. Which, now that I think about it, may not have been totally true. I'm referring to World War Two, by the way. She is…was American. She recently passed away and that's what led me to this revelation."

"Wait," I interrupted, "she just *recently* passed away? My folks died years ago. How old was she?"

"She was ninety-eight, rest her soul, spry and feisty as the devil himself. I guess she decided enough is enough and silently, painlessly died in her sleep two months shy of her ninety-ninth birthday. Her live-in housekeeper found her, sitting in her recliner, with the latest Peter Ash thriller in her lap. She had recently switched from reading Jack Reacher stuff. Don't know, though, if that's what did her in." And he chuckled.

All I could say was "Wow."

"Anyway, back to my story. Where was I? Oh, yes, World War Two. My father…well, yours and mine, that is…was wounded severely and was in hospital for some time. My mother was a very young army nurse, obviously working near the front lines. Sounds like I'm leading up to a cliché-ridden romance novel or a very poor Hemingway knockoff, doesn't it? Anyway, evidently she went arse over tit and things progressed from there."

"Excuse me?" I interrupted. "Arse over tit?"

Thackeray chuckled. "Sorry, lad. I believe you colonists say 'head over heels', right? Let me back up a bit here. I think I'm getting the horse before the cart. How did I discover about you? About us? Although my mother had several relationships throughout the years, she never married. She didn't return to the States for several years, electing to settle in England. Chiswick, to be exact, a district of West London. Her elder sister, also never married, lived in Vermont. Actually in the very house where I am now sitting. Her sister got severely ill a few years back. Victoria, my Mum, sold her place here in England and moved back to the States to live permanently with her and take care of her. Well, my aunt died, leaving this house to my mother, along with another small cottage on nearby Lake Dunmore. About three months ago my mother died, leaving everything to me. Bloody hell! What am I to do with this old rattletrap of a house and real estate, with me living in London? Don't worry; I'm not trying to diddle you out of money, or anything. That's not a problem for me. But I uncovered a dirty, dusty old trunk in the attic a couple weeks ago. Here comes that cliché shit again, my friend. There was a stack of old…and I mean *very* old letters in that trunk. The paper was brittle and brown with age. The letters dated from the mid 1940s to about 1950 and then they stopped. The postmarks were from Dover…veddy British, right? Not England, but New Jersey. I started reading. It took me a while but I began to piece things together. The letters were from a Corey Janus and, I must say, they were quite lovely letters, at that."

I think that my heart had stopped beating when he mentioned the letters. I knew I had at least held my breath.

"We need to pick up on this later today. Sorry to say that I have an appointment with a local realtor up at the lake cottage in about an hour. Can we schedule *(Pronouncing it 'shedule')* a call this evening? Can we do FaceTime or Skype so we can see each other?"

"Yes, yes, of course," I responded, trying to calm my nerves. "Can we do 7 or 7:30 this evening?"

"Certainly. No problem. Let's do 7:30. We have a lot of ground to cover. Perhaps you'll be able to answer some questions that I have as well."

We exchanged the appropriate information for connecting via FaceTime and clicked off. Now it was time for me to do a bit of investigating and fact checking. Google has become a good friend of mine. He casually mentioned that his mother's name was Victoria and I assumed her last name was Brecklyn. I did a search for recent obituaries in Pittsford, Vermont. Well, I'll be damned! There it was. Dying of natural causes at 98, her sole remaining relative was a son, Thackeray, of London, England. She was born in 1921, in Forest Lake, Minnesota. It mentioned that she had served as an army nurse during World War Two; resided in England for decades where she had worked as a volunteer tour guide at Stonehenge; and then published a series of best-selling mystery novels under the pen name of Vicky Jayne. She had repatriated five years ago. Holy shit! I had a feeling that my boring old age existence was about to be upended.

The witching hour – 7:30 P.M. and I didn't know how should I be feeling. Nervous? Apprehensive? Skeptical? Angry? But angry with whom? My father for doing what he did? Angry at Thackeray for interrupting my peaceful, boring retirement? Did Mom ever find out? Did Gram and Gramp know about this? If so, why was I never told, even after I had grown up?

Our respective images came into view on the monitors, hundreds of miles apart and decades of secrecy apart. We sat, momentarily silent, staring…studying each other. I could definitely see a great similarity. A few people have told me over the past years that I sort of resemble Daniel Craig. I suppose I do. Sort of. If you close one eye and squint with the other. I assumed Thackeray was probably about four or five years younger than me. He looked very distinguished. And he could be Daniel Craig's younger brother. He had dark blond hair (the same as my…our father), was clean-shaven and had a pronounced cleft in his chin. As did I. And our father. He was wearing a dark blue polo shirt; top buttons opened revealing a tuft of blond chest hair.

"How to begin? Well, I must say," Thackeray broke the silence, "I have a very handsome older brother."

"You're not so bad, yourself," I chuckled in response. "Although I'm jealous. You've retained far more hair than I have."

"It's clean living and not having to raise any children that does it." Thackeray said, shaking his head and laughing out loud.

"Oh, so I take it then, that I don't have any secret nieces or nephews across the pond?"

"No, none thank God! Just to be upfront right from the start and to get any uncomfortable facts answered, let's just say that you and I play on different teams."

"You mean...?"

"Yes, you got it. I'm gay."

"Funny, you don't *look* gay," I quipped. "Were you always gay or just since it's become popular?"

"Oh, I like you already!" laughed the Brit, arching an eyebrow. "A man after my heart with a droll sense of humor."

"Sorry," I responded, "but I can't take credit for that. I read that line in some book not too long ago and really liked it. Never had the opportune time to use it until now."

"Kudos to the original author!" chuckled Thackeray. "Right...well, then. Now that we've gotten that little tidbit out of the way...out of the closet, so to speak...let's talk family that neither one of us knew about. I will say, that with the wonders of the Internet, you were easy to track down. A professional photographer who retains his website despite being retired. Interesting. By the way, your portfolio knocked my argyle socks off, Baxter. Great work!"

"Thanks," I replied modestly. "And, please, you can just call me Bax. You, on the other hand, presented a challenge for me. Couldn't find you online. I thought you might be a piece of stainless steel."

"Excuse me?"

"Never mind," I laughed. "Let's proceed with this game of unanswered life history. What was your first reaction when you read those letters to discover that a sibling existed?"

He ran his fingers through his hair. "Well, bloody hell! I picked up the urn with my mother's cremains and shook it like an ice shaker filled with martinis and yelled at her. 'What the fuck?' I yelled. Why, why, why had she kept this from me? What would the harm have been to tell me? Years have gone by. Our father had died years ago, so what would be wrong with telling me the truth? I have no clue. Oh, in one of the letters I found an old black and white photograph. Two little boys were in it and I assumed that our father had sent it to show her how cute you were. One of them in the photo must be you. I have it here on the desk."

He held up the tiny image, bringing it close to the camera lens, and tears came to my eyes. Two little boys. One dark haired and one towheaded.

"That's me and my best friend, Ant. I loved him like a brother. Little did I know."

"Won't he be surprised to discover that you actually *do* have a brother after all these years."

I paused to regain my composure and to wipe away a tear before I responded. "When Ant…Anthony came home from Viet Nam he was in a flag-draped coffin. I was to be the best man at his wedding which, needless to say, never happened."

"Oh, dear. Tragic. Heartbreaking. I am so, so sorry," he responded, shaking his head. "Moving on then, I don't imagine that your father… damn, *our* father retained any photos that my mother may have sent of *me?*"

I suddenly remembered that mysterious old photo of a little boy in a sailor suit tucked away in that rickety roll-top desk that I cleaned out when my mother wanted to sell it to that sleazy antique dealer. But what had I done with it? Although it was rude of me, I ignored his question.

"You said that the postmark on those letters you found were from Dover, but what was the street address? I cannot imagine that my father would have been stupid enough to use that and have my mother get ahold of any of that correspondence."

"You're right, of course. But it was a post office box number. Very discreet, don't you agree? He obviously sent money to my mother every now and then based on what I can gather from his wording. He had a beautiful handwriting, didn't he?" I remembered that he did, indeed. "Who is or was someone named Chester? He was mentioned in just about the very last letter that my mother received"

"Chester Freemont was my maternal grandfather. Gram and Gramp lived just a few blocks from us in Dover. Why was he mentioned?"

"Ah, well, that explains it then. From what I can piece together from his words, evidently Chester encountered Corey at the post office, mere happenstance I presume, and somehow discovered the subterfuge. Morals, mores, and attitudes regarding indiscretions were a lot different back in the 1940s than they are now, remember. A deal must have been struck, then and there, to permanently keep the affair from your mother if the correspondence ceased. We have no idea, of course, what that deal must have been. Your grandfather must have had some clout, because, indeed, the letters stopped."

So *that's* why that feeling I got from both Gram and Gramp towards my father. The feeling of distrust and animosity. And that's why my dad seemed to be dancing on eggshells whenever they visited. Being that Gramp was a lawyer, it must have been an ironclad deal. The past is slowly revealing its secrets. Throughout the years I had kept the hope alive that, sooner or later, I would discover the reason why. And so, sooner or later has finally arrived.

"I wish that our father had secretly retained those letters he received from your mother," I sighed. "They must have been beautiful love letters. Heartbreaking, I imagine. Of course you have no way of knowing if she ever tried to track him down. You said that she came back to the States often to visit her sister. But that was long before the Internet and Google made life easier."

"I, too, came to the States often to visit my aunt. I traveled all around your glorious country. Yes, even Atlanta. Who knows? We may have been within a few short miles from each other at one time or another. Sooner or later, we *will* have to get together."

"Are you retired?" I asked. "What is it that you do or did? You're here now, but do you still maintain a home in England?"

"Yes, I retired a few years ago. Strange, but we're in a somewhat related field. I was a teacher of both art history and graphic design. Started out my career in London, and then was offered a splendid position in southern Spain. My partner and I spent several wonderful years there. Lovely spot. I taught international students at St. George's School in Malaga. I was thrilled to be there. Malaga. Birthplace of Pablo Picasso."

"Oh, I remember Malaga!" I exclaimed. "My wife and I visited Spain a few years ago and we flew into that airport. We rented a small villa in Marbella."

"Ah, yes. Marbella. Playground of the rich," Thackeray laughed. "The late, lamented Sean Connery once owned a beautiful villa there, overlooking the Mediterranean. He and his lovely wife hosted a party there one time that Todd, my partner, and I attended. It was for all the teachers at the international school. He didn't drink martinis, by the way, shaken *or* stirred."

Suddenly, a thought flashed into my mind. A distinct memory and a distinct mystery. There is no way, surely!

"Wait! You said you lived in Malaga for a number of years. I remember driving along the Costa del Sol, from Tarifa all the way up to Grenada, but how far from Malaga is Nerja?"

"Nerja? Hmm, I'd guess it's probably just short of about 60 kilometers, if I remember correctly. Why do you ask?" Thackeray answered with a quizzical look on his face.

I related the story to him about the little local restaurant and the maitre d' who seemed to recognize me.

"Well, then," he responded, "was it the Taberna de Pepe?"

"Oh, hell, I have no way of remembering the name of that damn restaurant. It was off the beaten path and definitely not in any tourist guidebook that I know of."

"Was it on a little, quiet back street, far up the hill from the center of town?"

"Yes, and it had several little rooms inside the place. Although it didn't look fancy-pantsy in any way, that maître d' wore a tuxedo."

"I. Will. Be. Damned!" Thackeray hooted. "Did he have a bright red pocket square in his jacket?"

"Yes! Now that I think about it, he sure did!"

"Ha! That was Alejandro. Todd and I went there often. It was one of our favorite dining spots. I simply cannot believe that you were there. It must have been long after we moved back to London, obviously."

My head was spinning. The past and the present were colliding.

"Please don't tell me that your favorite wine is Bodegas Mauro," I said. He stared at me.

"It's a tad pricy now, but, yes, that is one of my favorites."

We sat in silence for a few moments, simply staring at each other.

"The phone number you gave me," I began speaking again, "has a Vermont area code and not London."

"It's my mother's cell phone. I always use it when I visit. I keep mine turned the hell off. Todd and I communicate every day via Skype. He's being so patient with me while I'm here. He's holding down the fort, as you Yanks say."

"You know, " I said after a moment or two of silence, "this is so bizarre. I am just so damn comfortable, all of a sudden, sitting here talking to you…looking at you…as if we have known each other for years. The apprehension I felt when I first decided to reach out and respond to your letter has vaporized. If, indeed, you are trying to scam me in some way you're doing a damn fine job of it."

"Wait," Thackeray answered with an evil chuckle, "by the end of the call I will have you divulging your bank account information and the passwords to all your financial institutions."

"The fuck you will!" I responded, laughing as well. "By the way, how did it go with your realtor this afternoon? And what's going on with your mother's main residence there in Pittsford?"

"I'm at the mercy of these New Englanders up here. Not knowing the value of real estate in these parts I just have to go along with what I'm being told. I can Google certain things, of course, to see if I'm being diddled with but that goes only so far. My mother's house was in terrible disrepair and, slowly but surely, that's coming along. It is 108 years old, but has good bones, as they say. The whole interior is being renovated with very modern appliances and fixtures and what have you. She left me quite a bit of money and I am not a pauper by any stretch of the imagination anyway, so the expenses don't rattle me. Too much, anyway. I'm not afraid to negotiate with the contractors and you'd be surprised at how effective a long, hard stare with my arms folded across my chest can be. I've been told that it's a seller's market these days, so we shall find out soon enough, right? I'm also learning quite a bit about your tax laws here. Almost as bad as ours in the U.K. My head is spinning by the end of each day but a good gin and tonic remedies that situation straight away."

We both laughed at that. I like this man.

After I was silent for a moment or two, he asked, "What are you thinking?"

"I'm thinking that if this conversation were in a novel nobody would believe it."

"A month ago I wouldn't have believed it either. I thought that Brexit was the largest shock to my system. I was mistaken."

"So," I asked, "what do we do now? I mean, now that we have found each other, will our respective lives change that much? It would be nice to meet, face-to-face, but time and distance might prove a factor. I assume that once your mother's house is back in shape you'll head home, right? You don't have to stick around until both properties are sold, do you?"

"No. No, I don't have to remain in the States. So much can be done electronically these days regarding legal transactions. I've been told by the realtor that both properties should move very quickly. I have no idea if that's true or not, but we'll see. And besides, what with this damned ubiquitous maple syrup, I shall be two stone heavier by the time I get back home. Jesus, they put it on everything up here. Even in their coffee, believe it or not." He paused for a moment. "However, aside from all this real estate talk, I have left one very big question unasked of *you*."

"And that is...? I asked.

"What sort of man was Corey Janus? Was he a good father?"

"Let's each grab a gin and tonic for ourselves first, brother. This is going to take a while."

37

Tack scanned that little old photo of Ant and me, cleaned it up a bit in Photoshop and emailed it to me. I printed it out and held it in front of me, staring at it, for a good five minutes. I managed to dig out an old box of photos and memorabilia that I had lugged around with me from place to place for decades. I rummaged through it and almost at the very bottom I found those pictures that I had taken with Mom's old Brownie camera. Mom, Gram, Gramp and Mom's friend sitting in those big white Adirondack chairs at Lake Hopatcong…what was her name? Aunt Sophie? Yeah, that was it. There were the photos of Ant acting crazy, dancing around, making funny faces at the camera. I dug around a little more and uncovered my old high school yearbook. Flipped through the pages. There he was again. Anthony Joseph Bertoli, voted Best Looking. Yes, he was a very handsome guy. Dark, wavy hair and, what all the girls said, smoldering eyes. And there I was. Not a bad-looking guy. Just blond and bland. And I was voted Friendliest. Do they even still do that these days? Take Senior Personality Polls…in this age of everyone gets a trophy? Pulled out a couple more photos. A photo I had taken with my first brand new camera: a smiling young Ant in the kitchen with his parents, Angela and Joe Bertoli, all of them creating some wonderful dish. I can almost still smell the oregano and basil. Ant and his beautiful fiancée, Valerie

Panatone, arm in arm, with him in his army uniform. Ant, in his uniform, with my arm over his shoulder, the day he left for boot camp. In all my years, I have never had a friend like Ant. And I never will.

I picked up that older photo again, the one that Tack had sent. "I miss you so much, buddy, so much. You, your fabulous eggplant parmesan… and your fucking cemetery."

It suddenly dawned on me. It was something I'd thought Gramp had been kidding me about all those years ago, *"You're my favorite grandson, Bax."* Abbie came into the room and walked up behind me. She saw what I was doing, bent over and just wrapped her arms around my shoulder. Although I was silent, I know that she could tell that I was crying.

My emotions returned to somewhat normal a couple hours after my long conversation with Tack. Never knowing where in the world Darin might be, considering his hectic schedule, I texted him. *"Call me whenever. I have a surprise for you."* And I included an avatar of me laughing hysterically. There was an immediate reply. *"Actually, I'm home. What is it? Wanna Facetime?"*

His handsome face appeared on the screen, responding to my call. His on again – off again beard was off again, making him look years younger. His blond hair was again cut short. The length of which varies from month to month. There were the sounds of laughing children in the background and the two boys came running up beside their father and looked at the screen.

"Hi, Grandpa!" the boys called out almost in unison, both of them waving at me.

"Hi, yourself, you little twits," I called back. They both giggled and ran off again. Carson came up behind Darin, put her arms on his broad shoulders and leaned in to the monitor.

"Hi, Bax," she said, blowing me a kiss. "We miss seeing you guys," she continued. "I think that might call for a road trip, don't you agree?"

"Absolutely!" I responded with enthusiasm, returning the kiss. "I'm sure Abbie won't put up any argument either. She misses seeing her favorite son!" Darin, of course, was our *only* son and we had teased him about that "favorite son" thing since he was a kid.

"Where's Ma?" asked our favorite son, trying to look over my shoulder.

"She'll be here in a minute or two, don't worry. She wouldn't miss this golden opportunity to see your handsome face," I laughed.

"So, okay, Pop, what's that big surprise? Did you finally decide to write that scandalous tell-all autobiography, or what?" And he laughed as he picked up a cup of coffee.

"You have an uncle," I blurted out. His coffee cup stopped in mid-journey up to his lips and his smile turned into a look of confusion.

"Wait. What?"

Our conversation was winding down and we were about to say good night when a very sullen-looking Hayden came into the room and climbed up onto Darin's lap.

"Oh, you look so sad," I said, "what's wrong, little man?"

"I'm *not* sad," he responded with a petulant tone. "I'm mad, that's all."

Darin looked down at him. "Mad at whom?"

"Greyson," he answered. "I hate him! And I'm never going to talk to him again."

"No, no, no," I scolded, "you certainly don't hate your brother. That's not a very nice thing to say. Tell Grandpa why you're mad at him. Please."

Hayden paused and puffed himself up like he was filling with air instead of silent rage.

"He's been teaching me how to play chess. I must have made a bad move and he said it was stupid. He took my piece and laughed at me. So I knocked all the pieces onto the floor. It's a dumb game anyway. I'm never going to talk to him again. I'm going to bed now and won't ever let him in my room again." He folded his arms across his little chest.

I cleared my throat, stifled a laugh and shook my head.

"Can I tell you something, Hayden?"

His little head nodded.

"A long time ago, someone I loved very, very much told me that if the wind goes down with the sun, it will come up with the sun. I imagine the same thing might be true with anger, too. If you go to bed angry tonight, chances are that you'll wake up tomorrow morning still angry. Maybe even angrier because it festered and grew while you were sleeping."

I saw Darin smile. He, too, had been told this, years ago, for one reason or another. Hayden's little face looked up at me. He didn't look convinced.

"Maybe Greyson shouldn't have laughed at you. But that's really nothing to get so angry about, is it?"

His little head didn't move.

"You'll probably remember about that move in the future when you play chess and it will make you a better player, right?"

His little head nodded. Just a little.

"Greyson didn't call *you* stupid now, did he? He just said that move was stupid. Not a very nice word, I agree. But knocking all the pieces off the board was not a very nice thing to do either. I'm sure your father will agree with me when I say that you should go right back into Greyson's room and apologize. Make up with him, all right? You need to do it tonight, not wait for the morning."

I could see his little mind churning. He slowly moved away from Darin and left the room. Darin and I looked at each other and smiled. We waited for a couple seconds.

"I just heard him open Greyson's door," said Darin. He cocked his head, leaning back in his chair trying to listen.

"I'm sorry," I heard Hayden's voice say in the distance. "You big stupid butt-hole!"

And a door slammed.

Darin closed his eyes and put his hands to his face.

"I'll take it from here, Pop," he said, shaking his head. "I love you. Goodnight."

And we ended the conversation.

38

Thunder called and left a message on my machine. Then he texted me: *Let's do lunch. Tomorrow.* I answered to the affirmative. I hadn't seen or heard from him in well over a year, maybe even longer. One loses track of time when one is retired. We agreed to meet at the Vortex in Little Five Points, a favorite spot for both of us. And the best burgers ever!

We both pulled into the smallish parking lot at the same time and somehow managed to find two parking spaces side by side. We got out and immediately shook hands that melted into a great big hug. An old, white, balding guy hugging a huge, muscular, shiny-domed black guy...seemed the norm for Little Five Points. He looked great and I told him so. He returned the compliment but I knew he was lying. But what the hell? Ego is ego. I accepted it. It always puts a big smile on my face whenever I walk through that laughing skull of the front door to the place. A true landmark.

We exchanged the usual pleasantries and as soon as we ordered, he launched into the reason for our meeting.

"Your old friend and former client, Marty Howce, has long since left that packaging company he was working for, but he called me out of the blue the day before yesterday. He has a couple of good friends who own an art gallery up in the Buckhead area. They want to do a show completely with photography. I'm meeting with all of them in a few days and I suggested that they might want to include you, too. You have some amazing stuff, maybe even the stuff you did decades ago. You have some history there, mon."

I had to mull this one over. From time to time, friends and a few clients have asked about purchasing a print or two of some of my shots. I had to admit that the thought of having several in a large exhibit was intriguing.

"What the hell, Thunder? Why not? Could be fun. What else do I have to do in my lazy retirement, eh?"

We downed several more beers as he regaled me with horror stories from some of his recent shoots. Clients never change. Most of them are great but then you have your occasional asshole or two...or three.

Three days later I walked into the Brandson-Holliday Gallery in Buckhead and immediately realized one of the tragedies of old age: I was shrinking. Thunder, who stands a whopping six-ten, introduced me to Stet Brandson, an outrageously handsome guy who appears to stand a formidable six-six. Former client and friend to Stet, Marty Howce, was there as well. He stands about six-four. I *used* to be six-one. I was now five-ten. I was a fucking dwarf!

I chuckled to myself inwardly as I was introduced to Stet. I thought that I might be in trouble regarding Abbie. If she had thought *Marty* was hot, she would faint dead away upon meeting Stet, for sure. Not only was he a great-looking guy, what with his height, his beautiful black hair and his intense blue eyes, but, dammit, he turned out to be a heck of a nice guy as well. No pretentions about him whatsoever.

His gallery was impressive, as was the current show. I walked around gazing at all the paintings that, I had to admit, took my breath away. The artwork was a mixture of landscapes, abstracts and animals, but in color combinations I had never seen before. Wild, wild combinations, with the weirdest of color juxtapositions but damn, it all worked beautifully. Stet came up beside me and told me about this particular artist.

"She's color blind," he said, "and has problems with blues and yellows. She just squeezes the paint out onto her palette and goes at it. I have no idea, really, what *she* sees while she's painting, but her work is amazing, isn't it?"

"I have to admit, these are unique. I really, truly like all of them. I'm disappointed that the one I would really like to buy already has a red sticker on it. I love that purple goat!"

Stet laughed. "Don't worry, Baxter, she has painted that goat several times. Each one is a bit different, of course, but that damn goat seems to be a very popular one. She actually has a few of them as pets."

We finally got down to the business of going through my photos as well as Thunder's. We all sat around a large round table in Stet's office. First we went through Thunder's portfolio, which was extremely impressive. That big guy does incredible stuff with a camera. I could tell by watching Stet's face that he, too, was impressed.

"Oh, man," Stet sighed, "I see so many here that I would love to include. I have to be very selective, though, because I have a couple other local photographers coming in later this week with their portfolios as well."

He sat back, shaking his head as he looked from one print to the next.

"Okay, Baxter, let's take a look," he said, smiling at me.

I had rummaged through boxes and boxes of my prints. I'm a hoarder, I'll admit. There had been no need to show my portfolio for several years and a layer of dust had been cleaned off after I retrieved it from my storage room. Stet started leafing through the pages. He stopped abruptly at one that, obviously, held his attention.

"How old is this one?" he asked, turning the book for me to see.

"That one, my young friend, is probably about fifty years old."

"Well, then," he said, "obviously it isn't done with a digital camera. This might be a foolish question, but would you still happen to have the negatives?"

A broad smile came across my face. "That isn't a foolish question, but here comes a smartass reply. Exactly what kind of photographer do you think I am? Keeping fifty-year-old negatives? Ha! I probably have *sixty*-year-old negatives. I've probably carted more cartons of negatives and prints throughout all of my moves than I have furniture. Our homes have had so much incendiary material...i.e., celluloid...packed away that insurance agents would have had coronaries if they only knew. What was your question again?" Everybody laughed.

"Okay, okay," Stet continued after we all calmed down again. "Then how large a print can I get of this one. I want a few others of yours, definitely, but this one really intrigues me. Can it be enlarged to, say, thirty-six by forty-eight?"

I turned to Thunder. "Well, my towering friend, I no longer have a darkroom at home and no access to enlargers. You still have that projection enlarger at the studio? I know you are into things other than large format these days, but I was hoping…"

"Stop right there, Bax," Thunder interrupted. "Exactly what kind of photographer do you think I am? Shit, yeah, mon. Of course I still have it. And I know what you mean about film being so much better than digital. The crispness…the minute detail…the drama in this photo could only be captured on film."

"Well I'll be damned," said Stet, snapping his fingers. "You just gave me the title for the show. Thanks!"

The photograph that had intrigued Stet so much was, indeed, at least fifty years old. It was the handsome, rugged, craggy, forlorn, dirty face of a hobo named Jake. The one who had given me the good luck charm that I still carried in my pants pocket. The cupule had come off a number of times, only to be glued back on and re-glued throughout the years. But my studio's namesake remained with me. An acorn.

Stet selected six photos of mine to be included in the show, and suggested the sizes for each one. Five of the photos were in black and white, the one exception being a photo I had taken in Egypt. A little brown-skinned boy, perhaps five or six year old, wearing a dirty gallibaya, was peering at me nervously from around a massive column at the Temple of Karnak in Luxor. His big, inquisitive brown eyes were so expressive I couldn't help but snap his photo before he scampered away immediately following the click of the shutter.

Two months later, the opening night of the show was a gala affair. The gallery was packed and I recognized several of my former colleagues in the Atlanta world of photographers. A large placard on an easel just inside the front door announced the name of the exhibition: *Places & Faces – Captured Moments.* When I introduced Abbie to Stet I could almost feel her legs melt away and imagined an inaudible sigh. When Stet introduced me to his stunningly beautiful wife, Mary, I could almost feel *my* legs melt away beneath me. What a night! Thunder, also, had six of his photos chosen for the exhibit, all of which were color. And what glorious colors! Five of the photos were landscapes taken throughout the United States and one from near his hometown, Castleton, in Jamaica. That particular photo seemed to pop right off the wall, it was so brilliant. It had been taken in the Castleton Botanical Gardens, one of the oldest such gardens in the western hemisphere. His lovely wife, Constanse, could have stepped right out of that photo. She was wearing a traditional bright red quadrille dress along with a vibrant yellow headband. Both Thunder and their talented son, Blessing, wore a traditional Kariba suit, considered formal attire in Jamaica. They seemed to get as much attention as the photos. Needless to say, because of his stature, Thunder *really* stood out amongst the crowd. Literally.

I happened to notice that an older couple had been standing in front of one of my photos for several minutes. They looked as though they had stepped right out of the 1940s. He was a tall, dapper gentleman, wearing an ascot and sporting a well-waxed handlebar moustache. She was diminutive if slightly portly, and wore the largest, floppiest hat I had ever seen. I worked my way through the crowd to see which photo of mine had intrigued them so much. Then I understood. It was one of the last photos I had taken of Gram and Gramp. One of the series that I had taken decades ago up in my little attic studio in our house in Dover. The photo that I had loved but had saddened my beloved grandparents. Stet had suggested that I should crop the photo and zoom in on their handsome faces, which I had done. True, it showed their age but it also seemed to reflect the love in their eyes. Their love for each other. And the love for me as they faced my camera. So many years ago; so many tears ago.

When Thunder made the enlargements of my hobo Jake, he had made two versions. One in the crisp, stark black and white of the original and one in sepia tone, giving an older, softer impression of the shot. I liked the black and white version the best. Stet agreed with me. The photo generated a lot of interest among the crowd and several people asked me about the person depicted. They seemed to be fascinated by my story and they loved it when I produced the old acorn from my pocket. I may have started a new trend tonight: acorn collecting.

39

"So, tell me then, how did the show go?" asked Tack. "Those photographs of the opening night you texted look great."

This was our third Skype call since that initial blockbuster of a FaceTime call four months ago. I was actually growing very fond of this new, long-lost family member.

"Great," I responded. "I had no idea what to expect. There was such a conglomeration of photos from all my fellow shutterbugs. Hell, I was impressed. Stet, the owner of the gallery was very pleased, indeed, by the reception from his patrons and from the local press. He wants to make it an annual event. That large shot of my hobo friend from days gone by will now be in the permanent photo collection at the High Museum down here. I was flabbergasted."

"Well done, Baxter, well done!"

The conversation changed course at that point, turning to his progress with the two houses in Vermont.

"The house here in Pittsford has turned out beautifully and I already have a few perspective buyers chomping at the bit. I may have to face a bidding war. Not a bad situation at all, right?"

"Not at all!" I responded, "Not at all. The photos of the house that you sent look amazing. Obviously you lucked out with a great contractor. You've been fairly quiet about that cottage at the lake. What's going on there?"

"Ah, yes, right. Well, then. This is where the plot thickens, as they say. I want to…"

I thought I heard a door close somewhere in the house behind him.

"Oh, wait a sec. Todd is over here visiting the States for a couple weeks. He's been out shopping for more gin. You've not had the pleasure of meeting each other yet. Hang on," and he leaned back in his chair, calling out. "Toddy, please come in here for a sec, will you?"

A very handsome gentleman came in the room behind Tack and leaned in toward the screen, putting his hands on Tack's shoulders. He seemed, to me, like what Benedict Cumberbatch might look like in about thirty years or so. Tack made the introductions, we said the usual pleasantries and then Todd excused himself to go fix two gin and tonics.

"Well, damn," I said. "Now *you* hold on a sec. If I had known this was going to be a virtual cocktail party I would have come prepared. I'll be right back," and Tack laughed.

"Okay, I'm back," I said a few minutes later with drink firmly in hand. "Back to my question regarding that lake cottage."

We toasted good health to each other; Tack took a big swig of his drink, sighed and cleared his throat.

"Okay, hear me out on this one. I have, potentially, a proposal. Please let me speak my piece before you make any comments. Todd, basically, has no family whatsoever. He has been estranged from the lot ever since the day he first stepped forth from the closet at age eighteen. The few surviving members of his family aren't worth two shits. You, Bax, are my family now. The sole survivor. Todd and I were extremely well off before Mum passed. The royalties from her book sales continue to roll in, especially now since her death, for some bizarre reason. They have actually increased. Nothing like what that lady is making off her boy wizard books, mind you, but still! Bloody hell! The taxes here…I meant in the U.K., are killers. The sale of the house *here* in Pittsford will be taxed here in the States *and* hit me again back home. That I am willing to handle. I won't like it, but so be it. Okay, here comes the part where you may want to blurt out an expletive or two…but please don't. Yet. Hear me out. The same contractor who did the recent work on the house here made several extremely beautiful alterations to the lake house. My realtor made a startling suggestion to me late yesterday. I've been online researching all kinds of things. The house is lakefront. One hundred and fifty foot frontage on the lake, including a boat dock. It sleeps eight, possibly ten if everyone is friendly. The house is slightly more than thirty miles from the Killington Ski area. The house has prime rental possibilities both summer and winter." He paused to catch his breath and take another sip of drink. I did the same. "The way I've been figuring since early this morning is that the house has the potential of generating anywhere from ninety to one hundred-twenty thousand dollars per year in year-round rentals. I don't want to sound like an arrogant dolt here but, frankly, I simply do *not* need that money. I really don't! But now I don't really want to sell the house to some stranger who will continue to make profit on it. Sit still, Baxter. I see that you're beginning to squirm in your seat. Don't deny it. If I keep the house and use it as a rental, I will be hit with what I learned this morning is the Foreign Investment In Real Property Tax Act that exists here in the States. Bloody Hell, I don't need nor want more taxes. *However.* Yes, here comes the *however*, Baxter, get ready to soil your drawers." He took another sip and another deep breath. "If you are interested, I will sell that cottage to you for one U.S. dollar and a handshake. Non-negotiable."

I didn't soil my drawers. Nor did I clutch my chest and feign a heart attack…or even say "Wow, that's a fantastic offer." But I *was* taken aback. Abbie and I didn't need the money either. Our investments throughout the years had done well. Our respective careers had been extremely lucrative. I had led a charmed life as "they" say. A surprising gift decades ago from Gram and Gramp started my adult life off into a successful direction. That damn acorn worked, I guess. No, we certainly didn't need the "extra" income every year.

"I really need to give this some thought, Tack. Let me mull this over for a day or two, talk with Abbie about this and I'll text you as soon as we can come to a decision, okay?" He agreed and we rung off.

Our conversation, with this major proposal, ended before I had a chance to tell Tack that I located some of his mother's books at a local bookstore. I bought the first three in the series and enjoyed them very much. In fact, they were excellent. All the thrillers take place during the late 1940s into the early 1950s, in post-World War Two England, so they hadn't dated like some of the other thrillers I had been reading recently. Each one included a bit of actual, true history and ended with a surprising twist or two that I had never anticipated. I chuckled to myself in the middle of the second one when I recognized a character that could have easily been my—our—father. She depicted him as a handsome rogue. Indeed.

I was at the bookstore, searching for a couple more of her books when my phone chirped that I got a text. It was from Stet, at the gallery: *A patron, Ruut van den Graaf, wants to chat with you. Call me.*

I called him.

"You have a patron named Rut? Like stuck in a rut, Rut?"

He laughed. "His name is pronounced *root,* as in root canal. And he can be just as annoying. But he buys a lot of artwork from me, so I'm gracious about his behavior. He lives up around the D.C. area someplace but his son works down here at the Dutch Consulate, so he flies down to visit Vincent every few weeks or so. He has a pilot's license and his own little plane. Mary and I have nicknamed him the Flying Dutchman."

"His son is named Vincent, as in van Gogh?" I couldn't help but chuckle.

"You have no idea how proud Ruut is of his Dutch heritage. He claims he is a Count, but I've not been able to verify that in any way. Queen Maxima of the Netherlands infatuates him and a majority of the artwork he buys from me is presented to her as loving gifts. I have absolutely *no* idea how her husband, the king, feels about it. In any event, I didn't want to give him your phone number or email address until I had cleared it with you first. I certainly wouldn't violate your privacy in any way."

"Of course, I understand and I appreciate that, Stet. Sure, go ahead. I have no objection to him contacting me. Do you have any idea why, though?"

"Just wait, Bax. And be prepared. He's flying back in on...hmmmm, what's today? Oh, tomorrow. I have no doubt he'll want to meet with you. Just be prepared, that's all I'll say."

We finished our conversation a few minutes later and I sat down in the nearest chair confused and wondering.

Wondering whatever the hell happened to my quiet, boring retirement?

40

My cell phone played my jazzy ringtone shortly after nine the next morning. It showed an unfamiliar number and I was hesitant to answer it. Too many scams calls these days and I didn't give two shits regarding my vehicle's extended warranty. But I took a chance.

I had hardly gotten "Hello" out when a deep voice with a thick accent started right in. "Baxter Janus, this is Ruut van den Graaf," he said, rolling his R's almost theatrically. "I shall be leaving D.C. in a few minutes. Would it be possible to meet at three this afternoon at Stet Brandson's gallery?"

No *hello*…no *how are you?* Nothing else. He was waiting for a reply.

"I suppose so, Mister van den Graaf, but…"

"Call me Ruut, please, and I will call you Baxter, ya?"

"I have no idea what this is about," I continued, "you *do* realize that I'm a retired old guy, don't you?"

"You're not dead yet, right?" he retorted. "You still know how to click a camera, I assume. Meet me at three, please, I just received clearance for takeoff." And he clicked off.

Stet was just finishing a sale as I entered his gallery. He gave me a smile and a little wave. I sat in one of the black leather Barcelona Chairs in a small gallery off of the main room to wait for him. He joined me less than five minutes later.

"So, the Flying Dutchman didn't waste any time, did he?" Stet laughed. "He texted me thirty minutes ago. He had just landed at Peachtree-DeKalb and he should be here any minute, depending on traffic."

"What does he fly, an old Fokker? I've always loved to say that name."

"I haven't a clue what he flies. He was an officer in the Royal Netherlands Air Force years ago, so he's been up in the air for a long time."

The front door opened with a flourish and in walked a tall, reed-thin gentleman wearing a dark navy blue pinstriped suit, sporting a dark navy tie with pure white polka dots and a bowler on the top of his head. Stet turned to me and winked. "Show time," he whispered.

"Gentlemen," said Ruut, after seeing us in the side room. He approached us, removed his hat with his left hand, bowed adding a quick click of his well-polished heels and extended his right hand to me. He appeared to be in his late fifties, reddish-blond hair that was turning grey at the temples and a few freckles across his pale face. There were just a few wrinkles around his eyes but, aside from them, his face was smooth and youthful.

"Sit, sit," he said, joining us, "please sit. Baxter, it's a pleasure to meet someone of your magical talent." Just like his phone call earlier this morning, he jumped right in. No "how are you?" No "glad to see you, Stet"…nothing. He is blunt and to the point. Obviously not wasting time with frivolous chat.

That comment bemused me. What the hell did he mean: *magical*?

"Ya, truly magical. I stood and stared in amazement at three of your photos during the exhibit. You know which ones? Of course not. I tell you. That one of the little Egyptian ragamuffin, for one. That ragged, rugged man who looked like he was dragged yelling and screaming through life, for two. And that wonderful portrait of that handsome old man and, I assume, his wife. They all brought tears to my eyes."

"Well, that old couple were my beloved grandparents, Ruut. I took a whole series of them. I was very young when I did so and they were upset by the truth that the photos showed. It pained them both to truly see, through the camera lens, how old they were. They were very disappointed and I was distraught for weeks because I had upset them so much."

"Oh, no, no, no. But surely they were unaware how truly beautiful old age can be. They were both very handsome faces. I can only assume they were very handsome individuals as well."

I teared up and tried to conceal it. A customer entered the gallery and Stet excused himself to attend to her.

"What is it that you want from me, Ruut?" I guess I can be blunt as well. "I don't understand what you meant when you said something about my magical talent."

"Surely you noticed that the three photos I mentioned involved faces. Very expressive faces. But their eyes, Baxter, my god, their wonderful eyes. You captured their very souls by looking into their eyes...and their eyes looking back at us, the viewers, told us a lot. There was love...there was fear...there was hunger...all depicted in their eyes and you captured it. Captured it like I've never seen in any other photographer. That's your magical talent. You, your camera, your film, your talent captures souls."

Obviously I've captured his imagination. A very vivid imagination, for sure!

"Okay, so then I repeat my question, Ruut. Why am I here today?"

Stet finished with his customer and joined us again.

"I have a very beautiful wife," Ruut began, and I saw Stet nod in agreement behind the Dutchman. "And I have a handsome son. We are a very close, loving family. Toriel is a precious jewel to me, but she is ill. She is in the very early stages of a cruel, debilitating disease that will eventually rob her of her memory. At some time in the future, she will stare at Vincent and me and not recognize us. She will not even recognize herself. I want to capture the love in her eyes and beautiful face before she disappears. You, Baxter, can capture that in her eyes. You can capture the love that my family has for each other in our eyes. You can capture that like no other I've seen. But I already told you that, ya? I want a portrait of the three of us while that love is still alive and well. I want it on film, not digital. I want it in black and white. And I want it soon. I will pay you ten thousand dollars for such a portrait."

I was stunned...and saddened. I saw what that horrible disease had done to Gram and I knew what lay ahead for Ruut's family. Here I am, with plenty of money and people keep throwing opportunities at me, offering more.

"I will gladly do the photography you request, Ruut, but I cannot accept the money. It will be an honor."

"Oh, no, no, no, Baxter. That is unacceptable to me. If one is merely *given* something of value, then one cannot fully appreciate that value. There must be a price to be fully appreciated. That's my lifelong philosophy."

I scratched my head.

"Okay, one thousand dollars plus expenses. You know, film, prints, whatever else."

He scratched his head.

"Five thousand dollars, expenses included. Non-negotiable. And I will fly you up to our home in Virginia for the task. Please say yes, Baxter. You have no idea how much I love my little family. How much I want to preserve the look of love in all of our eyes."

Well, just damn, shit and throw in fuck while we're at it. How can I refuse a man so in love with his family?

"Okay, agreed. So, when shall we do this? I have to get some stuff together. I haven't used my camera that uses sheet film in ages, but that's what I want to use to capture the highest quality and the sharpest resolution."

"I can be back here one week from today, Baxter. I can fly in early, pick up both you and Vincent and have you back home in time for dinner. Well, maybe a late dinner."

"So, do you just fly your little plane back and forth between here and Washington?" I asked.

He laughed, but I had no idea why.

"Oh my, no, my friend. I cover a bit more territory than that. I own several pieces of property throughout the States and I visit them as often as I can. I like to see that they are being maintained and managed properly."

"Seriously? What are these places?" I asked, my interested now piqued.

"Nice little houses. One here in Georgia, for example, down on St. Simons Island. Another two on Cape Cod, a few more out west. One of my hobbies. I collect vacation rentals like little boys used to collect baseball cards.

41

It was a glorious early summer day, just perfect for flying. I assumed that Ruut would fly some sort of Piper Cub, what I call them. The only other name I could think of was Cessna. I'd soon find out. Careful about the amount of storage allotted on such a small craft, I had to be very careful regarding the equipment necessary for this shoot. Strobes, to be sure, bounce-lights, and reflectors, I loaded several sheet film cases and threw in several rolls of 35mm film as well. Two kinds of cameras were packed securely in a large case. Oh, and a tripod. I had no idea what kind of conditions there would be for the shoot. I hadn't asked if he wanted indoor or outdoor settings, but I was prepared for either. Kissing Abbie goodbye, I reminded her to have cocktails ready when I got back home. I'd text her when I was ten minutes from the house. She laughed, but I was serious.

I pulled into the parking lot at Peachtree-DeKalb Airport in the little town of Chamblee. This facility just happens to be the second busiest airport in Georgia. Although I've never been to the airport itself, Abbie and I have dined at a nice little World War Two–themed restaurant nearby. Ruut and his son were supposed to meet me in the terminal at seven and I was ten minutes early. He must have seen me park, because he came out of the terminal followed by a couple of teenaged boys pushing a luggage cart.

"Pop your trunk, Baxter, and these guys will load your paraphernalia into the plane," he said, snapping his fingers at the kids and motioning toward my car.

I did so, but wanted to carry the camera case by myself.

"Follow me," he indicated to me, "Vincent is at the Downwind Restaurant inside the terminal finishing his breakfast. We need to roust him and get on our way. Perfect weather today. Clear sailing all the way to Dulles."

As we entered the aviation-themed restaurant, a younger version of Ruut was finishing up and paying his tab. Ruut introduced us and I was amazed at the resemblance…all except for the attire. The elder van den Graaf was wearing a black pinstriped suit, crisp white shirt and a black necktie with white polka dots. No bowler this time, though. His son, who was, indeed, handsome, wore jeans, a bright orange Netherlands National Soccer Team jersey and sported a well-trimmed blond beard. He also appeared to be somewhat older than I had imagined considering the age I had guessed Ruut to be. His accent was slight, not as thick as his father's, and he spoke with a mellow voice.

"Let's go, guys," barked Ruut, snapping his fingers again. "I've already done the plane inspection and we're ready to go." And we hustled to keep up with his brisk pace. One of the many benefits of flying via private aircraft is that there are no security lines to go through. No restrictions about carry-on stuff, no taking off of shoes or having body scans. He led us down several hallways to an area marked FBO (Fixed Base Operator) and then turned and exited through a large door leading out to where small planes were parked. Looking around, I saw several of the planes I assumed were the types similar to what Ruut would be flying. All of them were little propeller-driven aircraft. We walked past them. Then I saw those two teenagers loading up a plane with my equipment. I stopped in my tracks.

"What the hell?" I said out loud. Ruut stopped and turned. His son laughed.

"What, you thought I'd be flying a Fokker?" laughed Ruut. "I love saying that word, don't you? Oh, I flew plenty of those in days gone by. I've graduated."

It was a small single-engine jet. As I soon learned, it was a Cirrus Vision Jet SF50…the smallest jet available for private use. It was beautiful! The body of the plane was bright, shiny white with a small stripe in orange beginning just under the cockpit windows and fanning out larger toward the end of the aircraft and then continuing up to cover the entire unique V-tail design.

"Haast je," barked Ruut again. "Time to fly."

Vincent leaned in to me and whispered: "He just said *hurry up* in Dutch. I hear it all the time."

I stepped up into the plane, carrying my camera case, and my jaw dropped once again. Yes, it was small, but it was more modern and far more beautiful than any commercial aircraft I had been on. I peered into the cockpit area. The screens looked like brilliantly colored websites on a computer. On one screen was a virtual real-time map of everything around us. The fanciest GPS I had ever seen. The white leather seats were so comfortable I'd soon forget we were on an aircraft. The panoramic windows took my breath away. Again. And the damn thing had push button starting. Aside from the pilot, it seats six passengers. It was so beautiful that I thought I surely must have been dreaming.

"Zitten!" shouted Ruut. Somehow I just knew that meant to take a seat and shut my mouth. Vincent and I buckled in. I watched as Ruut did a lot of fiddling up front. Airplanes have fascinated me ever since Ant and I played with our little balsa wood gliders in the back yard in Dover. I still have no idea how they get tons of metal containing hundreds of people up off the ground and keep it there. Some things are best kept to the experts. I pulled out my cellphone and snapped a couple photos to text to Abbie whenever I could.

I heard a lot of chatter coming from the cockpit area and static coming from the control tower and before I knew it we were airborne. It was an effortless ascent and I watched as the ground swiftly fell away beneath us as we climbed into crystal clear blue skies. Once we achieved what I assumed was cruising altitude, Ruut turned his head around to chat with us.

"Uh, shouldn't you be flying the plane?" I asked somewhat nervously. He shrugged nonchalantly.

"It can fly itself. As a matter of fact, it can land by itself in case of an emergency. You know, should I suddenly keel over dead. One simple button will do it. Even you could do it. See that little red button there?" And he pointed to a spot in the ceiling of the plane. "But, don't worry. I shall be in complete control."

On top of everything else that astounded me about this little plane, Ruut pointed out a huge, drop-down entertainment screen on the ceiling. If I so desired I could connect it to my laptop or even to Netflix to watch movies in flight. My mind was officially blown.

"Obviously you enjoy flying all over the place from what you mentioned last week. Do you ever get tired of it?" I asked, keeping an eye out of the cockpit window.

"Ah, ya, well…frankly, it's hours of boredom punctuated by moments of sheer terror." He must have noticed the look on my face. "I was teasing there, Baxter. That's an old cliché that most of my pilot friends have used for years. I've had far more moments of sheer terror dealing with people on the ground than incidents in the air. Sit back and relax. We'll be landing in a little over an hour. This is a short flight."

I sat back and semi-relaxed. Ruut turned back around and I struck up a conversation with his very personable but somewhat quiet son.

"I noticed that your accent is not as pronounced as your father's. Were you born here in the States?"

"No, no" he responded with a smile. "I was born and raised in Zaanstad, a bit north of Amsterdam. We moved to the States when I was a teen. By the way, Pa cultivates that accent. He could have lost it years ago if he really wanted to," and he laughed. "Ma and I tease him about it all the time. We accuse him of going to Berlitz to strengthen it. You'll see that my mother has an accent almost as slight as mine. Both of my parents have become U.S. citizens, I have not yet become one. I'm still thinking about it. Not so sure if I really want to stay here. I suppose something might persuade me to stay here, although at the moment I have no idea what that something might be. We'll see. Actually, I could have a much better paying job at the embassy in Amsterdam than at the consulate here in Atlanta. But I'm not a kid anymore, so I'd better decide what I want to be when I grow up." And we both laughed. "I enjoy politics very much, In fact, I have my degree in political science. I also love sports. A strange combination to parlay into a career, ya?"

"Well, pardon me asking, but how old *are* you, Vincent? Your father looks so young."

"I shall be forty-three in a couple months," he replied with no hesitation.

"That's not possible," I said in astonishment. "Your father looks like he's only in his late fifties or so, am I mistaken?"

Vincent slapped his knees and laughed hysterically. "He will love you forever for saying that. He tries to keep himself in excellent health. He eats well. He runs marathons all over the country. He's run the Boston Marathon for decades. He was seventy-four on his last birthday."

I was incredulous.

Before I knew it, we were coming in for a landing. One of the smoothest ever. Ruut is a fantastic pilot, even if he *is* an old guy! As we stepped from the plane, I swear it was the same two teenagers who loaded my stuff *onto* the plane who were now running to *unload* it. Hell, all teenagers look alike these days. Ruut took care of all the necessary paperwork, etc., required after arriving at Dulles and Vincent signaled me to follow him. The two teens had my equipment on a large luggage cart and were wheeling it toward a parking area. They pulled the cart up behind a car and, again, I was agape.

"Don't tell me that's Ruut's car," I gasped.

"That's one of them. Ma has the other one," answered Vincent. "We're just full of surprises, aren't we?" And he laughed again.

All of a sudden I was feeling like a pauper.

"What the hell is it?" I asked. "I'm not sure I've ever seen one like that."

"Oh, that's a classic and Pa keeps both his and Ma's in pristine condition. That's a 1975 Citroen DS. He's the past president of the local Citroen Car Club," Vincent said, almost proudly.

Ruut joined us shortly and we were heading off to his home in Lorton, Virginia, about a thirty-five to forty minute drive…or so he said. He made it in less than thirty minutes. No cops around. I didn't know, really, what to expect regarding his house. He was full of surprises so what was I heading towards? We pulled into a long driveway that led up to house that looked like the inside of a sauna. The entire exterior was comprised of horizontal wooden boards stained a deep walnut color. On either end of the building was a square-shaped structure, two stories tall. Each one had four tall vertical windows…two downstairs and two directly above them. These two "boxes" were connected by a wide, lower entryway with two huge sidelights on either side of the huge wooden front door. The roof appeared to be flat, but I soon discovered that it sloped slightly to the backside of the house. I have never seen anything quite like this but, somehow, I managed to keep my chin from hitting the ground. And, sure enough, in the driveway sat another Citroen. This one was white. Ruut's is black.

The front door opened and a tall, slender woman appeared, almost pushed aside by two standard poodles, one white and one black, that came running toward Vincent. He bent down and ruffled their ears as they bounced around, obviously excited to see him. The woman gave a whistle and the dogs immediately turned to run back into the house. Vincent then went to unload my equipment from the car. Ruut motioned for me to follow him up to the front door. The woman was gorgeous. Silver hair cut into a stylish, natural bob surrounded her face that had a few more wrinkles than Ruut's but was still youthful. She was wearing tight black slacks, and an untucked button-down white blouse that had very thin black stripes running vertically on one side of the buttons and horizontally on the other side. I have never seen such beautiful grey eyes that seemed to sparkle. She embraced Ruut and gave him a very warm kiss. Very warm.

"Baxter," said Ruut following that show of affection, "please say hello to my precious wife, Toriel. Toriel, please meet Baxter Janus."

She extended her hand to me and greeted me with a wide smile.

"Baxter, it is a distinct pleasure. Ruut has told me about your wonderful talent and I am thrilled to be able to sit in front of your camera."

Her voice, with its mild accent, was melodious. I almost felt as though I was in the company of royalty. But then, perhaps I was. Stet had mentioned that Ruut might be a Count or something like that.

"Please come in," she said, as she stepped back inside the door. "Ruut tells me he is flying you back home in time for dinner so we mustn't tally. Or is that expression dilly-dally? I can never remember."

Vincent was bringing in my equipment and he was helped by another man. He looked like Ruut. Vincent brought him over to me.

"Baxter, this is my uncle Fredrik. He's Pa's older brother. He's visiting with us this week. I shall make the introductions in Dutch. He doesn't speak English."

And he did so. Fredrik was very gracious, clicking his heels slightly along with a bow and extended his hand to shake mine. This family is loaded with good manners and good looks, for sure. Even the proverbial Dutch uncle.

"He's going to be your assistant for the shoot," said Vincent.

Seriously? How? The guy doesn't speak English.

I glanced around the living room as soon as we stepped inside. The walls were stark white. The dark hardwood floors were covered with white area rugs. The furniture...and I mean *all* the furniture, was black. There were countless throw pillows on the sofas and chairs and they were all in brilliant primary colors. Abstract painting of various shapes and sizes covered the walls. All of them in bright colors.

"Would you care for some coffee or tea?" asked Toriel. "I know you didn't get anything on the plane. Ruut's flight attendants are *so* rude," and she gave me a big friendly wink.

I laughed. "No, thanks, I'm fine. I may need a restroom shortly but I'm good for now."

"Ruut showed me photos of your exhibit. He took them with his cellphone and texted them to me. I am extremely impressed, as he is. How did you manage to capture such faces? Their eyes were so alive, and told so many stories."

"I like to talk to my subjects. Get to know them a bit. Let them get to know me...feel comfortable around me. Obviously, with my grandparents that wasn't a problem. With the others? Well, that took a little bit of time."

Toriel smiled. "Let's take a short walk, then, Baxter. Maybe we can get to know each other in a brief moment and make your task easier, ya?"

Ruut nodded at me and smiled. I followed his wife out into their spacious back yard. The lawn was well manicured and there was a large garden with row after row of roses of all varieties. She led me up and down each row, identifying each rose not only with its common name but its botanical one as well. Some of the roses were so fragrant that I could smell them just by passing by. We chatted and laughed as we walked. I had difficulty remembering that this poor, beautiful woman was afflicted with such a debilitating illness. To say that her personality was enchanting is an understatement. She stopped at one rose bush, with large white blossoms, and she grew pensive.

"I know my husband has told you about what we are facing…about my illness. I would *like* to tell you, now, that it is a lie. That it is simply not true." She sighed. "Alas, Baxter, but it *is* true, unfortunately. I am afraid. Ruut is afraid and my dear Vincent is afraid. I am afraid of what I will leave behind and afraid of what I will miss in the future. I'm not young any more, that is certain, but…" and her voice trailed off. She leaned over to smell the rose. "Ironic, isn't it? Roses are a magnificent creation…beautiful to look at but one must be careful not to be pricked by their thorns. Just like life. This one, a cultivar, is my favorite. It's called Moondance. It does not try to fool you with its beauty. The bush is practically thorn-free. I sincerely hope that when you look through the lens of your camera today that you do not see the fear that is in us. I hope that you can avoid the thorns and see only the love."

42

A few minutes later we headed back into the house. I heard quiet, mellow jazz being played, but I had no idea where it was coming from. Their sound system was very well hidden.

"This is where we need to be photographed," Ruut said, tapping me on the shoulder, as he led me to a plain white wall (wow, no paintings!) that had a very contemporary high-backed black leather chair in front of it. "We shall change our clothes while you set up, Baxter. Do you see any problems here? Will you need anything that you didn't bring?"

I looked around for the electrical outlets for my strobe lights and light ring. Might be tricky but definitely doable. I could set up my reflectors and bounce-lights to help eliminate facial shadows.

"No, Ruut, thanks. Get ready and we'll make magic happen."

He smiled and left the room. I quickly pulled out my cellphone and clicked several pictures of this expansive living room, which was more like an art gallery. I texted them, as well as the few photos I had shot onboard Ruut's plane to Abbie: *UR not gonna believe this!* Then I arranged my lights and my umbrella reflectors. I set up the tripod. I loaded my camera, first with eight-by-ten sheet film to start off with. As if on cue, ten minutes later, my three subjects entered the room and headed to that big chair. No wonder Ruut wanted the photo to be in black and white. The two men were dressed in tuxedos. Toriel was dressed in a full-length, sleek strapless white dress with a wide black sash around her slender waist. A simple, but stunning nonetheless diamond necklace and diamond studs in her earlobes completed the picture. No pun intended. The word *elegant* flashed through my mind. I thought perhaps they must have rehearsed this before today, because they all took their places like actors on a stage. Toriel sat gracefully in the black leather chair, Ruut stood by her side to her right and Vincent stood to her left. Truly, they were such a handsome family that it almost brought tears to my eyes. Especially knowing what lay ahead for all of them as, slowly, ever so slowly, Toriel would slip away from those two men.

I adjusted my lights and umbrella reflectors. Moved them some more. I was surprised. This really wasn't such a bad place to take their portraits. I looked through my camera. I had to admit, to myself, that this *was* going to be magical.

"Wait!" called Vincent. "Don't forget Aylin and Haghen!" And he whistled.

The two poodles came running into the room and headed for the trio by the chair. Uncle Fredrik came into the room as well and stood right behind me. *What the fuck?* I thought. *Dogs in this elegant photo?* The two canines were bouncing all around the chair, tongues hanging out and wagging their behinds. This is going to take forever! Maybe I *should* have accepted that ten-thousand-dollar offer. Ruut nodded in my direction, but it wasn't meant for me. Fredrik yelled out…so sharply that it made me jump.

"Blijf!"

And the damn dogs sat, one on either side of Toriel. The dogs looked directly at me (Fredrik was right behind me) and, I swear, those two fucking dogs were smiling. I quickly pressed the shutter release and the strobes went off. The dogs stayed where they were, allowing me to move my camera a bit, switch my film cartridges. And adjust the lights.

Two hours later, I had taken a dozen shots, with a few different placements of my elegant subjects…some with and some without the *honden*, as Ruut called them. Different film sizes and lighting changes altered the feel of the photos, but in each one the three van den Graafs looked directly into my lens and, yes, I saw it in their eyes. Love. This is a beautiful family, indeed. I have no idea where Ruut's wealth comes from. I don't care. He might be blunt. He might be somewhat arrogant. But he knows what he wants and, dammit, he gets it.

The family changed back into the attire they had been wearing prior to the shoot. A table had been set on the patio behind the house, so Ruut led me there while Toriel, helped by Vincent and Fredrik, brought out trays of various cheeses; an enormous bowl filled with fresh salad greens, and a bottle of Jenever…that I soon discovered was Dutch gin. Tossed in with the salad greens were dozens of jumbo shrimp.

Glasses were passed around and the gin was poured. I held up the bottle and looked at Ruut. He threw up his hands as if in surrender.

"No, no. Not for me. Remember, I am the designated flyer."

We ate, drank and laughed a lot for the next hour or so until Ruut looked at his watch and said that it was time to get back to the airport. The car had already been loaded with my equipment so all that was left was saying goodbye. Vincent was staying here for a few more days. I shook his hand and thanked him for his help. I did the same with Fredrik, with Vincent supplying the translation. I told them all during the luncheon that I would process the film as soon as I could. Thunder had already been prepared for my invasion of his territory. Toriel shook my hand, then leaned in and kissed me on both cheeks.

"I hope to see you again soon, Baxter Janus," she said with warmth. "Ruut needs to bring me to Atlanta sometime and we can dine together. I should love to meet your wife. She must be a very special lady."

One of the dogs came up behind me and licked my hand. The other one was aloof. So much for Dutch doggie diplomacy.

Before I knew it, after battling some traffic around the airport, we were airborne once again. It was only the two of us onboard. Ruut allowed me to sit in the copilot's seat this time and I was entranced by the opportunity. I was a little kid again flying, not a balsa glider, but a sleek little jet zipping toward a brilliant, blazing sunset in the distance.

"So, tell me, Ruut…" I started.

He fiddled with some instruments for a moment before turning his head to look at me. "Ya?"

"Are you at all interested in adding to your collection of vacation rentals?"

"Bax, hurry…come quickly! Hurry!" Abbie called from the living room. She was pointing at the television when I rushed in, thinking that the world was coming to an end. It was a newscast and the anchorman was telling of a state dinner at the White House. The camera bounced around, aiming at several of the arriving guests and then focused on the President and First Lady greeting the guests of honor. Right there on the steps of the White House stood King Willem-Alexander of the Netherlands, and his spouse Queen Maxima. No wonder Ruut was infatuated with her. She is gorgeous. I turned to walk away when Abbie told me to stop and look at the television again. Walking up the steps to greet the President were two people I recognized immediately: Ruut, in tails, and Toriel, in a long, flowing, strapless pale orange diaphanous gown with matching elbow-length gloves. To say she looked stunning was an understatement. She outshone the First Lady.

"Holy fuck!" was the only thing I could say. I can be truly classless at times.

43

It has been a little more than two months since I told Tack about Ruut via Skype, and vice versa, but there has been no information forthcoming from either one. Curiosity got to me so I texted Tack.

"Any word re Flying Dutchman?"

No response for about fifteen minutes, then: *"Facetime now?"*

Isn't technology wonderful? Two minutes later we were face–to–face and smiling at each other.

"Sorry, Bax, that I haven't gotten back to you sooner but it's been a bit frantic up here lately. I have a contract pending on the house here in Pittsford, contingent upon the buyer being able to sell his current home. Shouldn't be too much of a problem. Just a hassle, and the waiting game is a pain in the arse. My partner's been a bit narky around here lately too, which doesn't help."

"Narky?" I asked.

"Oh, right. Sorry, chap. I guess that sort of means ill tempered, moody...out of sorts. Toddy thinks I've been ignoring him. He'll get over it. He always does."

"Sooner or later I'll catch on to your slang, I guess. I hope!" I laughed.

"Yes, to answer your text query, yes. Ruut and Vincent have been up here three times within the last two months. His little jet caused quite a stir at that tiny airport in Rutland. He even made it into our local newspaper up here. Ruut's quite the publicity hound, isn't he?'"

"You have *no* idea! Ruut and his son, both of them? That must be a good sign, right? Is Ruut going to buy the house on Lake Dunmore?"

"No," was his succinct reply. "He is not."

"Well, damn. I'm sorry to hear that. I thought for sure that it would fit into his collection of rental homes. But it took three visits to decide not to buy it?"

"Ruut's not buying it. Vincent is."

"What the fuck? Are you serious?"

"Trust me, Bax, I was gobsmacked, too! The bloody thing turned into a bidding war. Seems as though my neighbor on the lake wanted to buy it as a rental. Had her eye on it for years for some reason. Yes, well… Vincent has applied for his citizenship here in the States, believe it or not. He absolutely fell in love with the place as soon as he set eyes on it. He's been doing a lot of research. As I said, it turned into a bidding war and I'm getting ten thousand dollars over my original asking price."

"No shit?"

"No shit."

"Well, I hope this doesn't become a contentious issue, with the neighbor and Vincent. That could turn ugly, I suppose."

"Oh, on the contrary, Bax, au contraire. Turns out my neighbor has a daughter a few years younger than Vincent. Kristen is a divorcee with a young son. There was definitely a spark when they first met. Almost knocked me over," and he chuckled. "The look in Vincent's eyes was laughable. I could tell he was smitten. This guy doesn't waste time, either. The deal hasn't been finalized yet and he already has two jobs lined up."

"Two jobs? But he's working at the Dutch Embassy in D.C., isn't he?"

"Not for long, he ain't…is that a proper Americanism? Apparently he's soon to get a job at the little community college in Rutland in the Political Science department. And he'll be a ski instructor at Killington during the winter months."

"No shit?"

"You seem to be stuck in a rut regarding your expletives this evening, brother," and Tack laughed again.

"Vincent must have been busy between his three visits, I assume."

"Actually, Bax, Vincent stayed up here after the first visit. Ruut has made the three trips, bringing clothing and books for his son. As I said, Vincent fell in love with the place immediately. It had never been his intention to stay or buy, but something about the place evidently clicked with the guy. Toddy and I invited him to stay with us after he said he wanted to find a motel while he did some exploring. He's a very pleasant fellow, really...smart as a whip, too. We've enjoyed his company."

"So, what happened to you saying you didn't want to sell to a stranger?" I asked. "I guess the fact that he doesn't want it as a rental changed your mind?"

"Well, yes, that, and the simple fact that Vincent is such a damn nice young chap. Oh, and pending the sale, Ruut has since promised to keep sending us a case of Dutch vodka every month when I get back home to London."

I started to say *"no shit?"* yet again, but realized I had probably met my quota for this chinwag.

It was an invitation way too good to turn down. In fact, turning it down wasn't even on the table. Tack had completed the sale of his house in Pittsford and was about to head back home to London. Todd had returned to the U.K. two weeks earlier as soon as the Pittsford house deal closed. Tack was temporarily staying with Vincent at the lake house, the deal being closed the same day as the Pittsford house. Vincent had decided to throw a huge party to celebrate his upcoming citizenship, the purchase of his new home and, last but not least, a bon voyage salute to Thackeray Brecklyn. Maybe calling it a party was an understatement. It was to be a weekend-long event. Ruut would fly Abbie and me up to Vermont on Friday afternoon. Darin, Carson and the boys, who were also invited, would drive up from Massachusetts early Saturday morning. Being mid-August, bathing suits were in order because everyone planned on staying in the lake and as wet as much as possible.

Although Tack and I have connected via Skype and Facetime often over the past several months, this would be the first in-person meeting with my half-brother. I was nervous and excited at the same time. Wanting to know as much as he could about his newfound family, Tack has also touched base, via Skype, with Darin and his family. Although he eschewed fatherhood, he seemed to relish the idea of being an uncle. Or half-uncle. Or whatever it's called.

It was a gray, gloomy day in Atlanta with threats of storms, but Ruut assured us when we met him at Peachtree-DeKalb Airport that the weather was fabulous up north. Abbie and I boarded his little jet and Toriel was waiting for us with open arms. She kissed me on both cheeks and did the same to Abbie after I introduced them. Ruut finished his inspection around the plane and climbed into the pilot's seat. He wasn't wearing his usual navy suit with polka dot necktie but his "casual" attire could have been featured in an L.L. Bean catalogue…for seniors.

"*Gesp omhoog!*" He ordered us from his seat. "Buckle up!"

Within minutes we were above the clouds and a brilliant sun shone through the windows. From that point on, there wasn't a lull in our conversation until we were making an approach to the little airport in Rutland. Toriel and Abbie had hit it off the moment they had met and were like schoolgirls chattering and laughing for the duration of our flight.

"I am so eager to meet Vincent's new lady friend," Toriel gushed. "Crossing my fingers that this works out. I'm hoping that he makes me a grandmother before I forget who he is," she laughed. But that gave my heart a tug. I glanced at Abbie and we both smiled.

We were cleared for a landing and Ruut was right. The weather looked just perfect. Not a cloud in the sky and the local forecast promised a glorious weekend. After deplaning, we grabbed our carry-ons and headed into the small terminal where we saw a smiling Vincent excitedly waving at us. Beside him stood a tall, blond man who I recognized immediately. Toriel rushed to greet her son and embraced him as though she hadn't seen him in years. Thackeray Brecklyn and I didn't take our eyes off of each other as we approached. Should we simply shake hands? Should we hug? Well, what the hell? We did both.

"I can't believe this," I said as we broke our embrace. "This seems so surreal, doesn't it? Or is it just me?"

"It is, indeed, a weird feeling, Bax," Tack said in response. "I still can't get my head around this situation."

He was a bit taller than I was, which surprised me. But then, I knew that old age had begun to shrink my once six-one frame. Obviously gravity loves to play tricks on us old guys.

I introduced Abbie to Vincent. Already being acquainted via Skype, Abbie and Tack greeted each other warmly.

"Let's get this show on the road, guys," called Vincent as he started walking toward the exit. "It's a great day and the lake is calling. We're forty-five minutes away from the start of a fun weekend!"

We all loaded what little luggage we carried into Vincent's Land Rover and off we went. As he said, it was a straight shot right up Route 7. The landscape was beautiful, with rolling hills and farms on both sides of the road. We slowed down a bit as the car drove through the town of Pittsford.

"The house I recently sold is just a couple blocks up that road," Tack said as we passed a side street. "It's kind of sad that I won't see it anymore. It's where you and I met, in a strange way, Bax. Seems like ages ago. So many secrets ago."

It took less than forty-five minutes, but eventually Vincent turned into a long winding road off of the highway. All the houses we passed had boats of one kind or another on trailers. The cottages were all well kept, at least they appeared to be, but they looked small. Just like I imagined lake cottages to be. My thought was, however, if Vincent's cottage is just as small, how will seven adults and two young boys all fit? Will we all be issued sleeping bags? Will tents be pitched lakeside? This could be a very cozy weekend. A left turn, then a right turn and I began to see water behind the houses. We had arrived at the lake, for sure. Vincent slowed down and turned into a long, tree-lined gravel driveway. His "cottage" came into view and my jaw dropped. The Land Rover rolled to a stop and we all got out of the car. Vincent acted like the perfect host...or a bellhop...and got our luggage out of his vehicle and started carrying it into the house. As soon as he opened the front door, Aylin and Haghen, their two poodles, came bounding out, their perfectly trimmed tails wagging at warp speed.

Tack and I walked toward the house. It was not at all what I had anticipated.

"This isn't exactly what I thought of when you called it a lake house," I said as we walked slowly up the driveway. "I was sure you called it a cottage when we first discussed this months ago. That is *not* a cottage!"

Tack chuckled.

"Semantics, semantics," he laughed. "You say tomato and I say tomahto."

"This is the place you were willing to sell to me, quote-unquote, for one dollar? Are you insane?"

Tack stopped walking for a moment. Started to say something but stopped again.

"We shall have further discussion about this before the weekend is over," he said, smiling like the Cheshire cat. "But not yet." And he continued walking.

The two-story gable-front house was obviously old but the recent refurbishments put a totally contemporary spin on it. A large gable faced the driveway, with a decent-sized balcony on the second floor coming from, what I assumed, maybe the master bedroom. Two other gables faced out from both sides of the house. The entire roof was a copper tin covering, offset by the warm brown clapboard siding and crisp white trim. It had a craftsman style look to it, yet retained the good bones of a decades-old lakefront residence. Surrounding the house were beautiful old, tall oak trees, with a smattering of balsams and some paper birches. Chattering, chirping birds swooped overhead as we walked. Something strange caught my eye. On one of the gable walls was a long rectangular window at a 45° angle matching the angle of the roofline.

I pointed up at it. "Funny," I said, "but I thought skylights were supposed to be on top of a roof, not on the side of a building."

Tack chuckled and shook his head.

"Vermonters…well, the old-timers, anyway, can be a superstitious lot I learned. That was an original part of the cottage before I started to refurbish so I kept it. It's not a skylight. It's called a witch's window. Apparently witches can't fly their broomsticks through angled windows such as that one, so they can't enter your house. Seriously. We haven't been bothered by witches since we've been here." And he let out a raucous guffaw.

I had to laugh too, and then I told him about the haint blue that was on the ceilings of many porches in the Deep South. He shook his head again. I didn't bother telling him about the acorn that I still carried in my pocket.

"Well, us Brits are a superstitious lot as well, I suppose. Black cats and all that crap. You know, in the U.K. if a black cat walks toward you it's bringing you good luck. But if the bloody thing turns and walks *away* from you, it's taking the good luck away from you. I believe all that shit about as much as I believe in the Almighty." He paused for a moment. "But, every now and then I begin to doubt my doubts...but that's neither here nor there. Sooner or later I'll find out, one way or the other."

We walked up three steps to the expansive front porch that was lined with huge hanging baskets containing the largest ferns I have ever seen. The heavy oak front door was arched and flanked by two narrow sidelights, also with arched tops.

"We're a couple of old dawdlers, aren't we, Bax? Looks like everyone has made it inside and probably swimming halfway across the lake by now."

"Oh, come on. We weren't *that* slow. And, by the way," I said, looking around to make sure I was out of earshot, "Ruut's older than me."

"No shit?" Tack exclaimed.

"Hey, that's *my* line!" I laughed.

We stepped past the front door, continuing through a small foyer and then into a huge living room. I couldn't help the ear-to-ear grin that came on my face. Hanging over the mantel of an impressive stacked-stone fireplace was that large black and white portrait of Ruut and his family... including the two poodles. It had been exquisitely framed and was flanked on either side by vases filled with roses. Toriel came up behind me as I was admiring it.

"You succeeded, Baxter," she said softly, "Succeeded beautifully. You captured the love. We shall be forever grateful."

I heard the toenails of the two poodles clicking on the dark hardwood floors as they came running up beside us. They sat, looking back and forth between Toriel and me. I gave each a quick ruffle behind their ears and they ran off again...toenails clicking.

As I soon discovered, this "cottage" had five bedrooms and six baths.

As Vincent was showing us to our bedroom I asked him "What in blazes do you plan on doing with all this room? This place is outrageously gorgeous but it's huge."

He laughed, shrugged his shoulders and replied. "Ya, well...I have a lot of friends, both in D.C. and back home. Not only will they all visit but also I plan on having lots of kids someday. Ma has already made me promise. Ha! And I'll try as hard as I can. No pun intended there, right?"

His elbow poked me gently in my ribs and he winked as he said it.

"I hope, too, that my parents will eventually come to live here when the time is right. Get yourselves settled. Be comfortable. I have already prepared a casual luncheon for us to have out on the deck facing the lake. Or, you can go for a swim first if you'd like. This weekend is for fun. And I can't wait to meet the rest of your family. My intention is to have your grandsons exhausted come Sunday evening! My girlfriend's young son, Lucas, will be very excited to have some playmates this weekend. You'll meet them both later today. Anyway, come out to join us when you're ready, ya?"

44

After tidying up a bit, and changing into shorts, Abbie and I headed out to join the others who were all out on the wide deck, enjoying the glorious day. We walked through the kitchen on the way out and were totally impressed. All the new appliances were the latest design trend: black stainless steel and a brilliant white farm sink. I could tell that Abbie was drooling. We stepped out onto the deck and Vincent stood to greet us once again. He was barefoot and now wearing orange swim trunks and a white t-shirt. Ruut and Toriel were still in the attire they wore on the plane and Tack had changed into shorts and a polo pullover.

"As I said," Vincent started, as he pointed to a long, rustic picnic table laden with a wide assortment of cheeses, cold sliced meats and various types of bread and muffins, "luncheon is casual today. Please, help yourselves. I have beer, wine and sodas here in the cooler. Whatever you care for. If you don't see what you want, just ask. If I have it, well, good. If I don't, well, you're shit outta luck!" And we all laughed.

We fixed ourselves a nice looking lunch and found some seats. I sat next to Tack and leaned into him whispering into his ear. "Man, it seems you spared no expense in fixing this place up. I'm so impressed I can't stand it. And, damn you! I already know that Abbie will be after me when we get back home to renovate *our* place. She nearly passed out when we just came through that kitchen." He smiled broadly and let out a loud laugh.

"I still have no idea why my aunt had this place," answered Tack. "It is so much nicer, and larger, than that little old house in Pittsford. Perhaps she had thoughts of using it as a rental before she got ill. Who knows?"

The hours seemed to melt away as we all talked and laughed, simply enjoying the atmosphere. No one had elected to go for a swim, although that water *did* look inviting. Suddenly Vincent glanced at his watch.

"*Schijten!* I lost track of time. I have to go pick up Kristen from work. Who wants to come with me? We take the boat to get her."

Abbie and I said that we'd love to go out for a boat ride; the others said they'd wait on the deck until we returned.

We followed Vincent down toward the dock. Obviously the two dogs were going to join us as they ran ahead, quickly got to the dock, and sat patiently waiting. Laying on the lawn as we passed was one orange canoe and two orange kayaks.

"You Dutch sure like that color, don't you?" I chuckled.

"Ya, for sure," answered Vincent. "See up ahead?"

There, moored at the dock, was a sleek Manitou pontoon boat. Its canopy was a brilliant, almost blinding, orange.

"It was custom made," Vincent said proudly. "Very easy to spot out on the lake, yes?"

"I'm sure it's easy to spot from the International Space Station!" I responded.

"You're funny, Baxter," he laughed. "Very funny."

We got onboard and he took his seat behind the wheel. The poodles jumped onto the boat and sat by Vincent's side.

"Is this going to be a three-hour tour?" I asked.

Vincent laughed again. "Oh, no, not that long. I promise."

"Your middle name wouldn't be Gilligan, would it?" I joked.

"Excuse me?" he asked, with a puzzled look on his face.

"Never mind. Weak attempt at local humor."

"The little hotel where Kristen works is just up ahead a little ways, around that bend to the right," he said, as he pointed his finger ahead of us.

The boat picked up speed and the breeze felt great. Abbie and I smiled at each other as we enjoyed the scenic tour. It was a gorgeous afternoon and we were looking forward to Darin, Carson and our grandsons joining us in the morning. There were other pontoon boats out on the lake and everyone waved at each other in passing. A large black dog was on one of the passing boats, walking back and forth, from front to back, wagging his tail and barking loudly. It actually looked as though he was enjoying the ride. The poodles paid no attention to the barking. There were a few small sailboats here and there, and we spotted a couple kayakers. We rounded the bend and a small peninsula jutted out into the lake with a small, very rustic two-story hotel not far from the water's edge. Vincent slowed the boat as he headed toward the long dock extending out into the lake. The hotel's sign came into view: Whitt's End Lodge.

"Whitt's End?" I asked. "Seriously?"

"Whitt's End has been the name of that little peninsula for decades," answered Vincent. "The Whitt family has owned a good portion of that lakefront since, I think, the late 1890s. A grumpy old man, Jonathan Whitt, owns and runs the hotel now. His name may be mentioned at some time over the weekend. Believe only part of what you might hear. Ah, there she is! That's Kristen, running toward the dock now."

Indeed, a strikingly beautiful, very trim woman was running down the grassy slope to the dock. She started waving as soon as she caught sight of the pontoon boat approaching. Vincent maneuvered the boat alongside the low dock so the young lady could step aboard. She was sun-tanned, contrasting nicely with her long flowing blonde hair and had an ear-to-ear grin, which I knew was for Vincent and not necessarily for us. Vincent got up to help her step onto the boat and they gave each other a gentle kiss. She bent down and ruffled the dogs' ears. One responded by licking her on the face. She giggled.

"Baxter and Abbie Janus, please meet my lovely friend Kristen. Kristen Whitt."

Say what? Abbie and I exchanged quick glances.

"So nice to finally meet you both," gushed Kristen with a melodic voice. "Oh, I just *love* that photo of Vincent's family," she said, looking right at me and holding my gaze. "Vincent tells me that his mom gets tears in her eyes every time she looks at it."

We all shook hands and the huge smile never left Kristen's beautiful face. I may have had a strange look on *my* face.

"Baxter," said Vincent after clearing his throat. "Yes, you heard correctly. Kristen Whitt. Her father owns the hotel and Kristen is the General Manger."

"Oh, that's...nice," was all I could muster.

I was almost certain that Tack had told me that his next-door neighbor at the lake house had wanted to buy the house that was now Vincent's for a rental property. I was confused.

"Let me clear up a little confusion you may be having now, " said Vincent with a smile. "Kristen's parents are divorced and..."

"*And*," Kristen interjected, shaking her head, "my mother got into a bidding war for that fabulous house. She wanted to turn it into a B&B, to compete, sort of, with my dad."

Now I *really* was confused. I thought about remaining silent but let's face it, that's not my style.

The boat slowly slid away from the dock and headed back out into the lake. The two poodles went to the front of the boat, sat, and quietly watched each passing boat. Perhaps on the lookout for that barking dog.

"But..." I started to say. I thought about it for a silent moment more. "Okay, I'm just a visitor here and we just met less than two minutes ago. This is really none of my business. You can flat out tell me that if you wish. I won't be offended. But I can be a nosy old guy whose imagination can run away with me on *rare* occasion." I saw Abbie bite her lip and stifle a laugh. "Well, okay. Just what *is* going on with all of you?"

Both Vincent and Kristen laughed. Kristen moved away from Vincent's side and sat on the side seat across from us, looking back and forth between Abbie and me.

"For several years my dad was cheating on my mom with the lady who owned the house Vincent just bought."

"With Thackeray's mother?" I asked, aghast.

"No, no, with her sister. Tack's aunt. Before she got really ill. And before Tack's mom came to live here in Vermont. It was a very bitter and contentious divorce. They haven't been civil to each other since. Oh, you'll get to meet my mom. She's joining us all for dinner tomorrow night."

Oh, swell!

"Alright…" I started again. "Your last name is Whitt. We were under the impression that you are divorced."

"Oh, I am. *My* husband cheated on *me* while I was pregnant with Lucas. He and my best friend had been secretly meeting back at the hotel. I divorced him before Lucas was born and I retained my maiden name."

She must have noticed the dazed look on Abbie's face and I was certain my eyes were spinning in opposite directions.

"You have no idea, Mr. Janus," Kristen said with a shrug and a laugh. "It's a regular Peyton Place up here!"

I once thought that my retirement was getting boring. Hell, I *should* write a freakin' book!

"Almost time for cocktail hour!" announced Vincent as he slowly pulled the boat up to his dock. "I know that, by now, Ma has prepared some tempting hor d'oeuvres for us and later I'll be grilling the juiciest of steaks. Let's get this celebration under way, ya?"

Although it was still hours until sunset, the sun was lower in the sky, on the far side of the lake, leaving a blinding reflection on the rippling water and casting long shadows as its rays hit the trees. The rest of our group was seated on the wide deck at the back of the house, facing the water, and we could hear raucous laughter as we approached, the poodles running ahead of us. Yes, this weekend was just getting started. What other surprises lay ahead?

45

10:37, the following morning. Toriel and Abbie, together, had prepared a sumptuous breakfast of French toast, lots of sausages and fresh fruit. Following it, they were now cleaning up in the kitchen. Tack and I sat on the deck, each enjoying our third cup of coffee as we were slowly recovering from our alcohol indulgence from last night. Somewhere, not too far away, a rooster was crowing. Or was that just my imagination? There was an empty bottle of Ketel One Oranje vodka standing on the picnic table. I stared at it for a moment.

"Wasn't that a brand new bottle last night?" I asked.

"Oh, you're quite correct. And there's another just like it lying on its side *under* the table," Tack answered as he nodded in that direction. "But who the hell is doing all that confounded hammering? Why are they making all that racket so early?"

I looked all around.

"Uhh, if I'm not mistaken, I believe that might be a woodpecker," I snickered.

"Oh," was his embarrassed reply.

We watched as Vincent and Ruut swam together out in the lake. A few minutes later Vincent pulled himself up onto the dock, his orange swim trunks catching the early morning sun. Ruut climbed up the short ladder and stepped onto the dock, following his son. Oh, my god…he was wearing navy blue swim trunks with tiny white polka dots. I couldn't help but laugh. One could tell by their trim bodies and muscular legs that they are definitely runners and both in very good shape. Ruut looked like he could be Vincent's older brother and not his father. I was jealous. My phone chirped, alerting me to a text. I knew from whom without even looking. I was correct. Even in my semi-stupor I can make brilliant deductions.

GPS eta 25 mns

"The kids are getting closer," I called in to Abbie. "I'm not sure if our hosts are ready for the whirlwind that's about to hit this place." Abbie laughed and shrugged her shoulders.

11:02, another text. **2 lttle tornados about to hit**

Abbie and I walked around to the front of the house and watched as Darin's car turned into the driveway and came toward us through the trees and over the crunching gravel. Vincent came up beside us to greet his newest guests. It suddenly dawned on me that he and Darin were the same age.

We could see two silhouettes bouncing around in the back seat. The car came to a stop and instantly the back doors flew open as those two little tornadoes were about to bowl us over.

"Grandma…Grandpa!" they both yelled almost in unison, arms held wide. This was their formal greeting. We're usually Gram and Gramp. It was *our* turn for those monikers.

'Hey, I warned you!" Darin called as he got out. By this time Carson was walking around in front of the car, also with outstretched arms, ready for our embrace.

When they were younger, Greyson and Hayden would leap up into our arms and wrap their legs around us. That was not going to happen this morning.

"What the hell have you done to our two little grandsons?" I laughingly asked Darin, winking at the boys. "Have you exchanged them for a newer, larger pair?"

The two boys giggled and hugged us tighter.

"You boys have gotten so big!" exclaimed Abbie. "Have you started driving yet?"

That sent the two of the kids laughing again. Hayden was eight years old and Greyson would soon turn ten.

I introduced Darin and Carson to Vincent as we watched the two excited boys run down toward the lake, followed very closely by two poodles. Evidently somebody was *really* ready for a swim! We all went inside the "cottage" and introductions were made all around.

Darin and I were standing side by side as Tack entered the living room.

"Obviously the acorn doesn't fall far from the oak, does it?" exclaimed Tack as he glanced back and forth between Darin and me. The past few months have been one Facetime session after another with all of us acquainting each other.

After Darin and Carson got situated in their room they joined us out on the deck. Ruut and Toriel had been relaxing out there and waited for the greeting hubbub to die down. They arose and graciously greeted the new arrivals. There was the sound of loud clumping as Greyson and Hayden run up the long wooden stairs.

"Is that your boat, mister…mister…hmmm.?" Hayden asked, looking up at Vincent.

"Just call me Vincent, little man, okay? Yes, that's my boat." "Boys, please call him *Mister* Vincent. Let's be polite, alright?" I told the boys. They both nodded.

"Mister Vincent, that's a super-duper cool boat. Can we take a ride?" Greyson asked.

"Ya, sure, we will all go for a nice long ride around the lake later if you want."

"Is that the name on the side?" Greyson continued. "It sure looks like a funny name."

I hadn't even noticed the name. I guess I never paid any attention to it. I guess I just thought it was the make of the pontoon boat. I'm normally observant but that slipped right by me.

Vincent chuckled and Ruut and Toriel laughed out loud.

"Ya, well," started Vincent. "That name, ORANJEGEKTE, is Dutch. It means orange craze. Ha!…us Nederlanders go crazy over our sports over there. All their uniforms are orange. So, okay, here comes a little history lesson for you." He kneeled down and looked both boys in the eye. "Orange is the color of the Dutch royal family. You know about royal families?"

"Kings and queens and stuff like that?" answered Hayden.

"I'm very familiar with queens. Royal or otherwise," Tack whispered into my ear. I gave him the squinty-eye.

"Very good, Hayden. You are so smart, ya? Well, it goes all the way back to our long-dead king Willem van Oranje. All the *way* back to 1581. Don't worry. I won't bore you with anymore." And he stood up again.

"But," interjected Tack, "He'll quiz you on it before you can get off that boat again!"

The boys looked concerned.

"Just kidding, lads…just kidding," Tack assured them smiling broadly.

A few minutes later, Kristen Whitt and her son Lucas came running through the trees to join us. Again, more introductions. Lucas was a couple years younger than our grandsons but they seemed to hit it off right away. Kids. Get them around water and boats and they speak the same language no matter the age differences.

"Okay, the itinerary is open, guys," Vincent announced. "As long as we all keep the party atmosphere going, the activities are up to you. Is it too early for luncheon? Do you all want to go for a boat ride first? Swim for a while? Hey, don't forget we have a canoe and kayaks, too. By cocktail hour this afternoon we should all be exhausted or I won't consider this event a success,"

"Boat ride! Boat ride!" all three boys seemed to yell in unison.

"Okay, boat ride it is. But everybody get your swimsuits on. There are a couple nice coves just perfect for splashing around. This will be a party boat, all you *big* kids. I have a full bar all loaded and ready to go."

Tack's eyes lit up.

"*What will we do with a drunken sailor? What will we do with a drunken sailor?*" he sang as we all wended our way to our respective rooms to change.

"*Shave his belly with a rusty razor. Shave his belly with a rusty razor,*" sang Darin, as he lifted his T-shirt revealing his hairy midriff.

Oh, Lordy. What a group!

It took the group almost thirty minutes to get ready---the kids were getting restless---but finally we all managed to get onboard the ORANJEGEKTE. I haven't even tried to pronounce it, but who cares? The mood, in a nutshell, was ebullient. The sky was a brilliant, cloudless blue and the sun rippled across the water. Sunscreen was passed around and we all soon smelled of Neutrogena. Vincent started the engine and the dogs, Aylin and Haghen, started barking. Their tails were wagging like little flags in the wind. We cast off and started to head out into the lake. Ruut and his family were in orange bathing suits. No surprise there. Toriel looked amazing and nowhere near her age. Although I had been trying to pay close attention, I hadn't noticed if her illness had progressed. It wasn't discussed and I was not going to approach the topic.

"Look over there boys," called out Darin. "See that big bird on the tree in the water? That's a great blue heron. Isn't he beautiful?"

As if on cue, the bird took flight and it was, indeed, beautiful. Its silvery blue feathers caught the early afternoon sun as he swooped overhead and he almost seemed to glisten. A deep blue streak extended from his orange beak, over his eyes and flowed out into a long feathery crest behind his head. Yes, I had my camera ready and I captured him perfectly.

Aside from the bar onboard, Vincent and Kristen had quickly made up several small sandwiches of thinly sliced cold meats, and a couple trays with various cheeses and crackers. It was turning into a fabulous little cruise, with Darin pointing out several types of birds that we saw either overhead or along the banks. Although it disappeared too quickly for me to point it out to the young boys, I was sure I had seen the masked face of a raccoon peeking out from behind a tree. Of course, it could have been that second gin and tonic that did it. I wasn't quick enough with my camera to prove me wrong or otherwise.

As promised, Vincent pulled the boat into a quiet little cove on the far end of the lake.

"Jump in if you'd like," he announced. "This is a great little place for a swim."

Toriel elected to stay back on the boat, but the rest of us took up his offer and soon we all were splashing around like little kids. Tack and I swam a little further out into the lake and Vincent came up and swam along side of us.

"This is usually where I take my pee break when I come out to this cove," he said, winking, as he passed us.

Tack and I quickly decided to head back toward the cove.

"Love you, Gramp!" shouted Greyson as I swam toward him. "Love you, too, Gram!"

Abbie and I splashed and played with our grandsons, making them laugh and giggle as they tried to splash us back. Lucas joined in and soon we were all splashing each other. Our laughter seemed to echo off the surrounding trees along the shoreline. Images of little black and white snapshots floated through my mind. Images of *my* Gramp, splashing and laughing with Ant and me a whole lifetime ago at Lake Hopatcong. I wondered—and hoped--- that Hayden and Greyson would have the same fond memories to look back upon years from now.

One by one we pulled ourselves back up onto the boat. The dogs greeted us with barks and tried licking the dripping water from our legs. The boys giggled as the dogs licked their faces. Abbie and I sat at the very front of the boat, enjoying the slight, cooling breeze as Vincent slowly headed us back to his house. We noticed that Carson and Kristen were sitting side by side in animated conversation. Darin was sitting next to "Captain" Vincent, also in deep conversation. Toriel, wearing a big floppy hat, was lying down with her head in Ruut's lap. He was gently massaging her shoulders.

As we passed Whitt's End, I noticed that Vincent pointed out the hotel to Darin. I couldn't hear what he was saying, but by the way Darin's eyebrows went up I knew it must have been the story about Kristen's father.

A few minutes later we saw a woman sitting on a folding lawn chair near the end of Vincent's dock. When she saw us she hoisted her arm in salute. She was holding a wine glass and a bottle was resting at her feet… in an ice bucket.

"Ya-Ya!" Lucas shouted when he saw her. He jumped up and down, waving his little arms.

"Ya-Ya with the ta-tas," Tack leaned into me and whispered in my ear. I assumed by 'ta-tas' he wasn't meaning the British *'goodbye.'*

Ruut caught my attention, winked and shook his head slightly. "It's show time, folks," he said softly.

As soon as the boat docked and was secure, Lucas jumped off and ran into the woman's open arms as she stood up. Tack wasn't kidding. Lucas was buried in the woman's very ample bosom. She looked to be about our age, meaning Abbie and me, and was very fit. Toned and tanned, with short spiked hair the color of Cabernet.

One by one we carefully disembarked, carrying our drinks with us. The two poodles ran up toward the house. One of them watered a shrub. Kristen introduced us to her mother, Rebecca Whitt, and I got the feeling that there might be just a slight bit of apprehension there. On Kristen's part.

Rebecca appeared gracious, if a tad woozy. Abbie and I exchanged quick glances and smiled at each other.

"Well, well, well, just look at you," she said to Tack, standing back and eyeing him up and down. He was on the dock, shirtless, his bathing suit dripping wet, and nibbling on one of the last pieces of cheese. He stopped chewing. "It's too damn bad you're pitching for the opposing team there, Tack. Haven't seen you in a bathing suit before. You're just a big bundle of hotness, aren't you?"

Well, well, well, indeed. This might be a very entertaining and eye-popping dinner party ahead of us for sure!

A few hours later, after all of us who had been out in the lake and on the boat had showered and refreshed ourselves, we gathered once again on the expansive deck. The casual attire of shorts, T-shirts or pullovers and bare feet was universal. Vincent started to fire up his grill in anticipation of another sumptuous meal.

Hayden ran up to Darin and tugged on his shorts.

"Daddy, I have *(hic)* the hiccups and can't get rid of them *(hic)*," he said plaintively.

"Oh, I have the perfect solution for that, lad," interjected Tack. "Hurry off the deck and run around this house three times without thinking of a purple fox and they'll be gone! Promise."

We all laughed, Hayden looked at Tack as though he was a crazy person, but then he was off like lightning, running around the house. Greyson and Lucas were running close behind him with two barking poodles in hot pursuit. Two minutes later he was back up on the deck, facing Tack. He put his little hands on his hips.

"Hey, mister, there's no such thing *(hic)* as a purple fox!"

Behind him, Rebecca suddenly let out an ear-piercing scream. We all jumped and I nearly spilled my drink.

"What the fuck?" I blurted.

Rebecca looked down at Hayden. "Well?" she asked.

There was silence.

"They're gone!" squealed a delighted Hayden.

"You're welcome," answered Rebecca.

Vincent was a master at the grill. Juicy, sizzling steaks last night and thick mouth-watering bone-in pork chops tonight. He also had the kids in mind with hot dogs and hamburgers. Kristen and Toriel had worked side-by-side preparing a huge fruit salad and Rebecca's contribution was the best potato salad I have ever tasted.

And the drinks continued to flow.

"I suppose by now," Rebecca said as she sidled up beside Abbie and me at the long picnic table, "that someone has filled you in on the story regarding this house, right?"

We acknowledged that claim.

"Well, I'm just glad it worked out the way it did. Vincent makes my daughter very happy. Tack's harlot of an aunt made my life a living hell!"

"Hey, hey, hey, I heard that," said Tack as he made his way to jostle in between Rebecca and me. "The way I heard it was that your scum-bucket of a husband seduced *her*...right here on this very deck."

I cringed. Rebecca huffed.

"Oh, Jonathan was a prick, no doubt," Rebecca moaned with a sigh. "Ha, he could never keep that pecker of his in his pants. I'm surprised he hasn't had the clap by now." She took another long swig from her wine glass.

"Mother," admonished Kristen, momentarily turning away from her conversation with Darin, Vincent and his parents. "Let's keep this a friendly party...and your feelings toward Father corked, okay?"

"Yeah, yeah, sure," Rebecca answered with a slight slur. "Did you all salute him as you sailed by that frigging hotel this afternoon? If only I could find a voodoo doll somewhere I'd stick the largest pin I had right into its crotch. The old fucker."

And then she because melancholy. Wine will do that, I suppose.

"Oh, Thackeray, I'm so sorry. It's the wine talking. I'm such a shit, aren't I? Hell, I'm certainly no saint either. The day I caught him with your dearly departed aunt I flushed his Viagra down the toilet. Little did I know he didn't really need it. What the hell. Anyway." And she sighed and waited a beat. And then she continued sotto voce. "Anyway," she repeated, shrugging her shoulders, "I stormed out and fucked the brains out of his sous chef over at that fucking hotel of his."

She quickly looked around.

"Shhhh...Kristen never found out about that." She paused for a moment, and then sighed. "I guess...no, I *know* that I'm just lonely, that's all. A lonely, abandoned old bitchy woman. And then, Tack, handsome you comes along. I got my hopes up again. Until you introduced me to Todd. If you stay here any longer I just may work my wiles on you and scare you straight!"

"FYI, Rebecca," said Tack, leaning in very closely to her, "dear heart, I'm a catcher, not a pitcher."

"I have no fucking idea what you mean by that, darling,"

Tack laughed and I rolled my eyes. Abbie had no idea what that meant either.

"Oh, sooner or later I'm sure someone might tell you about that," snickered Tack.

I was glad, at this point, that Darin and Carson were deeply involved with a conversation with Ruut and Toriel. The kids were running around like little Indians chasing fireflies that had all of a sudden appeared. When had the sun gone down?

"Yes, and then you started to renovate this glorious house, Tack, and my enthusiasm was renewed. Enthusiasm for revenge, of sorts, and enthusiasm for perhaps a new career late in life. I thought, at first, about this place becoming a nice rental property. It would have been the best rental on this side of the lake, no doubt. Then, the more the renovation took on bigger and better features, I began thinking about turning it into a fabulous B&B. It surely would outshine that shabby shack that Jonathan nit-Whitt the Prick calls a hotel. It's past its prime. Way past."

She paused to collect her thoughts and refill her glass. She was a tough old broad, crude, uncensored, with a mouth like a sailor, drunken or otherwise, but I was actually beginning to feel sorry for her.

"Your contractor, Tack, was simply amazing. And, yes, I know most of the end result was because of your creative input. You're a genius, my friend. A fucking genius. Then you send along that other charmer," and she nodded in Ruut's direction. "Shit, he can charm the pants off…well, no need to go there. I never met anyone so suave. And he drags along that other charmer. The one I know will surely be my son-in-law before too long."

Maybe, maybe not, I thought. Marriage still hasn't entered into the vocabulary of my own son!

"Oh, shit, Baxter! Abbie!" exclaimed Rebecca, slapping her head. "My god, we just met, what…four, five hours ago? I've been ranting and raving like a mad woman. You must think I'm the bitch of the century."

I had judged her from the moment she uttered that comment about Tack out there on the dock.

"No, no. Don't be silly. I'm certainly not judging you. That's not my style," I tried assuring her.

"Lucas?" she called out. "Come give Ya-Ya a kiss. I'm going home."

Her grandson ran up the stairs to the deck and, as he gave her a big hug, she bent down to kiss him on the top of his head.

"I'll see you whenever," she said to us, waving her hand. "Maybe I'll be back tomorrow. Or not. Maybe I'll drive over to the nearest convent and see if they could use any new nuns. I have to atone for my sins somehow! Good night, everybody! Vincent, you throw one hell of a party!"

We watched as she disappeared through the darkness until eventually we could see the motion-sensors on the floodlights on her house pick up her arrival back home. Somewhere an owl hooted.

Tack stood up, stretched and yawned. "I've had it," he said. "All this fresh air and frivolity takes its toll on us Brits. But I'll be ready for more come the dawn. Cheers, everybody!" He waved and sauntered back into the house.

Abbie and I joined in the conversation that Darin and Carson were having with Vincent and his parents. Kristen had gone into the house, carrying a stack of dirty dishes and could be heard loading them into a dishwasher.

"You've kept yourself fairly quiet tonight, Ruut," I said. "The day's activities get to you, too? Are you winding down?"

"Ya, well," he said, slowly looking around to see who might be in ear shot. "That lady next door is a bit much to take sometimes. Sorry, Vincent, but you already know how I feel. At least she didn't get going on one of her political tirades. Not pretty…not pretty."

Toriel patted his arm.

"I don't want to say she's endearing," she said even more softly than Ruut. "That's not the term I was looking for, but she has many good qualities and she's had some mean things happen to her. She can be sweet. Be nice, Ruut. Be understanding, Vincent. Be tolerant."

We assumed, correctly, that Kristen and Lucas would be spending the night here. The three kids, now fast friends, were going to be in sleeping bags out here on the deck. The weather was absolutely perfect for a sleep-out, with a full moon casting its brilliant reflection on the lake a few yards from us.

It had been a long, full day and everyone was ready to call it a night.

Kristen had done a great job of cleaning up and putting away the leftovers. All three boys came running out onto the deck with their summer pajamas on.

"Are the dogs going to sleep out here with us?" asked Greyson.

"No, no," answered Vincent. "Too much wildlife out there at night. I wouldn't want them to run off chasing anything and not come back."

"What do you mean 'wildlife'?" asked Hayden. "Bears? Wild cats? Mountain lions?"

"Oh, ya…all of that." Said Vincent with a smile. "Even Bigfoot, you know?"

"Stop it!" admonished Kristen, slapping Vincent on the shoulder. "He's just trying to scare you boys. Nothing will get you out there. But we'll leave the backdoor unlocked anyway, just in case."

"In case of what?" asked Greyson.

"In case you might have to pee during the night," I answered.

We all said our goodnights and went to our assigned rooms, leaving a small light on in the kitchen for the boys. I stripped and slid, naked, between the cool sheets. Abbie joined me a few moments later, turning out the light as she did so. The bright moonlight cast long shadows across the ceiling. I lay there admiring the patterns for a second or two. *How romantic* I thought.

"You don't think there really might be bears around here, do you?" I asked. Silence.

And then a little snort. Abbie was asleep already. Snoring softly. So much for romance!

46

The sun couldn't have shone any brighter when we all awoke Sunday morning. An almost blinding light replaced the moonbeams that had danced through our bedroom window last night. The aroma of cooking bacon and sausages does something to one's senses that cannot be defined. I was out of bed, showered and shaved within less than ten minutes. Being that I was alone in the room when I first opened my eyes, I made the assumption that Abbie was already outside or helping in the kitchen. Good assumption.

I walked down the hall from our room and glanced into the living room. As if it was in a spotlight, that huge portrait of Ruut's family glowed in the sunlight. An idea flashed into my head. I stared at it for a moment, and then turned toward the kitchen. I knew it was Vincent doing the cooking. I walked up behind him and whispered something into his ear. He stopped what he was doing, hesitated for a second, turning to look at me.

"Wonderful! That's a wonderful idea, Baxter. I know my parents will be thrilled. We do it right after breakfast, ya? Or do you mean now?"

"No, no. After breakfast will be fine. I'll have Darin help me with the chair. I have a feeling the sun will be in a better location then anyway."

Darin came in from the deck after playing with the boys out in the yard. I motioned for him to follow me. We both lifted the large, heavy white Adirondack chair and carried it down from the lawn to the far end of the dock. I looked around, trying to position it for the best effect. The sky was a crisp, cloudless blue and the lake was as still as glass.

By the time we got back inside, breakfast was ready and Vincent had told his parents my idea. Toriel came up to me, hugging me and then planted a big kiss on both cheeks. She turned to Ruut.

"Why didn't you think of this?" He shrugged. "I love this idea. So thoughtful, Baxter...so thoughtful."

The scrambled eggs were done to perfection. For that matter, they may have been the best we've ever eaten. Whatever Vincent's recipe is, we want it! I had never seen bacon and sausages disappear so quickly. After three cups of coffee I looked out at the sky and sun.

"I think the light is going to be just perfect by the time we get out there. Let's do it. Let's make magic."

I had suggested that they all be dressed in their very best orange swimwear. This portrait would be the antithesis of the so very formal portrait hanging in the living room.

"Sorry, Ruut, but this one will be digital. I don't really use much film these days."

He waved it off.

The three kids pushed back their chairs and made a bee-line for the back yard.

There they were. Whatever royalty they might be—was Ruut really a count? --- Vincent and Ruut stood, bright orange trunks, shirtless, barefoot, behind a seated Toriel, who looked fabulous in her one-piece orange bathing suit. Without too much direction, they struck the exact same pose as they had done while wearing formal wear.

This would make a striking portrait. This time in color, not black and white. The brilliance of the blue sky above, the shimmering water behind. I was able to arrange them so no boats were in the background, no other house along the water's edge. They looked like they, alone, were in Paradise.

"Wait!" called out Vincent. "The dogs!" He whistled and the two poodles came charging out onto the deck, their toenails click, click, clicking on the wooden planks. They were frisky and bouncing all over the place.

"Where's your Uncle Fredrik when we need him?" I laughed.

"Ahhh…ya…wait here!" Vincent answered and made a mad dash back into the house.

He was back in a flash, holding his smartphone aloft. He began scrolling through it.

"Ah, here it is. Good. Get ready, Baxter. Now we make magic, yes?"

He held his phone so I could see the screen. It was a video, on pause, of Ruut's brother, Fredrik.

"Okay," I said, somewhat doubtful. "I'm ready to shoot. Let's hope the dogs don't mess up the shot."

Vincent smiled and pressed *play*. He had the volume turned up. He quickly put his hand down to hide the phone from the camera's view.

"Blijf!" blasted Uncle Fredrik's voice.

Holy fuck! I'll be damned. Instantly the dogs stopped and took their places, sitting, flanking Toriel who was posed graciously in the Adirondack chair.

We made magic. Lots of it. I clicked away until I thought I had the perfect shot. Hell, I had a dozen perfect shots.

"Ahhh, beautiful," I said with my faux Russian accent as I lowered my camera.

The audience behind me, Darin, Carson, Kristen, Tack, and the boys all broke out in applause when the shoot was finished. Abbie had been right by my side as I shot. The poodles ran off to chase a squirrel.

"You did it again, Baxter," whispered Toriel, almost in tears. "Look. You captured the love once again."

We were scrolling through my photos on the camera back. I had to admit, each shot was a beauty. But then, I had some great-looking subjects. Ruut leaned in over my shoulder looking at the photos as well.

"You might be retired, Baxter, but you sure haven't lost your magnificent talent. That last ten minutes out there on the deck might just be the highlight of my entire weekend, yes?"

Actually, I felt overwhelmed by their emotions.

"I'll have some enlargements made and sent to you as soon as I can. Let's pick out whichever one or ones you might want. I'll make sure Vincent gets some, too. This was fun!"

"No need for that, Baxter," said Vincent. "Come on in and transfer those files to my computer. I'll take care of everything else at my end up here. You're the best. The absolute best!"

"Hey," called a bored-sounding Greyson, "when can we go out on the boat again?" He was sitting on the lawn with the poodles lying down by his side.

"I have a better idea, young man," said Vincent kneeling down to him. "How about going for a race?"

"What kind of race?" Greyson answered, perking up. "I can run really, really fast!"

"No, no," laughed Vincent. "I'm sure you run fast, but I was talking about on the water. By the way, did you know that my father and I run marathons? Maybe not as fast as you, but…" and he trailed off laughing.

Greyson looked embarrassed and I had to stifle a snicker.

"Have you ever paddled a canoe?" Vincent asked Greyson.

"A couple times, yes, sir. It was called an outrigger, though. We were someplace way out in the Pacific Ocean on an island. It was a couple years ago."

"Well, great!" responded a surprised Vincent. He turned to look at me.

"What do you say, Bax? You, Greyson and Hayden in a canoe against my father and me in our kayaks, ya? A race?"

"You're on! Let's do it, kiddo!" I said to Greyson, who now had renewed enthusiasm.

We got our respective boats down to the water's edge. I gave a few quick paddling instructions to Hayden who had *not* done it before. But, as it was, Greyson and I would actually be doing the work while Hayden just enjoyed the ride. Hopefully. We lathered up with sunscreen once again and stepped into our launches.

"How far are we going?" Greyson asked Vincent.

"Oh, just to the end of the lake and back. Six miles total, round trip." Vincent said, with a sly wink to me.

"Holy sh…!" Greyson started…then, wisely stopped.

"Just kidding, ya?" laughed Ruut, who was also ready to go.

"No," answered Vincent. "See that tree leaning out into the water down there?' And he pointed to a spot about a hundred yards away, on the far side of the lake. "How about to there and back, okay?"

"It's a deal," smiled my eldest and wise grandson.

The Flying Dutchman and his son were in their kayaks. I was positioned in the rear of our canoe, Greyson in front, with Hayden in the middle. We were ready.

Darin stood by, probably thinking that his old father would fall out of the boat within the first minute. Or tip it over. Tack used his finger as a starting pistol, holding it high in the air and started the countdown.

"Three…two…one…BANG!" he screeched. And we were off!

"Let's go, Gramp!" yelled Hayden.

To be perfectly honest, it really wasn't a race. We appeared to be a flotilla, three boats cutting through the water side by side. Our canoe was in between the two kayaks.

"Can't you go any faster?" jeered Ruut. "Maybe one of you should get out and push, ya?"

The boys giggled.

We made it to the tree faster than I thought we would. I hadn't paddled a canoe in years. That time at Boy Scout camp decades ago…a century ago…flashed through my mind. The part about canoeing.

All three boats turned around at about the same time and we started back to Vincent's place. We were slightly ahead. Then Vincent slowly overtook us. Then we were in the lead again and then Ruut overtook us. I knew they were just playing with us and giving the boys a good time.

"Oh, I'm getting *so* tired," moaned Ruut theatrically. "My arms are about to fall off."

"Me, too," called out Vincent. "You boys are just too good. I think I have to rest."

"Fakers!" yelled sweet, innocent little Hayden. "I think you're fulla shit!"

I nearly fell outta the canoe!

Our canoe pulled up to the dock just slightly ahead of the kayaks. I admonished Hayden for his choice of words and made him apologize to the Dutchmen. Although initially shocked by what the little twit had called out, they both had busted out laughing.

"I like your spirit, Hayden," said Ruut, chuckling, as he pulled his kayak out of the water. "Maybe not that word so much, but we had fun, ya?"

"Good job, kids," Vincent chimed in. "And you know what? My Pa *is* fulla you-know-what at times."

"*Let op je mond!*" answered Ruut, laughing harder. "Watch your mouth!"

I hadn't paid much attention to this before, but as we were all walking back up to the house for lunch I realized that Vincent's place was surround by several oak trees. Looking around on the ground as we walked, I found what I was looking for. I kneeled down.

"Boys," I called to Greyson and Hayden, "I have something for you."

They stopped and came over to me. I opened the palm of my hand to reveal two perfectly formed acorns.

"Yeah? Acorns. So what?" said that little smartass Hayden.

Darin came up along side of us.

I told the boys about that hobo friend of mine when I was about their age. And told them about the good luck that acorns can bring.

"I still have one in my pocket all the time," I said. "Well, not here in my bathing suit, but you know what I mean. I gave one to your father decades ago, when he was a little twit just like you. I don't know if he ever believed me but…"

I turned to look up as Darin reached into the pocket of his shorts and pulled out an old acorn. He looked down at me, nodded and smiled.

"Wherever I go, Pop, all around the globe, this has been with me since that very first day you gave it to me."

"Even when you were on stage as that…what's her name…Polly-Anna or,…er, whatever…Poly-Ester Pantsafyr?"

"Ha! *Especially* then!" He answered throwing his head back in laughter.

I smiled back at him as the boys picked out an acorn for themselves and scampered back into the house for lunch.

47

Sunday evening. The sun was setting behind the trees on the far side of the lake and the sounds of a summer night were slowly beginning. The beautiful symphony of crickets and katydids. Greyson and Hayden, both totally exhausted, had been put to bed in preparation for an early morning departure heading for home. Vincent and Ruut were out in their respective kayaks again, with Carson, Kristen and Lucas following close behind in the canoe. I knew that they'd be hauling them back up out of the water shortly. Abbie and Toriel were chatting and laughing on the deck. Tack approached both Darin and me and suggested that we come sit with him on the Adirondack chairs on the lawn, almost at the lake's edge. I wondered why. We each held our respective favorite adult beverages as we sat down. We stared out across the serene water. He finally broke the silence.

"This has been a most remarkable weekend," he started, "wouldn't you agree?"

"One of the best, in *my* book," I replied.

"I couldn't agree more," responded Darin.

Three smiling faces looking at one another. Tack cleared his throat. I thought I saw tears in his eyes, but it could be the light from the descending sun.

"I want you to bear with me, gentlemen," Tack said, with a slight catch in his voice. "And, please, do me the favor of not interrupting what I am about to say. I have learned, by now, Baxter, that you are very outspoken. But, bloody hell, this time just shush."

I laughed, Darin rolled his eyes.

"What I have observed this entire weekend has been both heartwarming and heartbreaking. The affection between Vincent and his parents is overwhelming. I shudder to think what lays ahead for them. The love, Baxter, in *your* family is palpable. I lost count how many times those precious little grandsons of yours called out to you and Abbie. 'Love you, Gram!' 'Love you, Gramp!' Brought tears to my goddamn eyes. Oh, how I miss never hearing a father tell me that he loved me. How I longed for it. But I'm too old for pity nor do I seek any…and that's *not* what this conversation is about. Todd and I have discussed this at great length and he is in total agreement."

Darin and I exchanged confused glances. What the hell was coming next?

"Here comes the part where you will need duct tape over your mouths. As I mentioned to you months ago, Bax, when we first chatted long distance, …and please don't take this as bragging, I'm not intending it as such…but I am very well off. You are the only family I have, so to speak. Toddy hates what's left of his wretched family and, frankly, he's well off also. Not only have I come out far ahead of what I had expected with the sales of Mum's two houses but since her death her book sales are skyrocketing and the royalties continue to add up. Don't pass out when I tell you the next bit. My lawyers are now in the final discussions with Netflix about adapting them to a television series. Bloody hell, there will be millions pouring in to my already full coffers. It's a pisser, ain't it?"

I know my jaw had dropped to the ground at this point. Tack took a short pause to take a breath and a sip from his vodka and tonic.

Jesus H. Christ, this man is a freakin' money magnet! King Midas reincarnated.

"The reason I wanted to chat with you both here, in private, is a simple one. And one that I hope will not offend you in any way. While I certainly missed having a father, I never missed having kids of my own.

Although, lord knows, I've taught hundreds of them! I have grown very fond of your family in a very short time. Frankly, it surprised the hell out of me. It's been obvious, from our many discussions over the months that you, Baxter, had a lucrative career. And you, Darin, are successful in your extremely interesting career. That being said, I would very much like to be considered your rich old gay uncle from afar. I have checked into your tax laws here…"

Where is he going with this? An owl hooted not too far from where we were sitting.

"…and I know that one can receive a 'gift' of fifteen thousand dollars yearly, tax-free, from an individual. I propose to you, Darin, that you set up an account for each of your two handsome sons and I will make sure that, by college age, they will be able to afford the very best that they may want. I also propose that you all come to visit me as often as you'd like. Toddy and I love to entertain and we make exceptional hosts."

Darin and I sat dumbfounded. What the fuck? How does one respond to a proposal such as that one?

"Wait, wait, wait," I stammered, "Surely you can't be serious? Your generosity is mind-boggling to say the least." I turned to look at Darin whose mouth was still open as wide as his eyes.

"I don't know whether I should hug you, slug you, or declare you insane," gulped Darin finally. "That offer is, at first, preposterous. This came straight out of left field and I'm not sure how I should react. Should I say that I simply couldn't accept such a generous offer? Or should I simply acquiesce in stunned silence?"

"I half expected the kind of reaction from you both that I see right now," Tack answered with a huge grin. "I'm sincere in my offer. Seriously, it sounds ridiculous doesn't it? This old sot giving away tons of money. But look at it from my viewpoint. Please. The money keeps rolling in. Todd and I give huge sums to charities every year and then, throughout the year, those greedy charities keep asking for more. Fuck 'em. Oh, we'll still give to a few worthy causes. But now I consider your sons, Darin, a worthy cause. They are bright, energetic, and I've picked up that they are exceedingly happy little twits, as you call them, Bax. Sounds so British." And he smiled again.

Good luck, in one form or another, has followed me all throughout my life. Ever since that hobo…what was his name? Jake! That was it…gave me that fucking acorn. I'm going to make sure that when my time comes I'm going to be buried with it in my pocket. Who knows what luck I might need in the hereafter.

"I don't want this offer to offend, nor do I want it to seem intrusive. There are no strings attached, naturally. I won't insist that the boys attend Oxford or Cambridge," and Tack laughed again. "Just accept it as an insurance policy to relieve some possible financial upheavals in the future. Who knows, really, what may lie ahead, eh? In all honesty, Darin…and Baxter…I could 'gift' the same amounts to you both as well. But, at this point, my generosity extends only so far," as he roared back in laughter once again. "No need to answer tonight. This offer won't expire at midnight."

It was almost completely dark by now. Music was coming from somewhere across the lake. It sounded like smooth, mellow jazz, perfect for this setting tonight. Someone over there has great taste in music. The outside lights on the deck had been turned on, casting shadows of trees all the way down to the water's edge. We heard a lot of laughter and animated conversation as Vincent and Ruut carried their kayaks toward us, with Carson and Kristen hoisting their canoe. Lucas ran ahead, on the lookout for the lightning bugs that were glittering through the air. The three of us guys stood up and joined them in their trek back up to the house. A unique bond had been formed this weekend. That could not be denied.

48

A foggy mist rose up from the lake, dissipating lazily as it reached for a crisp blue and pink early morning cotton candy sky. The honking of six Canada Geese broke the silence as they flew in through the mist and splashed down, one after the other. I stood at the end of the dock and watched them for a while. Tranquility personified. The sun was rising to my back, throwing my shadow across the remainder of the dock in front of me and out into the mist. Out of the corner of my eye I saw another shadow coming up behind me.

"Good morning, Pop," said Darin with two coffee mugs in his hands. "Thought you might like this, right?" as he handed one to me.

"Hell, yes, thanks," I answered, clinking our mugs together in a toast. We each took long sips.

We both stared out across the water. At this moment, I was the luckiest guy on the planet. Darin has gotten more handsome with each passing year, and I never loved him more than I do right now. His brilliant and perceptive mind continues to amaze me. He and Carson are rearing two wonderful, energetic, love-filled sons. Abbie and I did a damn fine job raising him. Well, probably Abbie influenced him more, but I was there to help on occasion, right? At least I inflicted no noticeable harm to his psyche.

Two other shadows slowly padded up from behind us.

"Good morning, gentlemen, care to join us?" asked Ruut as he and Vincent, both just in their swim trunks, headed for the end of the dock.

"Won't that water be a bit cold this morning?" I asked as I sipped my nice hot coffee again.

"Ya, sure will be. And your point is?" answered Ruut as he dove headfirst making a splash and disturbing the mist. Vincent laughed and followed his father into the water. They both let out a couple of playful hoots and hollers, which echoed across the lake frightening the geese who then responded with loud honking and flapping of wings.

"Almost time to head back to reality, eh, Pop?"

"I'm at that age where I try to eschew reality as much as possible. Don't tell your mother." And I laughed.

"I'm sure she already knows that," and he laughed in response. "We've suspected as such for years."

"Smartass!" was my reply while pretending to swat him across the face. "While we're on the subject of reality, what about Tack's proposal? Have you and Carson come to a resolution?"

"Yes and no. I'm going to contact a lawyer friend of ours shortly and run this situation by him. Neither of us feels right, just to arbitrarily either accept or deny Tack's absurdly generous offer. I told Tack a few minutes ago back up there in the kitchen. He understands."

The sound of giggles and the pounding of young bare feet running up behind us on the dock suddenly interrupted us.

"Hi, Daddy! Mornin', Gramp!" exclaimed Greyson loudly as he zipped past us, almost falling off the end of the dock before coming to an abrupt stop.

"Love you, Gramp," said Hayden as he wrapped his arms around my waist. "Can we go for another canoe ride before we go home, Daddy?"

"Afraid not, young man," answered Darin. "Your mom is packing things up right now and we have to head out right after breakfast."

Hayden's head drooped and he jutted out his lower lip. "Aw, poop!"

Darin arched an eyebrow.

"He could have said 'aw, shit', you know," I snickered.

Darin gave me that squinty-eyed look.

"Hey, we'll come back sometime soon." Darin quickly said to brighten the mood. "We've become good friends over this weekend with Vincent and we have an open invitation."

Hayden jumped up and down, clapping his hands. The two boys scampered back to the house.

"Carson and I have always wanted to learn how to ski, but have never taken the time. Guess who's going to teach us?" and he winked.

An hour later we were all standing around Darin's car, as they were ready to head back to Massachusetts.

"Wait! Wait a minute, please!" called Rebecca as she ran through the trees toward us.

"Run for cover!" I playfully said to Tack. "She'll convert you yet!"

Rebecca was carrying two large gift bags, with colorful tissue paper extending out from the top.

"I overslept and was afraid I'd miss all the goodbyes. Here, Darin and Carson, this one's for you and the boys. And Baxter and Abbie this one's for you guys. I just couldn't let you leave Vermont without some of our famous maple syrup. There's a big jug for each of you. The stuff will rot the hell outta your teeth but it's soooo good! Darin, there are several little bags of Maple Drop candies in your bag there for the boys. Should keep 'em on sugar highs for days on end. You're welcome!" And she laughed.

I glanced at Tack who was standing behind Rebecca. He put his finger into his mouth and faked gagging.

We all thanked her profusely.

"See you all again, soon I hope," she said. "Shit, I gotta go. I'll miss my hair appointment. Roots are beginning to show."

And she started to run back toward her house.

"Ta-ta," waved Tack.

I snorted.

There were lots of hugs, kisses and handshaking when the time came for our respective departures. We were making more noise than those damn honking geese.

The last thing I heard as Carson was closing her car door was "Mommy, can we get a dog?"

We stood and waved as Darin's car headed up and out of the driveway, tooting the car horn as he disappeared around the bend. It must have been the bright morning sun that made my eyes glisten. Tack patted me knowingly on my back.

"Ya, well, who's ready to go flying?" asked Ruut. "The weather looks good. Toriel and I have a dinner date tonight on St. Simons so we need to get going, yes? Can we all be ready in half an hour?"

What a weekend this has been. So much fun…so many laughs…so much Dutch vodka!

Thirty minutes later we were all congregating around Vincent's Land Rover, saying our goodbyes, as he loaded the luggage. Years of traveling abroad taught us how to pack sensible and pack light. Vincent hopped up into the driver's seat with Kristen by his side; Lucas would ride in the back with us. Ruut and Toriel climbed in beside him. He started the engine and I felt a lump in my throat.

"How much longer will you remain stateside?" I asked Tack. "I assume now that your business is concluded here you'll be heading home, right?"

He nodded his head, looking around at the beautiful serene setting. He shrugged and sighed.

"Yes, although I'll miss this place, homeward bound I shall be. I'm taking a puddle jumper from Rutland to Boston early on Wednesday and then onto a pond jumper to London that evening. It's been an amazing year, hasn't it, Bax? Who could have imagined what friendships would develop from a stack of moldy old letters, eh? Life will seem rather boring after all this excitement. I shall have nothing to do, now, but just sit around counting my money," giving me an exaggerated wink and a slap on the back.

Vincent gunned the engine giving us a very obvious hint. Abbie gave Tack a huge, tight hug and a kiss on the cheek, stifling a sob as she hopped up into the car. Tack grabbed my hand and gave a firm grasp. We stared into each other's eyes and then embraced. What a strange, twisted, almost unbelievable year this had been, indeed. We slowly pulled apart. It must have been the bright morning sun in Tack's eyes that made them glisten as well.

"I shall keep the doggies company," said Tack, patting one of them on the head. "Better get going, Captain Ruut will get cross if you aren't airborne soon. Oh, wait. Listen," he said, cocking his head and holding a cupped hand up to one ear. "Can you hear that? A gin and tonic is calling my name!"

I glanced at my watch. Barely 10:15. "Starting a bit early, aren't you?" I laughed.

"Just practicing getting back on London time," he snickered.

49

It's not that Abbie and I never argued throughout our marriage. Oh, we did. I can never remember any big knock down, drag 'em out stuff, but tempers flared, voices and blood pressures were raised. There were times when emotions just floated dangerously on the surface, ready to explode. I know, too, that there were times when one or the other bit their respective tongues to avoid histrionics. Although I seriously doubt that it ever would have escalated to that level.

Just like most marriages, I would guess, early on the arguments were about money. Ironically, not for the lack of it in our case, thanks to Gram and Gramp. But I liked to *spend* it. Abbie liked to *save* it. To this day, Abbie is still the frugal one. The one who still has no conception of what being a millionaire should feel like.

All that being said, we've reached that stage in our old age when it doesn't seem to matter any more, you know, those simple stupid little irritating things. Well, almost. Abbie can get irritated if I arch my eyebrow a certain way when she says something. Or if I roll my eyes in a non-too subtle way when she's bidding at bridge. I can get pissed off, albeit silently, when she starts talking to me from another room. Yes, I now have hearing aids, but her voice from afar still sounds garbled to me. It's all stupid, inconsequential stuff but, nevertheless, I guess it's all part of being together for decades and *finally* getting under each other's skin. There are days when we might feel that we're together way too much. And then there are other days when we almost come to tears realizing that our time together is growing shorter. I can't imagine life on this planet without her in it. And she rages at me at the thought that, eventually, I may be the one to go first.

"Don't you *dare* leave me here alone, dammit!" she might yell. "That would be just like you, you selfish bastard!"

It's a strange, morbid race that we're running. Neither of us wants to die, yet neither one wants to be the surviving runner. The reality, and everyone knows it: the finish line gets closer every day.

Still, our undying love is always evident. Evident to our family. Evident to our friends. Just, sometimes, it might not always be evident to ourselves, although we truly know it's there…merely sleeping for an hour or two.

To make matters worse, following our respective cataract surgeries we each discovered far more wrinkles and facial blemishes than we thought we had. Oh, and my pectorals are sagging. Growing old is a bitch! Dylan Thomas certainly knew what he was talking about: *Do not go gentle into that good night.*

Among the myriad lessons I've learned throughout my lifetime is that whatever we say or do makes a difference to someone else. We just have to decide what kind of difference we might want to make. And that, my friends, is not easy.

What a world Abbie and I have endured. From the end of World War II through the horrors in the Middle East, political and social upheavals, the Cold War, assassinations, the various ups and downs with the economy, successes and tragedies in the space program, Y2K…9/11…social media of all kinds, the COVID-19 pandemic, the contentious election debacles of 2020/2021 and then the riotous violence that threatened our democracy afterwards. But there is always the bright light of hope and optimism. Hell, we even survived quite nicely, thank you very much, the raising of a son. That may have been the most challenging, yet rewarding of all. But, damn it; we *did* survive, didn't we? Wars are still raging. Politicians are still (and always will be) corrupt. Hatred still finds safe haven in far too many hearts and minds. Maybe all is not right with the world yet, and probably never will be, but it is with *our* little world. Almost. We avoid looking into those damnable mirrors as often as possible; they remind us what we *really* look like. *Old age should burn and rave at close of day.* But, in our minds, we are still those two young kids commuting into the city, exchanging reviews of thrillers. We still read thrillers. And we still exchange reviews.

50

LATER: For some strange reason, I have never really been affected by jet lag. No matter which direction our travels have taken us, I'm ready to go like gangbusters as soon as we deplane. My philosophy is that if I'm on a long airplane flight, I must be going to or coming from someplace very interesting and I don't want to waste a minute.

Two days ago we returned from visiting with Tack in London. Our first visit with him, two years ago, was just a quick stopover as we headed to Paris to hear Darin deliver a speech at a huge international conference on the environment and climate change. This time we spent nearly two weeks with them. He and Todd are gracious hosts and we all toured around the country for several days. We stopped off at the White Cliffs of Dover. I swear, I almost heard Vera Lynn singing in the background but with nary a bluebird in sight. While there, we were able to watch as they filmed a couple scenes for season three of the Netflix series *Vicky Jayne's Murder Mysteries*. I hadn't recognized the actor portraying the role *very* loosely based on my father. Abbie told me the guy used to play Captain America. I guess I don't watch enough movies. All the vintage cars and costumes enthralled me. The art direction was spot on.

Tack was thrilled to hear that Greyson and Hayden, now in high school, had selected their respective college futures...thanks, in part, to "Uncle" Thackeray.

The unpacking was done, laundry washed and put away and groceries had restocked our fridge. Abbie grumbled, as she always did following our many journeys, that I took *way* too many photos and now I'm spending *way* too much time on the computer arranging them...cropping them... fawning over them. (Her words).

The weather forecasters were wrong. Again. Dire predictions had blared earlier in the day, warning us of a severe storm heading our way, capable of producing tornadoes. But, just like most politicians running for re-election and every known televangelist, it was a lot of sound and fury signifying nothing. I glanced outside and breathed a sigh of relief. It was turning into a pleasant mid-summer evening. Soon the crickets would be singing to me.

"Abbie, want to join me in a cocktail hour out on the deck?" I called into her from the kitchen. She was finishing the book she had started reading on the plane.

"I have just a couple more pages to go. Go ahead, make me a margarita and I'll be right out," she responded.

Make me a margarita? I was tempted to wave my magic wand and say "*Poof!* You're a margarita," but thought better of it. Some days I can sense when my humor might not be appreciated.

The storm has passed without a drop of rain. Just a lot of blustery wind, crackling lightning and some window-rattling thunder. I went out onto the deck to enjoy the remainder of the evening. The sun broke through the clouds in the west and silently kissed the tops of the trees around our place as it dropped further down, taking the wind along with it. *Rage, rage against the dying of the light.* Ice tinkled and sparkled in my glass as I sat down in my comfortable chair. The air smelled crisp and clean. Crisp and clean, just like the gin and tonic I had just sipped. I leaned back, resting my head on the soft chair and slowly glanced up into the darkening sky. Just enough light left to see the clouds parting but not yet dark enough to reveal even the brightest stars. Then I saw it. And then another. Oh, and there's another! A lazy smile came over my face and I could feel the tears beginning to swell in my eyes.

"Fledermaus," I whispered to myself. "Fledermaus."

(Slow Fade-To-Black)

(Curtain)

In Loving Memory
Sara Derry Akeroyd and Clifford Paul Akeroyd
Gram & Gramp…Forever in my Heart

ACKNOWLEDGEMENTS

"Sometimes a new beginning is even better than a happy ending."

I began writing this book during the self-quarantine period caused by the COVID-19 pandemic. Every day brought new tragic news from around the globe. Bad things were happening to people. Very bad things. I wanted to write about optimism and hope. Where (mostly) good things happen to people. Outrageously good things. Perhaps unrealistically good things. That's called escapism.

Confession time. I have been *extremely* cavalier with the time frame of actual events and some product placements. I moved certain things forward or backward to accommodate my narrative and that's not meant, in any way, to alter history. Time is fluid, after all, right? That's called artistic license and this *is* a work of fiction. So if you bother to take the time to fact-check any of the situations written about in this book, you may come up short. *"Liar!"* as a rude old parrot might squawk.

No fact checking required here, however. Without hesitation I acknowledge the love and support I have received for decades from my beautiful wife, Gaylin. Without her gentle, yet firm hand guiding me (almost since the day we first met) I surely would have ended up more of a scatterbrained mess than I currently am. She's my absolute best friend, my strongest, severest critic, and the best travel companion in the world. We still read thrillers. And we still exchange reviews.

Our two incredibly successful sons, Gregory & Christopher, survived my parenting skills, such as they were, to become loving parents themselves. Regarding our handsome grandsons, Devon, Jacob, and Peyton, I love them to the nth degree (no, I *don't* have a favorite grandson) and our gorgeous granddaughter, Alexis, has always been a joy...oh, and she is a fabulous photographer!

To all the photographers, graphic designers, art directors, food stylists, marketing directors, and other "nut cases" with whom I've worked throughout my career, thanks for the inspiration. And thanks for the memories.

(Fade Out...with "Ac-Cent-Tchu-Ate the Positive")

Printed in the United States
By Bookmasters